MW00882227

Advance Praise for
The Plans We Made

Deftly told and beautifully written, *The Plans We Made* is a story that explores the bonds of family, the power of forgiveness, and God's amazing work of redemption in our lives. Hats off to Beccue and Cushman for penning such a lovely tale!

Katie Ganshert
Award-Winning Author of *No One Ever Asked*

The Plans We Made is a beautiful illustration of how God can use disappointments in life for our good and His glory. A beautiful unfolding of what it looks like to walk with courage through life's curveballs. With layers of past and present and characters we can all identify with, this book will encourage you in whatever you might be facing in life today.

Kate Merrick
Author of *And Still She Laughs* and *Here, Now*

In *The Plans We Made*, Katie Cushman and Lauren Beccue carefully weave the stories of three lives in crisis into one beautiful tapestry. Set among charming mansions of Newport, Rhode Island, the story overflows with lavish details, light-hearted moments, and page-turning secrets and revelations. At its core is an engrossing inspirational message of value and worth that readers will treasure. Highly recommended.

Julie Carobini
Author of the *Sea Glass Inn* series

A beautiful story that explores complicated issues with grace, tender moments and a touch of humor. Endearing characters that will touch your heart. Don't miss this one!

Catherine West
Award-Winning Author

To this adoptive mother and caregiver to a child who battled cancer, *The Plans We Made* is a story of love and forgiveness, touching the deepest places of the heart. Cushman and Beccue remind the reader that God can be fully trusted in the preserving pain that past secrets lend, that mistakes can result in miracles, and that when our plans fail, God never does. Hope for healing will linger in the reader's thoughts long after turning the last page.

Shelli Littleton
Author of *A Gift Worth Keeping: It Goes With My Décor!*

BOOKS BY KATHRYN CUSHMAN

A Promise to Remember
Waiting for Daybreak
Leaving Yesterday
Another Dawn
Almost Amish
Chasing Hope
Finding Me
Fading Starlight

BOOK BY KATHRYN CUSHMAN AND SHEILA WALSH
Angel Song

THE PLANS WE MADE

KATHRYN CUSHMAN AND LAUREN BECCUE

To Carl and Alisa Parrish
I am so blessed to have such an amazing family.
Thank you both for being wonderful.

—K. C.

In memory of Laura Krimmel
"God had painted her soul with colors reserved only
for her."

—L. B.

CHAPTER 1

Caroline Chapman wanted to say yes—shout yes, actually—but a pesky dose of reality seized her vocal cords. "I haven't told my fiancé I applied for this, and I don't think he'll want to quit his job and move" didn't exactly seem like the right thing to say to a potential boss.

She pulled her SUV into the small-town center parking lot and racked her brain for a more professional reply. Before she could come up with anything decent, Audrey Brooks's voice came through the car speakers. "We'd appreciate a swift response. Summer is our busiest season, so we'd need you out here no later than the end of May, preferably sooner."

That gave her—them—seven weeks, give or take, to move from Los Angeles to Newport, Rhode Island. It was tight but doable. "Of course, I understand. Thank you so much for the offer. I'll get back to you in the next day or two, if that's okay?"

"That would be fine. Your experience at the Huntington Library would make you a valuable asset to us, so I definitely look forward to hearing from you."

Caroline ended the call, then shut off the engine. *Valuable asset.* Audrey's words reverberated in her mind, and she couldn't help but squeal.

She could see Dillon sitting at a patio table in front of her favorite restaurant in San Marino—the rosemary-currant bread alone was worth the drive through LA traffic—but she took a minute to peek in the rearview mirror and freshen her lip gloss. Sparkly pink, just like the bliss of this moment, as long as Dillon didn't squash it with his practicality. This two-becoming-one thing was already proving to be tricky, and the wedding was still a month away.

She shouldn't complain. It was his practicality that made him so dependable. Secure. He probably had her taxes done and waiting for her now, unlike their friend Nicole's husband who couldn't even manage to make a dinner reservation.

But the Newport Preservation Society was the epicenter of Gilded Age opulence. The mere thought of it made her insides dance. She'd perused their website so many times since she graduated from Westmont, but the fantasy never materialized beyond her screen. Until now. And she'd earned the job on her own, not because her fiancé's mom was on the board. No one could hint she didn't deserve it.

Was it completely impractical to want to move to the East Coast for it? Or ask Dillon to do the same? Caroline got out of her car and walked over to him. Thankfully, she managed not to skip.

"Hey there." He stood when she approached, then leaned over to kiss her cheek. "You look nice."

"Thanks. You look…" The dark circles under his ocean-green eyes were bigger than in recent days. "Tired. Are you okay?"

Even when he was tired, his eyes were still the most striking she'd ever seen. It was the first thing she'd noticed about Dillon when she met him four years ago, and soon they'd be the last thing she saw every night before going to bed.

"It's that busy time of year." He let out a long exhale as they sat, then he slid an envelope toward her place setting. "Here, your taxes are ready. Mail this in by the fifteenth."

"You're the best. Oh, we also need to tell Zach and Emma we're coming to—"

"I texted him this morning and said we'd bring chips and dip. I can pick it up if you don't want to."

"Thank you." She reached over and squeezed his hand. "Anything I can do to help you relax? Just think how nice it will be to unwind on the honeymoon."

"Actually, about the honeymoon...We need to iron out a few things."

Her body tensed. Dillon had already expressed concern that it was too long, and the way he scratched his chin didn't scream, "Let's add a couple's massage to the itinerary."

"Before you get into that, I have some news." She bounced a little in her chair. "On my drive over I got a job offer. I didn't tell you I'd applied because I didn't think I'd even get a response, so I figured what's the point. But I've been asked to be the director of special events for the Newport Preservation Society, responsible for everything from lecture series, concerts, children's events, the annual fundraiser..." As the words spilled from her mouth, Dillon's face didn't exactly mirror her enthusiasm.

"I wasn't aware Newport Beach had a preservation society."

"Well no, I don't think it does. I'm talking about Newport, Rhode Island."

A snort of a laugh burst from his nose, causing other diners to look their way. When she didn't respond, Dillon's eyes seemed to double in size. "Oh, you're serious?"

"Is that so hard to believe?"

"Caroline, I don't know what you expect me to say."

"'Congratulations' comes to mind." She wasn't exactly expecting leaps of joy, but a dash of enthusiasm would have been nice.

He nodded. "Yes, congratulations. Of course. I'm sorry, this is just coming at a really bad time. Something's come up at work, and I can't even entertain the idea of moving to Rhode Island."

She sat back in her chair and crossed her arms over her fractured hopes. "I moved to LA for you."

He gave a warm smile, then took a sip of his water. "But here's the thing, my company is moving the upper-level staff to Plano, Texas, in May, and they've offered me a great position there. Unfortunately, we'll have to pack up and move right after the wedding."

"Excuse me?" Her appetite for the rosemary-currant bread disappeared.

"I promise, I'll make it up to you. We'll take a honeymoon as soon as …"

The rest of Dillon's attempt to compensate for the bomb he'd just dropped was drowned out by the red-hot panic building inside her. "You've agreed to a transfer without telling me?"

He stared at her for a moment. "I'm telling you now. And you knew it was a possibility."

"I meant, without discussing it."

He leaned forward and placed his forearms on the table. "You applied for a job in Rhode Island without telling me."

"Getting an offer and accepting it are two very different things. Can't you say no?" She clenched her hands in her lap.

"I'd get stuck at my current level. And I did discuss it with you, Care Bear. I sent you that email, remember?"

A fairly recent email, analyzing the differences between costs of living, taxes, potential retirement age, and links to a few houses on the market, puffed through her memory. Caroline had read it after her last dress fitting, but since

Dillon didn't bring it up again, she figured it was no longer an issue.

"Dillon, I don't want to move to Texas. If we're going to leave LA, I really want to take this job. What about a CPA firm in Providence or starting your own business?"

"That's not realistic."

Her heart fell and her imagination provided no alternatives. "Then let's just stay in LA. I'll keep working for the Huntington and you can get another job here."

"Caroline, I understand you don't want to go and, obviously, I can't force you."

"What?" Her pulse pounded in her ears, getting louder and louder. "Are you suggesting…?"

"I'm not suggesting anything. I'm saying that I'm being offered a big promotion in Texas—something no one in their right mind would pass up—and I hope you come with me."

Cold rushed through her, as if he'd dumped his ice water on her head. "I don't—" Her voice hitched. "I don't understand."

"I don't either. I expected you to be behind me, 100 percent. For better or worse, right?" He shook his head and stared at her.

"I am behind you." Leaving her life, her job, her friends and family in Santa Barbara wasn't enough? All the little things she'd done to make his world better, like the Dodgers tickets for his birthday she really couldn't afford, the party she organized when he passed the CPA exam despite being swamped at work herself. Did he remember?

She twisted her engagement ring—Dillon's grandmother's—around her finger. His grandparents' fifty-three-year marriage, being chosen to follow in that legacy, the promise of forever—it all swirled through her and she started to get a little dizzy.

Her soul was screaming, but she couldn't say anything besides, "I don't like where this is going."

He shifted his weight in his chair but offered nothing more than a long sigh.

"It seems," her voice was small, but she pressed on, "that we both have some serious thinking to do."

She stood and grabbed her purse, then turned toward the parking lot. She could feel him, and everyone else at the restaurant, staring at her as she left, but she didn't look back. Instead, she got into her car, started the engine, then pulled away.

And he didn't try to stop her.

CHAPTER 2

Linda Riley screamed at the top of her lungs, "Go Maddox, go!" She jumped up and down, in spite of her precarious position on the edge of the bleachers. "Go!"

The coach waved her son around third base, and she watched as Maddox pumped his arms and legs at incredible speed, making his way toward home plate. The fans in both sets of bleachers roared with excitement as the throw from the shortstop came in fast and hard.

Maddox dropped to the slide as the catcher stretched forward and snagged the ball on the very tip of his mitt—less than a second after Maddox crossed the plate in a cloud of dust.

"Safe." The umpire swung his arms wide.

The team erupted from the dugout and piled on top of Maddox. The game winning run, scored in the eleventh inning, in front of home-side bleachers packed with Portsmouth Patriots fans—every varsity player's dream.

Linda's best friend, Kristyn, grabbed her by both shoulders. "He did it!" She threw her arms around Linda and pulled her in for a celebratory hug. Thumps of congratulations across the back, shoulders, and arms came from every direction as people made their way down the stands. "He did great." "Well done." "That kid of yours."

Linda looked toward Brent, who like most of the fathers eschewed the bleachers in favor of pacing the fence during games. Plenty of high fives and back thumps were being exchanged among all the guys, too. Brent wore his bright-red Portsmouth Patriots hat, which clashed with the dress pants and shirt he'd worn straight from work. Was the ball cap motivated by school pride or his thinning hair?

Probably a bit of both. Brent had never given a thought to his appearance until his hairline began to recede. She had assured him the change accentuated his square jaw and dimples, which was true. Even the salt and pepper in his hair served to pull out the mischievous glint often present in his hazel eyes. Men. So unfair that aging seemed to work for them, not against them.

A glance at her watch brought her up short. Marshall would be finished with chess club in ten minutes, so she needed to rush. After catching Brent's eye and exchanging gestures toward watches, cars, and dugouts, Linda headed out. Brent and she had agreed on a plan whereby she would pick up Marshall, he would wait for Maddox, and they would all meet at the house afterward. All this had been communicated without one word being spoken—a practice perfected through twenty-one years of marriage and the chaos of raising two teenage boys with very different schedules.

She hummed the Patriots' victory chant as she drove. What a shame Marshall had missed all the excitement. Then again, maybe it was for the best. The boys were as different as two brothers could be for more reasons than Maddox's tall frame and thick black hair versus Marshall's small build, fine light-brown hair, and Harry Potter glasses. Maddox was outgoing, goofy, and naturally athletic. Marshall was introverted, serious, and naturally academic—and got way too many comparisons to his popular older brother. Yes, it probably was a good thing he had missed it.

An hour later, as they sat around the dinner table, Maddox was far too quiet. Over the past few weeks this had become more and more common—a heavy class load and recent breakup with a girlfriend seemed to have exacted quite a toll. Tonight, however, Linda assumed the adrenaline rush of today's win would be sufficient to bring out a little of his old spark.

"Maddox, you're not getting sick again, are you? You're so quiet, and you look pale." And he did look pale in spite of his natural olive complexion.

"Nah. Just tired." He took a sip of water, then sprinkled Parmesan atop his marinara sauce.

Linda glanced at Brent to see if he, too, was perceiving red flags here. If he noticed anything, he gave no indication. He took a bite of salad and then said, "Of course you're tired. It took every bit of the energy you had to make that incredible run to the plate today. I'm tired just from watching it."

Maddox smiled, barely. "Yeah, that's right." His hair, still damp from the shower and neatly combed, provided another clue of something amiss. Maddox prided himself on looking as disheveled as possible and normally commenced tousling within seconds of washing.

Linda couldn't help herself. She leaned forward and put the back of her hand on her son's forehead. "Maddox, you're burning up. No wonder you're so quiet. I can't believe you're sick again."

"I'm fine." He twirled the spaghetti around his fork but did not pick it up to take a bite. "It's just a little cold. No reason to make a big deal."

"You're not fine. This is the third time this month you've run a fever. You're pushing too hard these days. Tomorrow you need to spend the day in bed and rest so your body can heal properly."

"No, Mom, I can't miss school tomorrow. I've got a test in pre-calc, and Coach won't let me play in the next game if I miss a day of school."

"Maddox you're not—"

"I'm fine, Mom, really." He stood, then loaded his utensils onto his mostly full plate and made his way toward the sink.

She turned to him, ready to scold him for interrupting her that way, when she saw his leg. "What is that?"

"What's what?"

"That bruise on your leg. What happened?"

Brent paused his spaghetti twirling and turned at the same moment Maddox glanced down. "That's weird." He pulled up the leg of his baggy athletic shorts, and the higher he pulled the worse it looked. A huge black bruise on the outside of his thigh. He shook his head. "Must be from where I slid into home plate today. It doesn't hurt or anything. I guess I just landed the wrong way."

Linda waited until the last plate had been cleared and everyone else was out of the room, then she picked up her phone to call Dr. Klimt, an old friend of Brent's father and an elder at the church. She'd phoned him at home many times about church or social events but never in a professional capacity. But something inside her was uneasy enough that she moved past the feeling of impropriety.

He, of course, was very kind. He listened as she explained what was happening, then said, "My schedule is packed full tomorrow. Why don't you bring him by around seven thirty, and I'll take a look before we open for the day."

"Thank you so much." As Linda hung up the phone, she couldn't decide if she was more relieved that he was taking her seriously or more concerned because he had taken it seriously enough to open his office early.

CHAPTER 3

The LA Bridal Expo had exploded in her living room, or so it appeared. Caroline had spent the last week at her parents' house in Santa Barbara, crying what felt like every last tear in her body, but seeing her apartment for the first time since Dillon's declaration of independence induced another round of despair. Everything around her brought another reminder of the wedding that was supposed to be the happiest day of her life but was officially called off late last night.

Sure, her mom had soothed her with phrases that are nice and uplifting when you see them on Pinterest like "Everything happens for a reason" and "All things work together for good for those who love the Lord."

Her dad told her how treasured she was and anyone willing to give her up didn't deserve her anyway... blah, blah, blah. She always figured those things were true, but at this moment, her throbbing head and her bleeding heart begged to differ.

Caroline flung her shoes off one at a time, not caring where they landed or what they hit on the way. She trudged through the hall and into her bedroom, where she pulled the curtains over her windows. Even though it was a warm April afternoon, all she wanted to do was hide in bed. Her boss kindly told her to take some extra days off before she returned to work. Their annual fundraiser was now behind them, and the rest of the events on the spring calendar were well under control. Thank the Lord, because she didn't have an ounce of energy to spare right now.

Before she pulled the covers up over her head, she grabbed her phone from her purse to do the same thing she'd done about a thousand times since she woke up this morning—check to see if Dillon called, texted, or emailed. Any hint of him coming to his senses and apologizing for the whole stupid thing.

Nothing. Not a whisper. Same as the last 999 times.

How could this possibly be the same man who'd tirelessly moved her stuff into this apartment? Watched every single episode of *Downton Abbey* with her? Without complaining! Helped her sift through invitations, napkin colors, and personal insecurity when she was planning events?

The only silver lining in all of this was she was now completely free to take her dream job in Rhode Island. She'd put it off until she knew for sure what Dillon was going to do, but with his emphatic assertion that it was Texas with or without her, she could proceed with peace. Sort of. She blew her nose again, cleared her throat, then called the Newport Preservation Society.

"Audrey Brooks," came a high-pitched voice over the sound of shuffling papers as soon as they were connected.

Caroline sat up straight on the bed. "Oh, yes, Hi Audrey. It's Caroline Chapman." Her throat was raw, and she sounded more like a Muppet than a viable candidate for employment.

"Caroline, hi." She sighed. "I was expecting to hear from you several days ago."

Great. She's already mad at me. This is not how I wanted to start. She tugged at the quilt on her bed. "I'm sorry, I was trying to sort out some details on my end. But everything is settled now, and I would be so honored to accept the job."

"Oh." A long pause followed, and the last shred of optimism left in Caroline's body plummeted into oblivion. "I've already offered it to another candidate. I really need to have this filled ASAP, and I interpreted your silence as disinterest."

A wave of nausea washed over Caroline and she couldn't breathe. Finally, she forced herself to speak. "Of course, I understand." Hopefully Audrey couldn't hear the lie fall through the crack in her voice.

"I'll tell you what. If this candidate doesn't accept, I will give you a call back, okay? I should know by the end of tomorrow."

"I appreciate that. Thank you." Caroline ended the call then threw her phone to the floor. *If* the other candidate doesn't accept. What idiot would let that job go? Well, what other idiot would let that job go?

No, it was over. Everything good in her life was over. As a fresh supply of tears ruptured from her burning eyes, a groan escaped her lungs and she fell into the pillow.

They lived happily ever after. That's how it was supposed to happen, right? For everyone else, it seemed. Instead, her prince charming—the steady, reliable one—took her fairy-tale ending, dumped it in a blender, and hit puree.

...

The call came six days after the early morning appointment. "Doctor Klimt would like to see you today and go over Maddox's test results."

Linda, who only seconds ago had been settled at her desk in the Portsmouth High attendance office, surrounded

13

by a half dozen kids who had arrived late, gripped the phone tighter and leaned forward. She kept her voice low. "Can't he just tell me over the phone?"

"Umm ... sometimes he feels it is better to review these things in person."

Sometimes? "Of course." She said this calmly, as if it were all perfectly normal. How she managed this, she didn't know.

"He suggests that you bring your husband with you, if at all possible, but no need to bring Maddox, as this is an informational meeting only." She paused for just a second, as if working up her courage to continue. "Does eleven fifteen work?"

"Eleven fifteen? Well I ..." Linda glanced at the clock on the wall. It was eight thirty, but she didn't bother to check her appointment calendar. Of course she would be there. It didn't matter what else was scheduled. "Yes, that works for me, but I'm afraid my husband is out of town."

"All right, then. We'll be looking for you in a little bit." And just like that, the call was over.

The doctor wanted to see her.

In person.

With Brent.

Without Maddox.

There could be no doubt that the news was bad. The question was, just how bad?

Maddox had seemed to feel better after she forced him to spend Friday and Saturday lying on the couch and resting. He would miss two practices and another game, as well as a test and a quiz. Fortunately, the doctor had backed her, going so far as to quote the school rules that did not allow a child entrance until twenty-four hours after a fever abated.

Maddox sulked all weekend, then had remained silent on the drive in this morning instead of his usual nonstop narrative of plans for the day ahead. This left Marshall in the unusual position of attempting small talk to ease the tension. It hadn't worked, but Linda appreciated the effort.

Now she sat in the school office and busied herself checking in stragglers, sending them off to class with a tardy slip and something to the effect of, "Have a nice day." After the last of them had gone, she wrestled with the almost-overwhelming desire to call Brent. She needed to talk to him, to share her fears. It would lighten her load just a fraction by knowing that someone else carried it as well, but she refused to allow herself the luxury.

Brent's position as vice president of a public relations firm always carried a heavy workload. That had increased exponentially when he had learned about a start-up organization called Game Changers, which brought prominent professional athletes from all around the country to speak to young men about the importance of living lives of integrity. He immediately wanted to be a part of it, and used every ounce of energy to convince the president of his secular firm to take on this Christian organization, and with reduced rates until things were up and running. The president made it clear that if they were going to spend time and resources on this, it had better not fail.

Determined to prove the worth of investing in the lives of young men, Brent put everything he had into this new program. This morning he had a huge meeting, and there was no reason to concern him until she knew the facts. No, this burden was one she would bear alone, at least for now.

She prayed about it, or at least she attempted to.

But in truth, instead of deeply spiritual eloquence, all she managed was, *Help. Please help.*

...

The receptionist rose to her feet the moment Linda entered Dr. Klimt's waiting room. Did Linda imagine the odd look on her face? Of course she did. The receptionist was new, and in a busy office like this, there was no way this woman remembered her.

"Mrs. Riley, please come on back." She opened the door to the innermost hallway, leaving Linda to understand just how wrong she'd been.

Linda made her way through the waiting room full of mothers and their children who had not been told to "come on back." She felt their glares as she walked past, but what she wouldn't give at this moment to be frustrated because of the long wait with a fussy baby or a child with strep throat.

At the end of the hallway, the receptionist opened a door with a gold plaque labeled *Dr. Henry Klimt*. She motioned Linda inside. Two ancient-looking wooden chairs faced a battered desk piled high with charts, journals, and textbooks. "Please, have a seat. He'll be right with you." She nodded a farewell without meeting Linda's eyes, then closed the door behind her.

In all of the sixteen-and-a-half years she'd been bringing the boys to this facility, Linda had never once been inside Dr. Klimt's actual office. Never. It smelled of old books and floor wax, with the slightest hint of disinfectant. The walls were filled with framed diplomas and certificates of specialty training, with one single painting in the center. A fishing boat heading out to sea. On the right, a storm was raging, on the left, there were clear skies and smooth sailing. The boat was directly in the middle, its course uncertain. Oh, how she identified with that boat right now.

A bright-yellow box of Kleenex sat on this side of the desk. Were they always here, or had they been placed here for her?

God, please let me be wrong. Please let me be an annoying, paranoid, ridiculously overprotective mother right now. Please let me laugh about it with my husband when I tell him the story of my near panic attack in the doctor's office. Please. Please. Just do this one thing for me, and I'll never ask for anything again…

Those words stopped her cold, because she'd prayed those exact same words many years ago. Prayed them with all of her heart. How many "just one more thing and then I'll stop" kind of prayers would God answer? Or even tolerate?

The door opened and Dr. Klimt entered the room. In his sixties, his balding gray hair and little wire-rimmed glasses portrayed him as the kind and genius doctor he was. He glanced at the empty chair beside Linda. "Brent is out of town I understand?"

"Yes. Until late tomorrow night."

Instead of going around his desk, he sat in the chair beside her. "I'm sure you've realized by now there is a problem."

Linda stared down at her clasped hands, then forced herself to speak. "Yes, I realize that. The question is, how bad?" Her throat closed on the question. When she looked up and saw the expression on his face, she began to weep.

CHAPTER 4

"A cur mangoes legroom." Linda knew her words were unintelligible. They seemed to scramble in her mouth much like they did in her brain. Her phone, set to speaker mode and perched on Dr. Klimt's desk along with her notes, mocked her with its steadiness. Constant light, unwavering connection, unfazed and unbothered by any of this.

"Linda, I can't understand a word you're saying." Brent sounded annoyed, and of course he was. He was in the middle of one of the biggest days of his career and had no idea what was coming. She needed to pull it together.

Dr. Klimt had been so supportive, telling her to take some time alone, stay in his office as long as necessary, make calls, whatever she needed to do. She managed to wait until he closed the door behind him before she doubled over in her chair and lost all control. She had purposely delayed this call until the sobs had all wrenched themselves from her body, until there was nothing left to tear out. Or so she'd thought.

"I'm … I'm sorry." Anguish choked her words.

"Honey, what's wrong? What's happened?"

"Maddox…" She took a deep breath. Her husband needed her to be strong right now. "I'm at the doctor's office." She swallowed hard. If she couldn't even tell him what was wrong, how could he depend on her to help get their son, and the whole family, through this? One more deep breath. "Maddox has leukemia."

"What? How…I…that can't be. He's too young. And healthy. There must be some mistake." The words were little more than a whisper.

A long silence stretched between them, thick and deep and suffocating. Finally, he spoke. "I think we should get a second opinion. How could they possibly know with certainty so soon?"

Linda picked up her notes from the desk. She had written down the important points because her husband always wanted details. "Dr. Klimt is sending us to a pediatric oncologist for further testing. They want to do a bone marrow…" The thought of the long needle inserted into her son's bones stopped the word flow. She shook her head. "A bone marrow biopsy, as well as some other tests, to get more definitive answers."

"So they don't know for sure yet?"

"Last week, Dr. Klimt was concerned enough that he ordered an extra test, he called it a…" she looked at her notes again, "blood smear. It showed something called Auer rods, and these are almost always associated with a particular kind of leukemia, called…" she glanced at the paper, "acute myelogenous leukemia, or AML. Dr. Klimt said this kind of leukemia is common in older adults but not in children."

"Not common, so maybe he's got it wrong. We definitely need to see a specialist. You said Dr. Klimt recommended an oncologist—is he local? When do we see him?"

"*She* is in Boston, at the Dana-Farber Cancer Institute for Children. Her name is Dr. Stern. Dr. Klimt knows her and believes she is one of the best pediatric oncologists around, and he said that Dana Farber is the number one-ranked pediatric cancer hospital in the nation. It's the best of the best. He has already called and spoken with Dr. Stern personally. She will see us Monday."

Brent's flight home would arrive close to midnight tomorrow night, but it came as no surprise when he said, "I'll catch the first flight out in the morning. Don't say anything to Maddox yet. We'll sit down with him this weekend and tell him together."

She nodded. It took her a moment to realize he couldn't see this. "Yes. Thank you. I'll see you when you get in tomorrow. I love you."

"I love you, too."

She only needed to wait twenty-four hours, and Brent would be here to help her process all of this. It would be so much better once he was here. They would figure out the best way to tell their son, together.

But how could she possibly survive the next twenty-four hours? Not able to say a word to anyone? How would she feed her son his dinner and remind him to pick up his dirty clothes and question him about his homework? She knew far better than anyone that those things just didn't matter anymore.

...

Caroline emerged from her bedroom to face several days' worth of dirty dishes, wearing the same pair of sweats since...she didn't know when. It had taken her that long to clear her apartment of all the wedding paraphernalia. If only she could clear her heart of Dillon so quickly.

Perhaps she should stop wearing her veil around the house, but it was too beautiful to stuff away just yet. Plus a small part of her, small and shrinking, still believed Dillon would change his mind. Tax season always stressed him out. Once that was behind him, he would realize how much he missed her, right?

A shower, that's what she needed. And a cold compress for the bags under her eyes. Anything that would help improve her appearance before she went back to work tomorrow. Caroline grabbed a box of matches and a candle from her coffee table, then headed to the bathroom. Despite the Southern California drought, she lingered under the hot water until the bathroom grew steamy and took the time to enjoy the smell of her peony body wash. It was a gift from Dil— No, she didn't even want to think his name.

How was she supposed to move on when everything around her reminded her of him? A few of her closest girlfriends had loyally unfollowed him on Instagram, but aside from them, most of her friends in LA were also his. Moving on apart from him would prove more than an emotional challenge.

As she turned off the shower water, she could hear the faint jingle of her phone coming from the other room. Probably her mom calling again to ask if she needed anything. Nope, unless she knew a hit man in Plano who could make it look like an accident. Times like this it would be helpful to have a brother. A big brother with a temper.

She rushed out of the bathroom, then slid her wet finger across the phone to answer, hoping to catch it before it went to voice mail. "Hello?"

"Caroline, hi. Audrey Brooks here. How have you been?"

Her jaw dropped. She nearly dropped the towel as well. "Fantastic, how about you?" It wasn't exactly true, but the alternative was not open for discussion.

"Doing well, thanks. I'm sorry to bother you on a Sunday, but I thought I'd give you a ring and see if you're still interested in the position. Our other candidate declined just this morning. So, what do you say?"

Her heart felt like it would burst out like candy from a piñata. "Of course I still want it. I'm thrilled."

"Wonderful! Okay, so you won't have any problem with the start date we'd originally set forth?"

"No, I think that should be just fine." She could get to Rhode Island in ... how long did she have, a month?

"Perfect. I'll email you the other terms of your employment, some current events and issues here in Newport I'd like you to read up on, and the contract—please sign and return. I'm not sure what you're planning to do about housing, but the summer market here is quite hot. I suggest you get a jump on it."

"Absolutely, I will. Thank you!" Caroline hung up, and for the first time since the breakup, she actually wanted to jump in the air, which was quite an anomaly seeing as how all she'd eaten lately was either deep fried or covered in cheese. She let out a squeal and didn't care if her neighbors heard.

After getting dressed, in real clothes instead of sweats, she grabbed a pack of gum from her kitchen, flipped on some music, and with new energy started putting her belongings into piles of what she would take, donate, or leave at her parents'. Sweaters—take. Lingerie she was saving for the honeymoon—burn. No, return. They still had the tags on them. Her limited-edition copy of *Anne of Green Gables*—take. On second thought, Rachel had always admired it, maybe even more than Caroline did. She'd give it to her friend as a parting gift. Miscellaneous personal items stuffed in her nightstand drawer ... *hmm.*

Much of it went directly into the trash—old receipts she didn't need, hand lotion she had squeezed the last drop out of. As she tossed a Bible she hadn't opened in longer than she'd admit to her parents onto her bed, a photo fell to the floor.

She paused a moment, then leaned over to pick it up. When she turned it over, she saw the words, nearly faded from the print but not from her memory, *I love you. Never doubt that.*

Her shoulders slumped. She had never doubted those words before. In fact, she'd believed them wholeheartedly. But now, it settled in a different way. *"Anyone willing to give you up doesn't deserve you anyway."* Her dad's words echoed in her heart. Of course, he was talking about something completely different. Still, Dillon had said he loved her, that he wanted to spend his life with her, but at the first real test of said love, their relationship came crumbling down. An unfamiliar heaviness filled her. She tucked the photo back in her Bible, then laid it in the take pile.

If only Dillon were in the take pile to help her navigate the move. *Am I doing the right thing?* Doubt crept in without warning.

Never mind. Moving forward. Dillon had made his choice, and she had cried enough.

She grabbed a fresh piece of gum, then chewed vigorously as she organized the rest of her bedroom. By the time she'd finished, her gum was gone and every bit of doubt had vanished. Most of the doubt had vanished. Some of the doubt had vanished. There was a fair amount of doubt left.

But whatever success was available to her in this Rhode Island adventure, she would find it.

And then she'd throw it in Dillon's face.

Maybe.

Chapter 5

D r. Stern looked surprisingly young to be such a highly lauded expert. She wore her brown hair in a short bob that just brushed the collar of her lab coat, then curled slightly to frame her angular face. In any other situation, Linda would have thought about what a "cute girl" she was. At this point, cuteness wasn't even a consideration.

"I agree with Dr. Klimt's initial assessment. However, we are going to do further testing to be absolutely specific about what we are dealing with. Today, we'll draw more labs and then send him down to radiology to do some imaging studies. Tomorrow morning, we'll need you back here for a bone marrow biopsy."

Brent scribbled furiously on a yellow pad of paper, while Maddox tousled his already messy hair. "I have a game tomorrow afternoon. Will I be done in time to get back and play?"

Linda's mouth fell open. How could he even think about games at a time like this? Thankfully, before she had a chance to say something she would later regret, Dr. Stern stepped in. "I'm so sorry, Maddox. I know all this is hard enough to hear without it muddling up the things you enjoy. The problem is, even if it is done on time, you'll need to take it easy for at least a day or two. The biopsy site will likely be sore for several days, but for the first day anyway, it's important to limit your activity and keep the area clean and dry."

He turned his face toward the wall and folded his arms across his chest. "Let's just get it over with then." He mumbled it so low that Linda could barely make out what he said. At other times, she would have given him a warning about being rude, but today, her heart was so broken for her son, she couldn't have scolded him for anything.

She looked at Dr. Stern. "What else do we need to do?"

"I expect to get results back from all of these tests by the end of the week at the latest. Barring anything unexpected, you should be ready to check into the hospital by Thursday or Friday. Plan on being here for a while."

"How long of a while?" Linda asked.

Brent leaned forward. "We've had several friends take chemo as outpatients. We're hoping to keep his life as routine as possible, so we definitely would like to explore that option."

"I wish that were a possibility, truly I do. Unfortunately, the particular kind of treatment in Maddox's case will cause very low blood counts. It's imperative that he live in a closely controlled environment while we are in the induction phase."

"How long?" Maddox's voice had a slight tremor.

"Depending on your response and how quickly your body rebounds, it could range from several weeks to several months."

"Months? What about school? What about...?"

Linda knew he had stopped speaking because he was fighting tears. She reached over to squeeze his arm, but he jerked away from her. "Leave me alone."

It stung. A lot. Still, she was prepared to endure anything, and if her son's anger at the situation was sometimes directed at her, then that was just the way it was going to be. She would be here for him, and she would take whatever he might dish out.

"Maddox, you're..." She refused to say it. Her son was sick, they all knew it, so there was no reason to keep repeating it. She took a deep breath and turned back to Dr. Stern. "We will be here tomorrow for the biopsy and will be prepared to come back as soon as you tell us it's time."

The doctor nodded. "In the meantime, I would suggest that we test your entire family as possible bone marrow matches in the event that becomes a necessity."

"Of course we will. What about his friends? Should they be tested, too?"

She opened her hands, palms up. "The more the better, however, the chances are much smaller of finding a match in someone who is not a close relative." She turned her palms down at the conclusion of her answer.

"We will be tested immediately." Linda left the room, thankful that there was at least some way in which she might be able to help.

...

What was today? Saturday maybe? Had it truly only been a couple of weeks since Linda spent Saturdays doing laundry, fussing about the boys tracking in mud, and polishing the antique wood floors? Now, sixty miles and a whole other world from home, she promised herself never again to worry about mud-tracked floors.

Maddox's phone occupied his attention. This was a good thing, so she focused on remaining perfectly still, letting him live for a moment as if he were just an average teenage kid having average text conversations with his average friends. For her to make even the slightest sound would remind him that she was here, and where *here* was, and the horrors he had endured in the past week, as well as the ones still in front of him. No, it was best that he forget all that.

Inside this hospital room that had been home for the past week and a half, time was measured not by weekdays or weekends, but only by numbers of days remaining in this round of chemo. Three. Just three more days and his body would get a break from the daily infusion of misery-inducing chemicals.

His phone kept buzzing every second or so with texts coming in fast and furious. "Wow." "Huh." "Get out." After multiple mumbles of exclamation, he said, "Mom, you've got to come see this."

She made her way over to his bedside, then reached for the phone he extended to her. On the screen was a photo of the high school parking lot packed with people lined up, stretching around the gymnasium and past the science building. Linda put her hand to her mouth and shook her head. "I can't believe it."

"Keaton said there are people everywhere, and they just keep coming. Someone said they're afraid they'll run out of swabs before they get everyone tested."

"See, I told you everyone wants to help you."

"Yeah, I just didn't realize there were this many everyones. Looks like the whole town just about, doesn't it?" He grinned up at her, with a hint of spark in his tired chocolate-colored eyes.

"Yes, it does." And it did indeed. She handed the phone back to him, as texts continued to come in.

So strong was the urge to keep looking at the pictures, she powered up her own phone—something Linda rarely did these days. She had committed herself to being fully present for Maddox when he needed her and didn't want to be distracted by texts and emails. Only a couple of times a day did she turn on her phone and send out an update on Maddox's situation—an email to a large group of concerned people and a text to a much smaller group of close friends and family that contained more of the nitty-gritty details. There had been far too many of these.

She walked to the window as her screen lit with over a dozen text notifications. Her friends had sent pictures similar to the ones she'd just seen. Looking at them made her heart a little lighter, as if maybe they really weren't alone, that maybe there was help for them somewhere.

When word had circulated around Portsmouth that a sixteen-year-old was in desperate need of a bone marrow transplant, the response had been amazing. Posters and signs showed up in shop windows, announcements were made on the radio and at every church in the area, newspapers and even WPRI had done feature stories. So the fact there was a large turnout for today's bone marrow search wasn't all that surprising. But this wasn't just a large turnout. It was gigantic. Far beyond Linda's wildest hopes. There had to be a match for Maddox somewhere in that group of people. There just had to be.

His phone continued to ping, bringing a trace of a grin across his pale face. A few years from now, this would all be a distant memory—the mouth sores, the rashes, the nausea. Today's show of support would be one of the more poignant scenes in the rearview mirror. Linda was thankful for that.

She started toward her chair, happier than she had felt in a long time. Before she took the second step, however, the all-too-familiar sound of retching filled the room. From instinct borne of habit, she grabbed the emesis basin and rushed toward the bed.

Too late.

The sheets would have to be changed.

Again.

CHAPTER 6

It wasn't until the Uber brought Caroline over the Newport Bridge and dropped her off in front of a furnished rental on a gray May evening when the consequences of her decision really started to set in. Of course, she'd had plenty of second thoughts while she was packing and saying good-bye to friends and family, but she'd done a fairly decent job of powering through and keeping her focus. She was on to bigger and better things.

But now, her body ached from nearly ten hours of traveling, she was hungry, and she didn't know a single person within three thousand miles. It's not that she was expecting a welcome reception, but a card in her mailbox would be nice. She peeked inside. Nope. It was empty.

No matter. Minor speed bumps.

She took a deep breath, smelling the ocean a half mile away, and shook off the negativity that threatened to taint the significance of the moment. She found the key her landlord had left in a lockbox, then headed to the front door of the small two-bedroom Cape-style bungalow. The blue shutters and American flag flapping in the wind were indeed "quaint" as the advertisement had promised, and the landscaping was neat and tidy, but her ringing phone prevented her from inspecting the inside any further than just beyond the entryway. She plopped her two large suitcases and her purse on the floor, then answered.

"Hi, honey. It's me. Did you get there all right?"

"Hey, Mom. Yeah, I just walked in the door, actually."

"Oh, good. What's the house like, as cute as the pictures?"

Caroline walked into a small living room. "Well, I certainly wouldn't have chosen the paint color." She made her way into the kitchen. "But it's clean and has a nice beachy feel."

Mom continued as Caroline walked up the stairs. "Maybe the landlord will let you tweak a few things."

"It will be fine." Caroline looked into the smaller of the two bedrooms. "The guest bedroom is pretty cute. I'll have it all ready for you before you get here."

"Listen, I'll do my best to fly out for your birthday. Hopefully Gram Gram will be well enough for me to escape for a long weekend, but until then, we all love you, we're praying for you, and cheering for you from California, okay?"

Caroline didn't know where they came from, but as she stood at the top of the staircase, her vision became clouded by an onset of tears that was as unexpected as it was unwelcome. She was twenty-eight years old, for goodness' sake. But her mother's voice felt so much farther than three thousand miles away. "Thanks, Mom. I miss you guys already."

"Aww, we miss you, too, but we'll see each other soon. Call us often and send pictures. You know how much Gram Gram likes to see what you're up to."

"I will. Talk to you later." As soon as Caroline hung up, she wiped her nose on her sleeve, then hauled her suitcases up the stairs to her bedroom.

The house was small, but it was more space than she'd ever had to herself. Or that she ever thought she would have to herself. She fought off another threat of emotion.

Maybe I can get a cat to keep me company. Dillon was allergic, so she was never able to entertain the idea before now.

But as soon as she did, she groaned. Coming to grips with being an ex-fiancée was one thing. The cat lady image was quite another, and certainly not worth the risk, regardless of whether or not she wanted one. *No, no cat.*

Caroline grabbed a fresh pack of gum, then started to unpack. Soon, her pictures were on the nightstands, her clothes were in the closet, and tomorrow she would go to the grocery store and get food. It still wasn't exactly her home, but it felt more like it by the time her suitcases were empty. See? Everything was going to be fine.

She had a pizza delivered, and after a long shower, she finally settled into bed. Although she had no sense of what time it was. She grabbed her phone: 12:38 a.m. It was only 11:38 p.m. in Texas—yesterday.

Caroline smiled. She was living an hour ahead of Dillon. In a small way, she had moved forward, even if her heart hadn't yet caught up.

The hardest part was behind her... she hoped.

...

Caroline peeled her eyes open the following Monday morning but not by choice. She'd tossed and turned much of the night, still unused to the bed in her rental, and her alarm yanked her from the little sleep she had gotten with a blaring foghorn.

She chose a preppy yet professional hot-pink blouse and a pair of navy-blue business-casual capri pants for her first day of work. It was drizzling outside, but since her car was still being transported from California, she had no choice but to walk the half mile to her new office. Not ideal, but it would give her some time to wake up, sip her coffee, and tame the jitters of nervousness and excitement that had cemented themselves in the pit of her stomach. Not to mention stare at The Elms with her own two eyes.

She nearly gasped as she stood on Bellevue Avenue's sidewalk a few minutes later. She'd seen the majestic mansion on the Preservation Society's website and in books, but nothing could compare with seeing the home modeled after a mid-eighteenth century French chateau up close. When the Berwinds first opened the house in the early 1900s, they threw quite a party—with two bands so there was never an interruption in the music and monkeys running around the lawn. She'd read about it when she first applied for the job.

The house was spectacular and proof that a young, unknown professional from out of town—architect Horace Trumbauer, if she recalled correctly—could create something worth admiring. She'd have to take a tour as soon as possible.

A short while later, she walked through the wooden double doors of the stone mansion the Preservation Society had converted into their offices. Then she was greeted by a tall, blonde woman with not a single hair out of place.

"Caroline?" She extended a slender, manicured hand. "I'm Audrey Brooks. So wonderful to have you here."

Caroline smiled and returned the handshake. "I'm thrilled to be here. I can't wait to get started."

"Let me show you around." Audrey led her across the large entryway, the canary-yellow walls attempting to perk up the seriousness of the dark, six-foot wainscoting and deep-red carpet. She pointed out the staff kitchen, bathrooms, and the library and archives room downstairs, then motioned toward a sliding dark-wood door at the other end of a hall. "I've arranged a board meeting for this morning that I'd like you to be part of, so we'll wait to go in there. Your office is upstairs. Shall we?"

Caroline nodded and started to follow Audrey's brisk assent on the dimly lit, carpeted stairs at the back of the building when a voice thrust through the silence.

"Ms. Brooks, a moment?"

Audrey turned, then Caroline followed suit. A thin young man with a black goatee stood at the bottom of the stairs, holding a notepad, pencil, and phone.

"What is it, Aiden?" Audrey sighed but then stepped down a few steps and smoothed her navy pencil skirt. Did Audrey know him, or had she just read his name off the *Aquidneck Island News* name tag hanging from his neck?

Aiden cleared his throat. "Can you please comment on the Chadwick? They are on track to—"

Audrey's hands went up, silencing Aiden. "The issue has been settled in court. I have nothing further to say about it, except it was Mr. Chadwick's wish that his mansion, Chadwick Place, be donated to the Preservation Society, and that did not happen. It's a shame."

Aiden nodded and jotted on his notepad. "How do you respond to project manager Chris Stratton's assertion that the historical restoration is being done accurately?"

Audrey shook her head and snickered. "We'll see about that."

"What about his argument that if the property—*when* the property—becomes a hotel, guests will be able to participate in a historical experience rather than just look at a piece of property?"

Audrey squinted and stared at the ceiling. Caroline had read about this in the packet Audrey emailed her. Something about a dispute between Tom Williams's hotel group and the Preservation Society over a mansion and the lack of a will? She was fuzzy on the specific details, but what

Caroline remembered clearly was the cost—both of the renovation and to stay as a guest.

"One has to wonder how they'll be able to do that if they are charging one thousand dollars a night." The words emerged from Caroline's mouth before she remembered she wasn't the one being interviewed.

Both Aiden and Audrey looked her way, and Caroline wished she wasn't wearing such a brightly colored top. Should she keep talking, shut up, or excuse herself to find her office on her own?

She took Audrey's slight smile as a cue to continue, but her voice was unsteady. "Well, our goal is to make the extravagant history of Newport accessible to everyone. It seems unless you have enough money, the Chadwick will be something to appreciate from afar but not experience."

Audrey nodded and pointed a finger at Caroline, as if adding an exclamation point to the end of Caroline's argument. "Exactly."

"And you are?" Aiden's pencil was scribbling across the pad.

"This is Caroline Chapman." Audrey set her hand on Caroline's shoulder. "She is our new director of special events, from California, and the official spokeswoman on this matter. Any further questions can be directed to her. Now, if you'll excuse us?"

"Good day, ladies." Aiden turned and let himself out a side door near the bottom of the stairs.

"Well done. I knew I hired you for a reason." Audrey smiled, then glanced at her watch. "I'm sorry. We'll have to finish up the tour later. Let's head to the boardroom."

Caroline's mouth was dry. She smiled back, but all she really wanted to do was run out and tell Aiden there were undoubtedly far more qualified people for the role; it wasn't exactly in the job description. She followed Audrey and took a few deep breaths along the way.

As soon as Caroline walked in the door, eighteen bodies that looked as though they'd escaped from a Brooks Brothers' catalogue turned her way then settled into their seats.

"Ladies and gentlemen." Audrey sat at the head of the table and then motioned for Caroline to sit next to her. "I'm pleased to introduce you to Caroline Chapman. Caroline, the board of trustees."

She stuffed her nerves away and smiled a hello to each of them as two more women entered the room.

"Ah, thanks for joining." Audrey pointed to two empty chairs at the end of the table. "This is Gloria, our treasurer, and Ruth, our head of marketing. Caroline, you'll be working closely with both of them, so I've asked them to join us."

Ruth nodded, her black, curly hair held in place with a bit too much gel. Gloria offered a quick smile in acknowledgment, then flipped her short silver hair off her face before she opened a file on the table.

"Now, we're about to enter a new fiscal year, but last year we brought in quite a bit less than anticipated since we had to close several properties for overdue cleaning and restoration." Audrey seemed to be talking more to Caroline than the board—undoubtedly they were already aware of this. "In addition, losing Chadwick Place was devastating. A new property would have really helped. Now we have another major competitor for corporate events, social events, and weddings, all of which are significant sources of revenue."

Caroline made a mental note to look into the details of the hotel more thoroughly and to plan a visit. At least to see what all the fuss was about, if not to prepare for her new, albeit unanticipated, role.

Audrey continued. "Our summer calendar is set. Caroline, you will ensure everything goes off without a hitch, especially our annual fundraiser in August. That is crucial. But come fall, we're really counting on you to keep things going, to create some new and inspiring events." Her eyebrows rose at that last part.

"We can always have a Halloween-themed Clue party at one of the mansions. You know, Colonel Mustard in the ballroom with a candlestick?" She was about to tell Gloria she'd make a great Mrs. White, but after seeing her mouth fall open, Caroline opted to keep quiet. "Never mind..."

An older gentleman in a navy blazer leaned forward, then rested his elbows on the table. "We are a nonprofit. Revenue is not our end goal, but without it, we won't be able to keep the mansions up to standard. I hope you understand the seriousness of that."

Caroline swallowed. "Of course." *Oh, good heavens.* She could rattle off a list of ten events that had worked wonderfully at the Huntington Library, and she chose to make a joke about a Clue party? At least when she had suggested it in jest to the Huntington's board, they all got a good laugh out of it. Now she just wanted to crawl into the floor.

She spent the next several minutes—truthfully she didn't know how long—looking down at her lap and willing her hands to stop fidgeting. She could hear Audrey and several board members' discussion going back and forth, but it just sounded like the grown-ups in a Charlie Brown movie—*wha wha wha wha wha.* Her heart was pounding too loudly for her to really pick up on anything of consequence.

"Caroline, Ruth, and Gloria: thanks so much for joining us." Audrey's voice jolted Caroline out of her trance. "We will continue this meeting privately. Ruth, will you please show Caroline up to her office?"

It wasn't until Caroline exited the boardroom that she exhaled. She followed Ruth up the back stairs in silence and was content to do so, until Ruth interjected with a loud whisper, "I think a Clue party sounds wicked fun." Her deep-brown eyes glimmered as she spoke.

Wicked? Was that a good thing? "It was just a joke."

"I say we do it." This time, her smile seemed to cast its vote for the proposal as well.

"Really?"

"Why not? Gloria can be Mrs. White!" She followed this with a robust laugh, then pointed to a small room at the end of the hall. The wood floors creaked as she walked in. "Here, you and I share this room."

Caroline followed, then settled at her desk. It sat in front of a large window that overlooked the building's side lawn, and she could see a few sparrows in the birdbath.

"Not a bad view, right? On a clear day, you'll be able to see the ocean. Just a peek of it through those trees, but nice, nonetheless. You're from California so I thought you'd like that desk."

"Thank you."

Ruth flopped into her swivel chair facing the adjacent wall.

Ruth's welcome tamed her heart rate, and she was momentarily able to forget that horrendous first impression she'd made downstairs. As she pulled her laptop from her bag, she couldn't help but feel like she'd made a friend.

And eighteen enemies.

CHAPTER 7

Linda held Brent's hand as they sat across the conference table from Dr. Stern and two pediatric oncology residents. Dr. Stern's expression was serene, as always. Hard to imagine how she managed this in the midst of what she saw on a daily basis. Of course, she treated other people's children, not her own.

She looked at her notes for a moment. "The good news is, once we finally found the right cocktail of drugs, Maddox has shown an encouraging response to treatment."

Linda knew what she meant by the *right* cocktail, because there had been a couple of the wrong kind before now. This right mixture did not cause her son to have a seizure, or an allergic reaction, or his kidneys to shut down. But now his response was *encouraging*. That was a word she could latch on to.

"On the other hand, we have not found an acceptable donor." Dr. Stern clicked her ballpoint pen several times. "That is unfortunate."

Unfortunate?

Brent leaned forward, extending his hands as if arguing logic to a potential client. "Over a thousand people have turned out for the marrow drives. Surely one of them will be a match." He paused for a second. "And what about his brother?"

Dr. Stern shook her head. "Only about one in four siblings present as a close match, and regrettably, Marshall did not beat those odds. We are continuing to search databases, where new people are added on a daily basis."

Brent rested his forehead against his right hand in defeat. Six years ago, he had watched as his mother lost her battle with cancer. It hadn't taken long, but Linda knew that he still had pictures in his mind of her last month: thin and wasted and barely conscious. For his son to be headed in that direction—well, it was one of the things that gave him nightmares. His next words sounded thick and choked. "And if no suitable donor is found, what happens then?"

Dr. Stern took a deep breath and nodded, as if agreeing that it was a fair question—but perhaps one she didn't want to answer. "There is a high likelihood that his cancer will return." She paused for a moment. "There are a few other options for treatment, but a matched donor is his best hope at a long-term remission."

His best hope.

Brent didn't say anything. Linda suspected he feared he would break down if he spoke again.

He needed Linda. They all needed her. She somehow managed to speak. "Thank you for all that you're doing."

Dr. Stern reached across the table and squeezed her arm. Her smile was gentle. "We're going to fight for your son with everything we've got."

"I know you will." Linda heard the words coming from her mouth as if someone else was speaking. "We really do appreciate it—all of it."

The medical team stood and walked out, leaving Linda and Brent alone in the small conference room. The two of them sat staring at the table. Linda put her hand on his arm. "Things are going to be okay. Our friends are praying, the doctors are working hard, Maddox is fighting with all his strength. It's going to be okay." *Would it? Would anything ever be okay?* Regardless of the answer, she had a role to play, and that involved saying words that she wasn't sure she believed.

Brent stood. "I need to go make a couple of calls." He didn't look at her as he hurried from the room.

The emptiness hung heavy around her. There was only one thing left to do, one possible way to increase the chances to make things *okay*. She'd spent the past few weeks preparing herself for this, just in case, and now the time had come.

She reached inside her purse and removed a newspaper article, which she unfolded to reveal the sticky note inside. Written across the cheery yellow paper, in blue permanent ink, was the contact information that could potentially fix everything.

It also might destroy every good thing left in her life.

CHAPTER 8

Don't look down. Look up. The sky—it was the color of those blue hydrangeas that used to grow in the front yard back home. The ones that would bloom like crazy all summer and fill vases in every room of the house for three months straight. But from third-story scaffolding, Chris Stratton really didn't care what color it was.

"I need a break. I think I'm going to grab my lunch." He took off his Red Sox hat, then wiped his forehead with the bottom of his athletic shirt. They hadn't made much progress in the two weeks they'd painstakingly been removing the limestone facade from the Chadwick. The last three and a half hours weren't much different. At this rate, they'd be done by Memorial Day, all right … five years from now.

As he began the slow and steady descent, a faint voice came from ground level. "Chris, there's someone who wants to talk to you."

He forced his gaze downward, then spotted Miguel, the head stonemason, and a young woman standing nearby. Good, it wasn't one of the city inspectors.

He climbed down, grabbed his water bottle, then wiped another bead of sweat running down his cheek with his shoulder as he walked over to her. Standing next to Miguel, she looked about the size of a Chihuahua. A cute

Chihuahua, but still, it probably wasn't something he should say out loud. "Can I help you?"

"You're Chris Stratton? The project manager?"

"Yeah."

"Oh, I don't think I've ever seen a project manager that's so ..." She tilted her head to the side.

"Let me guess, young?" It was the only way anyone ever finished that sentence. At thirty-two, it was a fair statement, but after three years of being Tom Williams's project manager, you'd think people wouldn't care anymore.

"I was going to say 'hands on.'" She pointed toward the scaffolding.

"Oh, I'll take that as a compliment." He smiled, then drained the last of his water.

"I'm Caroline Chapman, Newport Preservation Society."

Chris nearly spit out the water left in his mouth. He couldn't believe it, but he would have preferred a city inspector. They were a pain, but at least dealing with them was in his wheelhouse. He reached out and shook Caroline's hand anyway. "What can I do for you?"

"I was wondering if you would take a moment to show me around." She looked directly at him, giving Chris the hint this wasn't optional.

Great, just what he needed. The uneasiness in his stomach grew but getting on this woman's bad side could create further problems he had no desire to deal with. "Sure, come on in."

As he led her toward the front door, he couldn't shake her name—it sounded familiar, but she hadn't been part of any of the court proceedings regarding the property. Then it hit him. "Wait, Caroline Chapman, as in NPS's official spokeswoman on the Chadwick?"

"I gather you read *Aquidneck Island News'* latest article." A whisper of a smile formed across her lips.

"It was about my project, wasn't it?" Judging by her flinch, he guessed he'd sounded as arrogant to her as he did to himself. He sighed, relaxed his shoulders, then tried again. "I try to keep up on the media—PR and all."

He didn't mean to be a turnoff, but he was plain sick of all the holdups NPS had caused. He'd just as soon move on and never give them another thought. Now their "spokeswoman" had not only drawn negative attention to the hotel's prices, she was standing in what was going to be the lobby. "Well, as you can see, demo is well underway."

Caroline stood on the exposed subfloors and observed the room. All the walls were open so at least she was too late to object about the original wallpaper being ripped out. It was hideous anyway. Then her attention seemed to shift to a pile of rubbish in the corner.

She walked over to the pile, then dragged out a large chandelier with a few dozen missing pieces of crystal. "Are you getting rid of this?"

"Uh, yes?" His phone chimed from his pocket, so he reached in to see what problem awaited him this time. He could hear Caroline objecting in the background but tuned her out as he focused on the text. One catastrophe at a time.

The garbage disposal at home needs to be fixed, and you said you'd take me to dinner! Love you anyway...

Chris let out a groan. He'd forgotten all about dinner and wished he could forget about the garbage disposal.

"Is there a problem?" Caroline looked at him again. He hadn't noticed how blue her eyes were before. Like those hydrangeas.

"The women in my life can be a little demanding, that's all." He smiled.

"Oh." Caroline pointed to the chandelier again. "Well, as I was saying, this can be refurbished. You're not going to reinstall it? I thought you were trying to keep the house historically accurate."

Chris shrugged. "The designer wants it out."

"If you're just going to throw it away, can we have it?"

"It's all yours." Perfect. That would save them a whopping ten dollars at the dump. Actually, NPS was a nonprofit. He could make this a tax-deductible donation. Even better.

"Great, let me get a few photos, and I'll arrange to have it picked up." Caroline reached in her purse and took out her phone.

"Chris, can you come out here a minute?" Miguel stood outside, leaning his head into the entryway. "I need you to look at something, pronto."

Chris nodded, then turned to Caroline. "Be right back."

When he and Miguel were standing in front of the Chadwick, Miguel pointed up to the scaffolding where the other men were still working. "Mold. Behind the stone."

Chris could see it from ground level. "Great." He let out a sigh and rubbed his hand along his jawbone, then down his chin. "This will set us back and we'll have to tell Tom." His mouth was dry, which gave him an idea. "Del's lemonade on me if you make the call."

"No way, man. That's why you get paid the big bucks."

It settled like bad sushi, but it was true. And he needed every cent. "Fine. Let's get a remediation expert out here as soon as possible. Better pray this doesn't delay things too much, or we're both in for it. And then you can go get the Del's."

As Chris walked back into the hotel, he pulled out his phone to lower the boom, then stopped. No, he'd better wait until after lunch, and after NPS's spy was out of earshot.

"Okay, I'm back. You want to go upstairs? Or check out the view of Easton's Beach?"

She didn't move. In fact, she resembled that garden statue they'd tossed last week. Was it the lighting, or was her face getting pale? "Hello? You okay?"

"I, um, I'm sorry, I need a minute." She stared at her phone for a few more moments, then put it in her pocket. "Actually, something's come up. I need to go. I'll get back to you about the chandelier." She turned, then walked, no, ran out of the room.

Well that was odd. By the time Chris headed back outside, she'd disappeared. Perhaps the nose fell off of Alva Vanderbilt's marble bust at The Elms or some such calamity.

...

Caroline ran the entire way home from the Chadwick, and by the time she made it to her front door, she had to stop a moment to catch her breath. She fell onto the sofa just as her knees were about to give way, then fumbled for her phone.

"Mom," Caroline practically shouted as soon as she picked up.

"Honey, are you okay?"

"I don't know. I just, I can't even believe this. One minute I was trying to salvage a chandelier from a construction site and the next—"

"Stop right now and calm down."

Caroline took a few deep breaths, letting each out slowly.

"Okay, good. Now tell me what's the matter."

"I got an email marked urgent from someone who says she's my birth mom, and her son ..." The words jumbled in her own head. How could she possibly communicate them to someone else? "I'll just read it to you." Caroline put her mom on speakerphone, pressed her email icon, then took another deep breath.

Dear Caroline,

My name is Linda Riley. You do not know me or, at least, it's been a really long time since we've seen each other—although we were once very close. The truth is, I am your birth mother.

I'm not sure how you feel about hearing from me after all these years. If you have any questions, I am happy to answer anything at any time. If this contact upsets you, please forgive me. That is something I would never intentionally do. But necessity has dictated that I reach out to you now, and that I do it immediately. There is something I must ask of you. No, I don't ask. I beg.

My son has cancer. His name is Maddox and he's sixteen, and he is such a good kid, and he desperately needs your help. A bone marrow transplant is his only chance at returning to a healthy life. Everyone we know has been tested, and there are no suitable donors. Since you are his half sister, it is possible you would be a match. Will you please consider being tested so we can find out? You are my only hope, and I throw myself and my son's life at your mercy.

This email must have come as quite a shock, and you clearly have a lot to take in. If you need to speak face-to-face, I will drive to wherever you want, whenever you want, just please, please help me. Even if you are angry at me, even if you hate me, that's okay. You most certainly don't owe me anything, but please help Maddox. His life depends on it.

Linda Riley
401-555-7642

"Wow." Mom broke the lingering silence, but her voice was quiet. "That's so sad to hear."

"Yes, it is." Caroline pulled her knees up to her chest and wrapped her arms around her legs. Her heart was still racing. "But...I thought Linda Newton was my birth mom. Do you think this is a mix-up?"

"Maybe Riley is her married name, I don't know. I kept in touch with her for a little while, sent her pictures of you, but when you turned one, she mailed me a letter asking me to stop. That's when she sent that picture you have and asked me to give it to you when you were old enough to know what happened."

The photo jogged her memory in her now half-functioning brain. Had she brought it with her? Was it at her parents' house? That's right, she'd tucked it in her Bible before the move. "Hold on, I'm going upstairs." When she made it to her room, she searched her nightstand drawer and found the Bible and photo.

There was Linda Newton or Riley or whoever she was lying in a hospital bed, holding a newborn—Caroline. She'd looked at this picture so many times when she was younger, but now, for the first time, it all hit her in a different way. She couldn't really make sense of it at the moment.

Caroline turned the picture over and read the words in that familiar handwriting she'd first seen when she was ten years old: *I love you. Never doubt that.* Her throat tightened, and her mind didn't know where to settle.

For practically her entire life, Caroline felt that Linda was just a woman out there somewhere—"selfless enough to give Caroline to good parents" as her mother had told her—and yet...uninterested in getting photos and updates after Caroline turned one? And now, an email from her was sitting in her in-box.

Asking to meet.

Caroline sat on her bed, then flopped her head onto her pillow. "So you think this email is real?"

Mom sighed. "It sure seems to be. I don't see how anyone else could get that information."

She stared at the wall and massaged her forehead for a few moments. "This isn't what I planned on dealing with two weeks into my new job."

"I doubt Linda planned on her son getting cancer."

Her mom's words shot through the phone and landed in a pit in Caroline's stomach. She closed her eyes and sighed. "That's not what I meant. I'll help if I can. I meant… the rest of it. Meeting. Getting involved."

The remaining shards of her heart post-Dillon started to ache. Now was time to move forward, not have the past come barreling into her life at full throttle, and with cancer. This felt like the time she had gotten caught in an undertow at Laguna Beach. Every time she made a sliver of progress toward the sand, another wave would topple her. And it was Dillon, junior lifeguard since he was eight, who pulled her out.

The air-conditioning kicked on. "Did you know she lived in Rhode Island? Twenty minutes away from Newport?"

"I had no idea. The last address I had was in Massachusetts. Peabody, I think." Mom paused. "I think you should take some time to process this. Pray about it. I'll let Dad know, and then we'll all talk more about it, okay?"

"Okay." Caroline ran her hand against the back of her neck.

"But if you do decide to meet her, please tell her thank you. For giving me the greatest gift I've ever received."

Chapter 9

*H*ey, *everyone, time for the daily check-in. I just sent out the larger group email, but on a more personal note, it's been a hard day for Maddox. He's been really sick and seems more discouraged than usual. Send extra prayers his way. Love to you all —L*

Linda had barely hit Send when she got the first response. *How are you? How can I help you?*

She fired back the usual answer. *Pray for Maddox. That's all I need. He's asleep now, so I'm going to take a little walk and get some fresh air.*

She would send a similar text at least five more times tonight. It wasn't exactly truthful, but it was what people wanted to hear. They all needed her to be solid and dependable and full of faith and hope. Not just Maddox, but Brent and Marshall, her friends, and people at church, too.

Maddox had fallen into an exhausted sleep, but Linda's "walk" went only as far as the cold tile of the bathroom floor adjoining her son's hospital room, where she fell to her knees and allowed herself to sob. She buried her face deep into a towel to muffle any noise. She couldn't disturb her son.

After the initial shock of the diagnosis, she had managed to hold herself together, to be strong for everyone else. She had done what she was supposed to—pretended, put on a brave face, conducted her life in what could only be called a fraudulent manner as she spouted out words of peace and optimism and perseverance—until now. Now everything seemed so hopeless, she couldn't fake it anymore.

After a while, she dried her eyes, sat back, and simply stared at the back of the door. At some point, she realized that she was banging her head against the wall behind her—not hard, but persistently. How long had she been doing it? Everything about her was so numb right now, it just didn't matter. However, the idea that the noise might wake Maddox was enough to make her stop.

She reached for her purse and pulled out her phone. Two texts and seven new emails in the past fifteen minutes. She clicked the envelope icon and held her breath as she scrolled down the list.

Nothing but the usual.

All of these emails were from friends and family on the update list. She knew they were full of the *we are praying for/ thinking about/ sending good thoughts* type sentiments, likely accompanied by the usual uplifting verses and quotes people sent at a time like this. And she appreciated them. Every one of them. Really, she did. But right now, there was only one email she wanted to see in her in-box, the same one she'd been both anticipating and fearing for two days now. The same one that still hadn't arrived.

She reached inside her bag and pulled out the news article she had printed several weeks ago, as soon as she heard that bone marrow donors would be needed. At the time, she'd assumed they would find a donor quickly, and mostly did this research because staying busy at something potentially useful helped keep her sane.

So, she had googled Caroline's name, something she had done thousands of times over the years. This time, however, she almost fell out of her chair when she found this article.

Caroline, it seemed, had just taken a new job and was now living and working less than half an hour away. When Linda had first seen it, before she thought this information would be necessary for Maddox's sake, she procured a hard copy of the newspaper, tore out the page, and put it into her purse where she planned to leave it untouched. She'd thought that maybe after this crisis was over, she would ... what? Contact Caroline? No, she hadn't seen how that could be the right thing for anyone.

By now, however, this article had been removed and unfolded so many times it was getting torn and dirty around the edges. The headline "Bringing New Life to a Grand Dame of the Coast" stood prominently at the top of the page. The article went on to detail the renovation currently being undertaken on a historic hotel and extensive interviews with the construction manager. "We're creating an experience. One where guests can step back in time and enjoy the glamor of the Gilded Age, without forgoing the modern luxuries and comforts of home they're accustomed to. Authentic restoration can be quite challenging, but we are off to a great start and expect the results to be worth the extra effort."

Beneath the cover story, a much smaller article had addressed the "authentic restoration" issue. The Newport Preservation Society was raising quite a few arguments against the project and the way it was being carried out. These issues were such a recurring event in this part of the country—historic renovation, fights with the preservation society, etc.—that Linda would not have considered the article in any way significant. Except for the newly appointed spokeswoman of the Newport Preservation Society.

Caroline Chapman.

What were the odds of Caroline being this close to her right now? Having moved here from across the country within a month of all this happening to Maddox? Astronomical odds. Unbelievable. Surely God had brought her here for a reason.

At first, Linda had hoped it was so she could perhaps catch a glimpse of the young woman her daughter had turned out to be. Just to allow Linda to feel the peace of knowing everything had turned out well for everyone. Now, though, she believed it had to be something else. *"For just such a time as this..."*

Esther may have saved an entire nation when Mordecai said those words to her long ago, but each life had value. Maybe Caroline's such a time was all about one life.

Maddox's life.

If that were the case though, why wasn't she answering her email?

CHAPTER 10

By the time Saturday arrived, Caroline needed more than a break, she needed a therapist. She'd been trying to focus on the plans for the annual children's tea party, but no matter how many packs of gum she chewed, she simply couldn't keep her thoughts grounded on her work. Her mind kept drifting back to Linda's email, inducing an inner debate over how to respond. Being tested to see if she was a match for Maddox was one thing—a simple cheek swab. A face-to-face meeting with Linda was quite another.

The only other people she could really talk to about this were her parents. Her close friends knew she was adopted, of course, but she always got the feeling that talking about it made them feel awkward. Like they didn't know what to say. Dillon? He'd probably have some good insight or suggest some pragmatic things to think about before she made an emotional decision. But the idea of calling him made her queasy.

She decided to walk down to Bellevue Coffee and at least begin her day with a therapeutic beverage. The morning clouds were thick, but with sun in the forecast for the afternoon, she grabbed her Dodgers hat on the way out.

She got her usual skim latte, then sat at the picnic table in the corner of the café's patio, next to a black flower box and the white picket fence bordering the parking lot. A blue jay landed on the fence a few feet away, its eyes fixed on the toddler's toasted bagel at the next table. Come to think of it, the bagel looked pretty good to her, too. No wonder the bird wanted it.

A family trip to Monterey emerged from her memory. She had been six, maybe seven. They were walking on the pier, and her dad bought her a carton of dead fish to throw to the sea lions down in the water. She was about to toss one over when a seagull swooped in and nabbed the fish, biting Caroline's finger in the process. Her mom held her as she cried, and her dad bought her some cotton candy. She'd forgotten about that until now, and a warm ache nestled in her heart. She rubbed her hands up and down her bare arms. Where's that sun her weather app had promised?

Just then, someone tapped the back of her shoulder. "Excuse me, ma'am, but I'm going to have to ask you to leave."

"What?" She whipped around. Chris stood behind her, breathing heavily as if he'd been running, with a mischievous grin on his face.

"There are no Dodgers' fans allowed in Red Sox Nation, so I'm afraid you'll either have to burn that or find another place to live." He pointed to her hat.

"Oh, well excuse me. If this town ain't big enough for the two of us, you're welcome to go. The Preservation Society will take very good care of your hotel."

He ran a hand through his short, dark-brown hair. "It's not my hotel. I just do what the boss tells me to."

Even if your boss tells you to steal from a dead person? "What are you doing here, anyway?" Not that it was any of her business or that she even cared.

Chris tilted his head slightly and pointed toward the café door. "Getting coffee." His grin returned as if to say, "duh."

"I mean, in Newport. On a Saturday. Do you live here or...?"

"No, Tom Williams has a house here. I've been crashing in the guesthouse while we're working on the Chadwick. I was actually planning to email you later this morning. You never came back for the chandelier, and I need to clear stuff out."

"Oh, yeah. I've been really busy this week." Truthfully, she'd forgotten all about it, and in light of Linda's email, it really didn't seem to matter anymore. "My car isn't arriving until Monday, and I don't know if anyone from the office is around to get it today."

"Well, let me grab a coffee, and maybe I can lower my standards to sit with you for a few minutes, see if we can arrange something. Preservation Society, Dodgers' fan—two strikes." He rumpled his nose, turned, then strode into the coffee shop.

A few minutes passed and Caroline glanced at the time, then the exit. She was really hoping for a quiet morning, maybe a jog down Cliff Walk, not sitting and chitchatting with Wreck-It Ralph. Before she could make up her mind, he came back, coffee in hand, and sat across from her.

"I'm going back up to Boston this afternoon and on Tuesday I'm going to St. Lucia. The Canary Beach Resort is getting a new pool, and I need to make sure everything is up to par." He took a sip of his coffee.

Caroline crossed her legs under the table but remained silent. Wouldn't that be nice if her only concern was getting to St. Lucia?

"Not that any of that matters to you. I'm just saying if I leave the chandelier, I won't be here next week, and someone else will dump it. Can I bring it by your place on my way out of town?"

Caroline shifted again. Judging by his tall and muscular physique, he'd have a much easier time moving it than she would, but the idea of giving out her address made her stomach clench a smidgen. One too many episodes of *Blue Bloods*. "How about the porch at the office?"

"That works. What time should I meet you? I'd like to leave Newport by two."

"Just drop it off at your convenience. I'll walk over this afternoon, and I think I'll be able to drag it inside." She took the final sip of her coffee, and out of the corner of her eye she noticed the blue jay flying away, then looked back at Chris. "Thanks for thinking of it, by the way."

"Sure." Chris nodded, then took another sip of his coffee, then another. Just as she was about to tell him to have a nice trip, he spoke again. "So, what happened the other day? The roof cave in at Rosecliff or something?" He chuckled and set his cup on the table.

If only that were the case. "Not exactly."

"Audrey quit? Your latest event get canceled?"

This was getting annoying. "It's a personal thing, actually."

His smile faded and his shoulders fell slightly. "Oh, I'm sorry. I didn't mean to make a joke of it. I hope everything is okay."

"If you consider a cancer diagnosis okay, then everything's peachy." She pinched her lips together and sighed. "Never mind. Sorry."

"You have cancer?" Chris sat up, his mouth agape for a few moments.

"No." She rolled her eyes. She didn't know if that would relieve or disappoint him, given that she already had "two strikes." Okay, that wasn't exactly fair...

His eyes softened, almost like he was inviting her to keep talking. Or maybe it was just her imagination, sparked by her inability to process this situation in her head or over the phone any longer.

She almost spoke again, then paused. Okay, maybe going a tad further wouldn't hurt. "A boy who lives in Portsmouth has cancer, and his mother has reason to believe I could be a bone marrow donor, but I haven't been tested yet."

"Are you going to?"

She sat up a little straighter. "Of course, but…" Again, her thoughts teeter-tottered over how much to say. "Well, his mom also wants to meet, and I'm not really sure I want to get involved to that extent."

He shrugged. "Simple coffee would be nice. It might mean a lot to her."

"Simple?" Her cheeks warmed. What gave him the right to an opinion anyway? And a wrong opinion at that.

"Sorry, none of my business." Chris put his hands on the table and stood. "I hope it all works out, okay? I'll drop off the chandelier in a bit."

...

Chris finished the last of his coffee as he walked away, then chucked the cup into the recycling bin at the street corner, ready to resume his run.

"Simple coffee would be nice. Might mean a lot." He mocked himself under his breath. His words of wisdom tasted bitter on the way out the first time. The second, he wanted to spit. Maybe he should stick to giving advice he was actually willing to follow.

Just as he returned his earbuds to his ears, a call prevented him from starting up his music again and his run.

"Hey, Tom. What can I do for you?" He paced down Bellevue Avenue, past the Tennis Hall of Fame and a few shops he wouldn't be caught dead in.

"Just checking on that mold situation."

"Well, I've got Miguel and his crew working overtime so we can fully assess the situation, and the remediation guy came out yesterday. He said he'll have a preliminary estimate to me by Monday, but obviously without knowing how much mold there really is, he won't know the full scope of work required."

"Too many unknowns, Chris. I need facts."

His neck stiffened. "And you'll get them as soon as I have them. Do you want me to scratch St. Lucia?" Thankfully, he managed to control his tone.

"No, I need your eyes on that project for the next few days. But as soon as you return, I want answers."

"I will get it done."

Tom sighed. "I know. You've never given me reason to doubt that. I've just had it with the delays on that project, and I don't want to miss any of next year's tourist season. Listen, if you finish this job on time, I'll throw in a 20 percent bonus."

Chris stopped walking. He nearly stopped breathing. "Really?" Between his salary and that bonus, he was just about one year away from affording long overdue restoration. Or maybe it was retribution. "We will finish on time." Even if he had to build the place himself.

"Good. We'll talk later this week."

Chris hung up, then started running again, the quick and steady rhythm of his feet echoing the fuel of his momentum. One more year and Stratton Construction Company would be his.

...

After five long days of waiting and receiving no response from Caroline, Linda could wait no longer. Several possibilities played across her mind. Caroline might be intentionally ignoring the email, for any number of reasons—anger, hurt, resentment. Regardless of which of those might be true, Linda needed to speak to her. She would apologize, explain, and grovel if necessary.

Another possibility that had begun as a faint idea but had grown louder in her mind as the days passed with no response—what if she hadn't received the email? What if the online email address from the Preservation Society website was incorrect? What if it went to junk mail? What if Caroline just hadn't seen it yet?

Since today was Saturday, Brent and Marshall had arrived this morning to spend the day with Maddox. This was the day she drove home, washed her clothes, did routine chores—although there weren't many to do. Kristyn had assigned herself Mondays and Thursdays at the Riley home. Nonfamily visitors were discouraged at this point in treatment, so Kristyn turned her energy toward helping Brent and Marshall. She cleaned and cooked and did laundry and anything else she could think of that might be helpful and encouraging. Brent said she even brought fresh flowers a few times—the effect being mostly wasted on Marshall and himself, but the thought behind it was very much appreciated.

Today, outside the hospital, Linda could do whatever was necessary without fear of being overheard. But what to do?

She drove toward home, still clueless on how to proceed until she arrived at her usual exit. The familiar sign jarred her—MA-138S/Middletown & Newport Beaches.

Newport.

It was just twenty minutes farther down the road. What if she went there now?

In a flash the decision was made, and she drove toward her new goal, knowing perfectly well this was ridiculous. According to the website, the Preservation Society's office hours were Monday through Friday. But since there were likely many events this time of year, someone could be there on Saturday, right? Even if it wasn't Caroline, maybe one of her coworkers could give her contact information. Yes, that seemed like the best place to start.

It was a quick drive. She pulled to the curb in front of the gray stone mansion with the Newport Preservation Society sign out front. Before Maddox got sick, Linda would have marveled at the beauty of the place. She spent hours leafing through magazines of historic homes, restoration, and refinishing, searching for inspiration as she restored the dignity of the "dilapidated" colonial she had talked Brent into buying a decade ago.

In fact, she had met Brent while she was volunteering on a project with Habitat for Humanity. The two of them were young and excited about helping others with the talents they possessed—his publicity, hers painting and staining. All these years later, this beautiful old mansion meant nothing to her but the potential link toward saving her son's life.

A young man in jeans and a T-shirt was carrying a large box up the sidewalk toward the building. A surge of adrenaline shot through her. This was her chance!

She hurried out of her car, but by the time she was half-way up the sidewalk, he had already deposited the box on the front porch and started back toward his truck. "Excuse me, do you work here? Is anyone here today?"

The man laughed. "No, I definitely don't work here, and they are closed on weekends. You should try again on Monday."

He started past her, but desperation kicked in and she couldn't let him get away. "But you ... do you know the people here? Caroline Chapman maybe?"

The question stopped him in his tracks, and he turned to look at her again. "Who did you say you were?"

"I'm, uh ... a friend of her mother's. I need to talk to her about something important."

The man studied her for a minute, then shook his head. "Sorry I can't help you. Like I said, try again on Monday."

Linda forced herself to paste on a smile. "Thanks anyway."

He smiled back from underneath his Red Sox cap. "Have a good day."

She didn't know if she replied or not, but somehow she made it back to her car. Coming here had felt so hopeful, and now ... She would just have to try something else. Maybe she should call, just in case someone was inside. Yes, that sounded reasonable.

On the second ring, a perky female voice answered and instructed the caller to try again during normal business hours. Was that Caroline's voice?

She leaned her head against the steering wheel. *I've come this far. I can't give up yet. But what else is there to do?* Maybe drive around Newport and hope to find Caroline walking down the street? Ridiculous. Still, Linda considered every possible scenario as she drove away. She saw the sign for Bellevue Coffee and decided a latte might be helpful as she thought things through.

A couple minutes later, she was ensconced at a cute little picnic table on the patio beside a black flower box and a white picket fence. She liked the contrast and found this place somehow calming. She sipped her coffee, her mind spinning. *God, please show me what to do. Please help me. Or at least help Maddox.*

No new ideas presented themselves as she watched a bluebird flit about the patio picking up crumbs from the ground. She finished her coffee. Nothing left to do but go home. She would call the Preservation Society on Monday. She took one last glance at her cell phone. Three new emails. She pulled them up.

> *Dear Linda,*
>
> *First, I'd like to say how sorry I am about Maddox. It was certainly a shock to hear from you, especially under such circumstances. Of course, I would be happy to get tested to see if I am a match. What do I need to do and where do they do the testing? Regarding a meeting to discuss things, please give me some time to think further about it.*
>
> *Best,*
> *Caroline*

Oh, dear Jesus, thank You! Thank You! She's going to get tested!

Linda pulled away and drove back toward her house. Things were going to work out now, she just knew it.

CHAPTER 11

Linda waited until morning rounds, her stomach tied in knots over what she was about to do. When the group of doctors made their way into Maddox's room, and the residents and fellows began their usual poking and prodding and talking through today's medical progress, Linda nonchalantly walked over to Dr. Stern and handed her a folded piece of paper. Dr. Stern nodded so slightly it was almost indiscernible, then walked out into the hallway.

Less than a minute later she returned, walked over to Linda, and handed her the piece of paper. Her heart racing, Linda slipped it in her pocket. As soon as the team made their way out the door, she rushed into the bathroom.

On the front side of the paper was her own note— *Urgent, I need to speak with you ASAP. Privately.*

On the back side, in Dr. Stern's fairly neat script—*Meet me in my office after rounds. I should be there by 9.*

At 8:45 Linda was patrolling the hallway outside Dr. Stern's ninth floor office, willing her to hurry up. Five paces, turn. Five paces, turn. Glance at watch. 8:46.

Five paces, turn. Five paces, turn. Still 8:46. Five paces, turn.

At 8:53, Dr. Stern emerged from the stairwell door. Linda rushed toward her. "Thank you so much for meeting me like this."

"Of course. Let's go into my office." She unlocked the door to a cramped little closet of a space, the desk piled with thick charts. There was probably no such thing as a chart that wasn't thick in the life of an oncologist.

Dr. Stern closed the door and motioned Linda to a chair. "Have a seat and tell me what's going on."

Linda took a deep breath. "I know someone who has ordered a swab kit to get tested as a match for Maddox. The kit should arrive by tomorrow, and I wanted to ask you about getting the testing expedited for it."

Dr. Stern's expression was sympathetic. "It's great that you are getting more people to come forward to be tested. And continue doing that. The more people we test, the better. Just keep in mind that outside the immediate family, the odds decrease to the point where it doesn't make sense to waste time and resources on rushing a sample. Although I do fully understand the urgency of your situation, I'm just saying in this particular case, we have to go through the normal channels. I know it's not what you want to hear. I'm just explaining that the system is the system, and these things take more time than any of us would like."

"Here's the thing. This one is not outside the immediate family."

Dr. Stern looked at her doubtfully. "Really? Your husband and Marshall have both been test—"

"It's my daughter." Linda blurted it out before she lost her courage. "I have a daughter." *Deep breath, keep it together. You're not helping anyone if you fall apart now.* "She was born when I was in college. I ... didn't tell anyone about her. No one. I was studying out of state at the time, and even my parents never knew. Her biological father doesn't know she's alive, and my husband doesn't know that she ever existed."

Dr. Stern's usual serenity evaporated, leaving her wide eyed and her jaw dropped. She plopped into the seat across from Linda and rubbed the back of her head. "O—kay. We will definitely want to get this one fast-tracked. I'll make the call now. They'll do the initial testing from our own labs to make it faster." She shook her head, her eyes seeming to stare into space. "Are you going to tell them? Maddox? Your husband?"

"I ... uh ... not yet."

Dr. Stern had recovered her usual neutral expression, likely perfected over years from delivering bad news to parents of sick kids. Still, Linda somehow had the impression that she disapproved and felt the need to offer something in the way of explanation.

"It's just that, with all that is going on with Maddox right now, things are so hard for everyone. I don't see the point in coming out with this kind of disclosure if she is not a match. It wouldn't help anything."

Dr. Stern nodded. "It's your decision about what and when to tell them. As for now, can you write down her name, birth date, and all other pertinent information for me?" She pulled out a small notepad and pen from the pocket of her white lab coat. Both the notepad and the pen had some sort of drug name written across them, large, indecipherable words like the kind that surrounded almost everything happening with Maddox right now. Linda's hand shook as she wrote her daughter's name across the page. Her daughter. It all seemed so surreal.

She handed the piece of paper back to Dr. Stern, who took it with a nod. "Whether or not she is a match, we will do everything we can to help Maddox."

"I know." But she also knew that the piece of paper in Dr. Stern's hand was the best hope they had right now. The only real hope anywhere on the horizon.

The child Linda had given up, had left to someone else to raise, presented the only chance for saving the son she had kept.

She couldn't bring herself to think through the emotional difficulties behind this situation, the things they would all have to work through when the truth came out. Before that, though, the only thing that mattered was a match. They would deal with the rest of it after they'd saved Maddox's life.

...

"Oh, that looks great!" Caroline leaned over Ruth's computer and examined the newsletter that would go out to NPS's subscribers that afternoon. "Maybe just make this a bit larger?"

"No problem." Ruth adjusted the event's time and date font size.

La Fête, the name Caroline had chosen for this year's annual dinner and ball, was the last major event of the summer and historically the biggest source of revenue for NPS. All of the proceeds this year would be going toward historical restoration at Chateau-sur-Mer, and Caroline was determined to have the event bring in more than it did last year.

Caroline inspected the updates. "Perfect. And then we'll send a follow-up invitation at the beginning of August. Okay, I'm meeting the florist at eleven, so I have to run. I'll be back after lunch, and maybe we can talk about some fall events?" She reached into her purse for her keys, but just as she was about to leave, Gloria burst through the office doorway.

"Have you seen this?" She held up a copy of the *Aquidneck Island News*, then handed it to Caroline.

"No, why? What's in it?" Caroline perused the cover. It was this week's edition and had a picture of Newport Vineyards on the cover.

"Page 5." Gloria leaned over Caroline's shoulder.

It took Caroline a while to find what Gloria was referring to, but just before she was about to ask, she saw it. There, at the bottom of the page, was a picture of Caroline and Chris at Bellevue Coffee, the headline read, "Frenemies?"

Her cheeks got hot as she read the article aloud so Ruth could hear. "'Just when we thought the clash between Tom Williams and the Newport Preservation Society couldn't get any hotter, two rival employees Chris Stratton (Williams Hotel Group) and Caroline Chapman (NPS) were seen together, chatting over what appeared to be a friendly Saturday morning coffee. What were they discussing? And why did Chris leave so abruptly?'" That snippet was all she could take. Her breakfast nearly resurfaced when she saw the article's author: Aiden Pierce.

Caroline slapped the paper down on her desk. "I was…it was just…" She took a deep breath and collected her thoughts. "It was a chance meeting, and he sat down to discuss the chandelier. The one I put in the artifacts and archives room. The one you thought was 'stunning.'"

"Are you sure?" Gloria adjusted her glasses. "I don't care what you do with your spare time, but Chris Stratton?" She gagged. "If I ever got within ten feet of anyone from the Williams Hotel Group, they'd regret it."

Caroline sighed. "This is nothing more than tabloid drama. I can't believe Aiden was even allowed to run it. I don't remember seeing him there."

"I'll email the paper right now." Ruth swiveled around in her office chair. "We're one of their biggest advertisers, and I have a good relationship with the editor in chief."

"Thanks." Caroline handed the newspaper back to Gloria. "Burn this. And please don't show it to Audrey."

"She's the one who showed it to me."

Caroline's forehead started to sweat. "Wonderful. I have to go."

She walked past Gloria, then down the stairs and just as she made it outside, her phone rang. Now what? She usually didn't answer calls from numbers she didn't recognize, but just in case it had to do with La Fête, she answered.

"Hello?" She didn't mean to sound so snippy.

"Caroline Chapman, please?" The woman's voice was drenched in a thick southern accent.

"Speaking."

"This is Sharon White from Be The Match. You submitted a cheek swab for a patient in need of a bone marrow transplant recently. Can you confirm that please?"

Her heart started pounding. "Yes, for Maddox Riley." She did her best to compensate for the snarky tone she'd answered with, but nothing could compensate for the surprise. She wasn't expecting to hear back at all, let alone so quickly.

"I'm calling to notify you that from preliminary testing, we believe you are a potential match. We'd like to move forward with the next round of testing, but first I need to ask you a couple of questions."

"Oh." Her breathing nearly stopped for a moment. "Okay."

"Are you willing and, as far as you know, able to proceed with the donation process?"

Caroline got into her car and shut the door, her thoughts scurrying all over the place. "I believe so, yes."

"Do you have any reservations whatsoever about donating if you are selected by the transplant team to do so?"

She looked at the car's clock, the radio presets, the air-bag icon, the windshield. "Um, no?" Her voice squeaked a tad, so she cleared her throat and said it again, this time with more oomph.

"Great. I will be sending you a blood kit via overnight mail. You will need to take this to your local lab or blood bank immediately, and we will contact you again if you are qualified to donate."

"Okay, will do. Thank you." She hung up the phone, placed it in her lap, then took a deep breath. Then a few more.

Oh, Lord, help me. She tugged the clasp of her necklace and placed it behind her neck. Well, this wasn't some bizarre hoax or crazy mix-up or a case of mistaken identity. She was a sister. She had a brother—someone she was connected to in a way no one else on the planet was.

And her brother had cancer. Her. Brother. Had. Cancer. It was as foreign a phrase as Caroline had ever thought in her life. So far from reality, yet the truth of it knocked her head to the headrest. And maybe, just maybe, she would be the one to save him. To give him the greatest gift he'd ever receive.

Despite the heat in the car, a chill came over her. *Okay, calm down. One step at a time.*

Chapter 12

Good morning everyone. Checking in to let you know that Maddox is currently sleeping soundly. As each day between treatments goes by, he gets a little stronger. I am so thankful for each of you and your continued prayers and support. I'm about to spend time with my prayer journal to prepare myself for another day of hope for healing. Love to you all!

Linda sent the text, then settled into her corner chair, prayer journal in hand. The heavy cardstock of the cream-colored paper normally felt soothing to the touch. Today, it stared up at her, waiting. Linda stared back, pen poised, and wrote … absolutely nothing. What could she possibly say that she hadn't written hundreds of times before?

Maybe she could write about this morning's incident. But no. Someday they would read this journal as a family, and she needed to keep it positive. There was no need to remember Janice, the perky young woman from Dec My Room who had stopped by this morning. "Since you're one of our more long-term residents, you are eligible for a free room makeover. Maybe you've seen Randy's room across the hall? Or Samantha's next door?"

Maddox snorted. "Really? Princesses and Buzz Lightyear? You think that's going to make me feel better?"

"Maddox!" Linda jumped to her feet.

Janice didn't seem to notice anything out of the ordinary. Perhaps she was used to the rudeness of sick teenagers.

She grinned at him as if he'd just told a joke. "I certainly would not expect that, no. But if you're into a sport—football, say—we could set up a New England Patriots theme or your favorite college colors, perhaps?"

Maddox folded his arms and turned away.

"Maddox, you are being rude." Linda's cheeks burned as she looked toward this sweet woman who just wanted to help. "I'm so sorry. My son knows better than to behave this way."

Janice waved her off. "Not to worry. I understand. It's hard to be young and sick."

"You understand? Really? When's the last time you had sores in your mouth, or vomited up blood, or had a needle stuck into one of your bones? I don't think you understand much at all. And I do not like football. I like baseball. But I don't want a baseball bedspread. I want a baseball diamond, and I want to be standing on first base."

"I'm so sorry." Linda walked Janice to the door. Even Janice seemed a little stunned now. Still, she answered very sweetly, then escaped toward the elevator. Linda attempted to reprimand him—which was hard, given how thin and pale he looked. He refused to answer her and had eventually fallen asleep in a huff.

No, she would not write about that. But what else could she say? Finally, she spelled out the single word *HELP*, closed the journal, sat back in her chair, and closed her eyes.

She startled awake some time later. How long had she slept? She shook her head to clear it, thankful Maddox was still asleep, and picked up her phone. The notification jolted her fully awake.

An email. From Caroline. She touched the icon and held her breath.

Linda—

I got notified today that I am a potential match. They are having me do additional blood work for further testing. Thought you would want to know.

Caroline Chapman

Linda clapped her hand across her mouth to keep from shouting, crying, or otherwise making a noise that would wake Maddox. A potential match! She had prayed for it, she had hoped for it, but even now she couldn't truly believe it.

Dr. Stern had told her that many people who are considered possible matches in preliminary screening prove to be incompatible with advanced testing. Still, this offered hope. The first they'd had in a long time.

She couldn't wait to tell Brent. She stood and started toward the door, planning to slip out and call him. Then she realized the problem with that plan.

Per protocol, the patient's family was not notified until a donor had successfully matched through the second round of testing and then confirmed that he or she was willing to move forward with the procedure. Brent knew this. If she told him there had been a potential early match, he would want to know how she knew. She would have no choice then but to tell him everything, and now was not the right time to drop that bomb.

This potential happy news would have to remain her secret alone.

...

Later that afternoon, Linda got a text from Brent.

My office staff took up a collection and is sending us out to dinner Friday night. I told them that you didn't like to leave Maddox for long, but they insisted. Truly, we haven't talked just the two of us since this all began, so I think it's a good idea. I've already spoken with Ken and Kristyn, and they will drive up with me and stay with Maddox while we are gone. Kristyn asked if Keaton would be allowed to visit—I told her to check with you.

Just the thought of going out for dinner made her feel guilty, but Brent was right. It would be nice to have more than a whispered conversation in the hospital corridor. Then it smacked her full force. This would be the perfect time to tell him about the potential match. About Caroline. About everything.

The knot in her stomach—a constant companion since Maddox's diagnosis—tightened. Brent didn't need anything else piled on him right now, and for that matter, neither did she. But Brent did need this potential good news as much as she did. He deserved it. And if Caroline was indeed a match, it was all going to come out anyway. Perhaps it would be better if it happened on a calm night at dinner rather than in the thick of a bone marrow transplant.

Yes, that was it.

She looked toward the ceiling, "Thank you." It was the closest thing to a prayer she had managed to get out in several days.

Dinner sounds nice. See you tomorrow night. LL

It was the first time she'd signed a text with their usual *Love Linda* initials since before the diagnosis was official. Would they ever go back to normal again? Especially after Brent found out the whole truth? It didn't seem possible.

...

"It's silly for you to stay here all alone. Come with us." Brent did his usual arguing-for-common-sense gesture—hands out, palms up, eyes wide. It had never worked on Kristyn before and would not start now, but Linda loved him for trying. She knew that he couldn't stand the thought of leaving Kristyn in the lobby alone.

She shook her head. "Absolutely not. Tonight is about you having some time together, just the two of you. The last thing you need is a third wheel."

"You are never a third wheel. You are a family member." Brent continued holding out his hands.

"Nope. And I wouldn't have made the ride up here if I thought this was going to be an issue. I brought my knitting and my Kindle, and I'm perfectly happy here. Ken will come down in a while so I can go up and chat with Maddox for a bit."

Only two nonfamily visitors were allowed in the room at any given time. Kristyn had declared that Maddox needed a boys' night, but she still wanted to come and at least say hello. So here she stood in the lobby, prepared to sit alone and wait. Linda hugged her friend. "You really are wonderful."

"Of course I am." Kristyn plopped down on a blue vinyl armchair, picked up her latest knitting project—a blue infant beanie—and made a shooing motion. "Get going you two, before I lose my patience."

"Well, we certainly don't want to suffer the wrath of Kristyn." Brent conceded.

"You're right about that." Kristyn didn't bother to look up from her knitting, but she quirked up the left side of her mouth in the grin of victory.

Brent led Linda through the lobby and out the front door. "It's a family-owned lobster joint and less than a quarter mile away, so I thought it would make for a nice walk." The upbeat tone in his voice was forced, but Linda appreciated it for what it was. He was trying to make this night seem as "normal" as possible. Just another dinner with his wife of two decades.

"Sounds good." She, too, tried to force an upbeat tone but didn't think she'd carried it off.

New England fresh-off-the-boat lobster in some small dive had always been their go-to for special evenings. As they made their way down the sidewalk, something about the open space, the towering buildings lining each side of the road—it all made her feel exposed and vulnerable. Perhaps it was because this was the first time she'd stepped outside the hospital in almost a week.

For several blocks, they walked on without speaking. Finally, Brent said, "Maddox seemed to be in good spirits tonight."

"Yes, he was excited to see Keaton. He's been talking about watching the Red Sox game and eating ice cream all afternoon."

Brent smiled. "Doesn't he watch the Red Sox most every night?"

"Yes, and he often eats ice cream, too—when he can keep it down—but apparently those things are better with another teenage boy instead of your mom."

Brent reached out and took her hand. "That right there tells me the kid's got a lot to learn."

Linda squeezed his hand, savoring this closeness, knowing that by the end of the evening these moments would not happen so easily. *Keep it going. Just a while longer. Keep this moment going.* "It's perfect timing for a visit. He feels pretty good right now, and this will give him a little emotional boost before ... well, next week."

Brent nodded. "Yes, that's a good thing."

What Linda didn't say, what they both knew, was that Maddox would start the third round of chemo next week.

It would be all they could do to keep nutrition of any form in him after that. His mouth would break out in new sores. His hair would continue to fall out—something he had been mostly covering with a baseball cap, but after this round, he would likely not be able to do so anymore. He pretended it didn't bother him, often making jokes about "starting to look like Dad." Still, he'd stopped his constant hair mussing. She suspected this was in an effort to slow the loss.

"Supposedly this is one of the best lobster places in this part of town, and with reasonable prices, too." Brent pointed at the Kingsman's Lobster sign on the next block.

"I'm not sure that telling your date about the restaurant with reasonable prices is the best way to start a romantic evening."

Brent chuckled. "Well, romance has never been my strong suit, now has it?" As much as his lack of romance had been an ongoing joke in their lives for the past twenty years, at this point, it just didn't matter. Still, they needed to pretend for a while. "And since the crew at work took up the collection to pay for tonight's dinner, I suppose the fact that I'm playing on the cheap is all that much worse."

"Yes, it is, come to think of it. I don't know why I keep going out with you."

Brent leaned toward her and waggled his eyebrows. "Because I'm so handsome."

Linda stopped walking, tilted her head to the side, and squinted. After a moment, she nodded. "Yep, that must be the reason." They resumed walking, and this felt so normal that for a moment they could almost believe it. Linda said, "That was nice of your coworkers to do this for us." And it was nice. They were nice. Every single one of them.

As they approached the door, he said, "I'm glad we have this time, because I do want to talk to you about something while we're here."

She swallowed hard. "I've got something I need to tell you, too."

He didn't seem to notice the sound of panic in her voice, because he smiled as he swung open the door. "It's nice to have some alone time to talk things through, isn't it?"

Linda wasn't so sure about that. Still, she nodded.

The restaurant was packed, and in spite of their reservation, they had to wait about ten minutes in a crowded alcove along with what seemed like most of Boston. It delayed any serious conversation for the time being. Linda was grateful for the extra time to work up her nerve.

Finally they were led to a small booth in the back corner. Brent slid in across from her. "Nice of them to give us the quietest spot in the house. So, tell me, what is it you needed to talk about?"

Linda's throat went dry. "You first."

He picked up his menu but didn't open it. "I need some advice, I guess. About Marshall."

"Marshall?" Whatever Linda had expected him to say, it wasn't this. "What about him?"

"He's been acting up a bit."

Linda snorted out of pure reflex. "Marshall? Acting up? What does that even look like?" She conjured up pictures of him turning in his homework only one day early instead of three. But since school was out for the summer, that couldn't be the problem.

Brent shook his head. "I know, it surprised me, too. But twice in the last month I caught him sneaking out of the house at night."

"Really? To do what?"

"Going to meet up with Gary."

That was a relief. If ever there was a kid who was as straight and narrow as Marshall, it was Gary. "What were they doing? Building a spaceship?"

"My thoughts were running along the same path until last week when Gary's mother found them attempting to smoke a cigarette. And I say attempting, because they each managed about two puffs before they became violently ill."

"Marshall? No way."

"That's what I said at first, too."

"Why didn't you tell me any of this before?"

"I've been trying not to worry you. There's plenty for you to deal with here. And I've tried to talk to him, but I get nowhere. I was hoping you'd give it a try."

"I'm ashamed to admit it, but I've been so wrapped up with what is happening with Maddox, that I haven't spent enough time talking to him about his own life. I'll have a chat with him when he comes to visit tomorrow."

"Good. You do seem to be able to talk him through these kinds of things better than I can."

"That's what mothers are for." She managed a light tone in spite of the guilt that weighed upon her. She couldn't believe she had missed any warning that Marshall was struggling. What kind of mother did that?

She opened her menu, but only because she needed a break in conversation for some time to process everything. Brent followed suit, much to her relief. She stared at the appetizer list unseeing, trying to think about how to proceed with the next part of their conversation.

Let's see, she could start with, "I'm just wondering, have I ever mentioned to you about the daughter I had while I was still in college?" Or maybe something like, "I hope you won't take this the wrong way, but I've been hiding something from you for the past twenty-one years." Or maybe something like, "Great news. You have a stepdaughter." She was pretty certain that none of those were the right way to handle this.

"Hello, I'm Sal and I'll be your waiter this evening." Sal was not much older than Maddox. He was tall, with dark wavy hair, and from his tan it was obvious he spent a lot of time outdoors. He probably played sports, like many boys his age—the ones who weren't locked in a cancer ward.

Linda shook her head slightly in an attempt to knock out the self-pity and focus on the task at hand. She admired her husband as he made small talk with the young man as if he didn't have a care in the world. Brent had always been good at that. He asked questions about the menu, and the weather, and how long Sal had worked here. Back and forth the two of them bantered, back and forth. Easy-peasy.

Then Brent and Sal were both staring at her. "I'm sorry, did you say something to me?"

"I asked if you were ready to place your order."

"Oh, sure. I'll have ..." She didn't look at the menu. "I'll have the same thing as my husband."

"Very good. I'll be back with your iced teas in just a minute."

Brent was watching her with a perplexed expression. "I've never seen you order lobster tail before. It's always a lobster roll for you."

Linda shrugged. "I ... uh ... thought maybe it was time to try something new."

Brent reached across the table and took her hand. "You okay? I'm worried about you. This is crazy stressful for all of us, but you are right in the thick of it, having to be the one who is strong for Maddox, and I know you can't be getting anything like restful sleep in the middle of that hospital room."

"I'm doing all right." She squeezed his hand a little. "It must be harder on you. Being in a different town, not seeing and hearing what is going on. Trying to carry on with your job and Marshall almost as if everything is normal."

"In some ways yes, but I think being separate from it and being busy helps keep me sane."

The drinks and food arrived in quick succession, thereby allowing her to continue to stall a little longer. She picked up her knife and fork, looked at her food, and remembered why she always ordered a lobster roll instead of the tail. It was the act of getting the meat out of the shell. She'd never been able to do it well, even when it came with the shell precracked. Her hands hovered above the crustacean as if they, too, wondered what was to be done.

Brent laughed and shook his head. "Send your plate my way and I'll take care of that for you."

She slid it across the table. "Thank you."

"Now, you told me you had something to talk about. What was it you wanted to say?"

CHAPTER 13

Chris's Boston condo smelled cleaner than any bachelor pad should. Probably because it was more of a hotel room than anything else lately. He tossed his keys on his kitchen counter along with a pile of mail. He hadn't been back here since just after he'd returned from St. Lucia weeks ago. And although he'd only be here for a couple nights, it felt good to be home.

He took off his sneakers and brought his duffel bag into his bedroom, where he started pulling out dirty laundry. A few moments later, his phone buzzed in his back pocket. Probably one of his Boston College friends texting to see if he wanted to hang out. He tried to keep in touch, especially with the handful of guys from the lacrosse team who still lived downtown, but with his schedule, he had little time for relationships. Of any kind.

The last two women he'd dated made that quite clear— he wasn't around enough, didn't call enough, hadn't contributed enough ... It wasn't completely inaccurate, but what could he do about it? They didn't seem to complain when his job afforded him access to VIP events at hotels he'd worked on or high-profile parties Tom threw. Only when he actually had to work for them. And as soon as he explained his intention to quit and run his own construction company one day, well, things seemed to fizzle pretty quickly.

He started the washing machine, then glanced at his phone. Nope, not a BC lacrosse friend. His gut simmered at the sight of her name on his screen.

Hi Chris. Just thinking about you and wondering if you'd be up for Sunday brunch?

Nope again. As much as he wanted to shoot back words that more accurately communicated how he felt, he opted for a tactful response.

Thanks, but I can't. It was sort of true. He was planning to go to Reality Church on Sunday morning—something he hadn't had time for in several weeks—and he missed the sense of connection he felt when he was there. Then he was heading back to Newport. He probably could have worked brunch into his agenda but definitely not into his ambitions.

He ordered a pizza from his favorite North End Italian joint. The Red Sox were playing, so he sprawled out on the couch and flipped on the game while he waited for it to be delivered. Bottom of the second, up one—zip. Nice.

Okay, if you change your mind, you're welcome. As always.

The text came just as Martinez struck out, leaving a man on third. Chris didn't know which was more upsetting, the obviously blind umpire, the text... or the fact that the only thing that came to mind now was that lame advice he'd given Caroline several weeks ago, "Simple coffee would be nice." He rolled his eyes and shook his head as he walked to the kitchen for a glass of water.

No, most upsetting was now that he started thinking about Caroline, that stupid article, the questions from Tom that came as a result—her eyes that matched her Dodgers hat—he couldn't seem to stop.

...

Linda took a sip of her iced tea as Brent slid her plate back. "I...uh...well, I wanted to tell you that..." She picked up the lobster pick and rolled it between her thumb and finger. Her eyes burned so she blinked hard, but a tear trailed down her cheek anyway.

Brent reached across the table. "Hey, what is it?"

"I wanted to tell you that..." *Work up your courage and tell him now. You'll never have a better time than this.*

She stared at his tired face. He seemed to have aged overnight, and of course he had, trying to keep his hectic work schedule, be there for Maddox, and unbeknownst to her until this minute, deal with Marshall's teenage angst.

She thought of Kristyn sitting in the hospital lobby, knitting beanies for the newborns at Portsmouth Hospital. She pictured the look on her face when she learned the truth about Linda, the humiliation on Brent's face when he had to tell Ken. Nothing would ever be the same. How could she do that to Brent?

"I wanted to tell you that I really appreciate the way you've been handling things at home, and I truly believe that Maddox will get through this. I'm ashamed to say that I've been full of doubt about it, but not anymore. I believe that we will find a donor, and Maddox is going to recover and live a happy life. I'm sorry I doubted before."

Brent squeezed her hand. "I believe it, too."

He continued to study her, as if waiting for her to continue, but in that moment she knew she could not bring herself to say even one more word. She dunked the piece of lobster in drawn butter, then stuck it in her mouth.

Conversation over.

CHAPTER 14

Chris was tempted to drive straight to the beach. The June air was thick and heavy, and on a day like today, it's where he'd prefer to go. But Attleboro wasn't exactly out of the way. As he headed back to Newport from his Boston condo Sunday afternoon, the persistent twinge in his gut drove him straight into the driveway of the two-story ranch-style home he grew up in. It wasn't right to put this off when he actually had the time to get to it today.

"Mom?" He made his way into the kitchen.

"Oh, Chris, it's you. So good to see you." Mom came out of the family room and pushed her chin-length blonde hair away from her face. She stood on her tiptoes to kiss Chris's cheek.

"You, too. Heard your garbage disposal isn't working, so I came by to fix it."

"It's been jammed for a while, but I've sort of gotten used to not having one now." She hummed a little halfhearted laugh and went to the fridge. "Want anything to drink? Diet Coke? Lemonade?"

"No, thanks. Sorry I didn't come sooner. Your garage doors could use a fresh coat of paint, too. I'll try to get that done in a couple weeks."

"Oh, I don't want to be a burden." She took a sip of her Diet Coke and placed her small frame on a bar stool. "Uncle Jim offered to send someone over." Her tone was more hesitant.

Chris clenched his jaw at the mention of Uncle Jim. "You're not a burden, Mom. I'll do it. Are Dad's tools still in the basement?"

"I haven't touched them, so if that's where they were the last time you were here, that's where they are now."

Chris trotted down the basement steps, then past a few bins full of all his old sports equipment—Rollerblades, a few hockey and lacrosse sticks, baseball bats. His golf clubs from high school were collecting dust in the corner. Next to his dad's. Chris had been meaning to help his mom clear it all out, but every time they came down, they spent more time filtering through old memories of family camping trips and game nights than storage bins. "Let's just leave it till next time," his mom would say.

He located a small toolbox on his father's worktable, sitting in front of the old Stratton Construction Company sign that used to hang outside the office back when his dad still owned it. Back when his dad was still alive.

He grabbed the toolbox, then made his way back upstairs.

"Chris?" Someone called as he got to the top and turned off the light. "Hey, Mom, is Chris here?" He opened the door and found his younger sister, Blythe, standing in the kitchen, her keys in one hand and her purse in the other. "There you are. Finally!"

"I know, I know. I'm sorry." He walked over, then pulled her in for a tight hug. "What are you doing here?"

"I came by to grab some pictures and saw your truck in the driveway. I nearly passed out from shock." Her dark-brown eyes lit up in amusement.

"I pulled out what I could find and put them on the kitchen table for you." Mom pointed across the room. "That box right there."

"Perfect. Thanks." Blythe pulled her shoulder-length brown hair back into a ponytail.

"What do you need the pictures for?" Chris set the toolbox on the floor, started pulling the dish soap and cleaning supplies from the cabinet, then eased himself underneath.

"Adam's parents need them for the video they're making for the rehearsal dinner," Blythe said, although with his head in the cabinet, Chris couldn't be sure he'd heard that correctly.

"Wait, the what?" He hit his head as he pulled it out. "Ouch."

"The rehearsal dinner. Oh, that's right. You've been MIA, so I haven't had the chance to tell you that I'm getting married!" Blythe's squealing kept getting louder until her feet were next to him.

"Are you serious? Congratulations! When did this happen?" He stood, took a better look at her ring, then hugged her again.

"Memorial Day. I really wanted to tell you in person, though, so I kept waiting for that dinner you promised me like forever ago."

"I'm sorry. Listen, come down to Newport whenever you want, and I'll take you to The Mooring. Mom, you should come, too."

"No, no. You kids go. I don't want to intrude." Mom waved her hand like she was shooing a fly.

"When's the big day?" Chris sat back down, then slid his head under the sink, more carefully than he'd pulled it out.

"March 9th. It's not ideal, but Adam's being stationed in Honolulu in April, and we don't want to be apart anymore."

"You sure you want to be a Navy wife?" Chris liked Adam, a lot actually, but how would his little sister hold up with her husband on a submarine, with limited contact, for months on end?

"I want Adam, so I'll take whatever comes with him."

"Even his last name? I'm sorry, but Mrs. Dingledine?" Chris couldn't help but laugh.

"What can I say? I love the guy. At least my initials won't be B. S. anymore, thank goodness."

"It was Dad's choice, not mine," Mom cut in. "Oh, that reminds me, I got you a little something."

"Blythe, have you told Addie Beth?" Chris pulled a wrench from the toolbox.

"Yes, and she's driving me crazy. She's already opened up a registry for me at Williams Sonoma and filled it with all these gadgets I don't even know how to use, and some device for making baby food. As if that's happening any time soon. Will you please call her and tell her I'm capable of picking out my own cutery?"

"You mean cutlery?" Chris laughed again. He wasn't surprised Blythe and Addie Beth were clashing or that Blythe asked him to mediate. It was the way it had always been, with Addie Beth being ten years older than Blythe, and Chris stuck in the middle. "She means well."

"I know. I don't want to hurt her feelings, but advice is one thing; takeover is quite another."

"Here." Mom came back into the room. "This is for you."

"Tiffany's?" Blythe's voice was considerably higher than normal. Chris's stomach sank in proportion. "What's this for?"

"A little engagement present."

"Oh, it's adorable. I love it. Look, Chris." Blythe walked over to him and held out the small silver circle pendant with BHD, her future initials, engraved on it.

"Nice." He meant it, but his tone might have suggested otherwise. Why was Mom shopping at Tiffany's? She couldn't afford that.

"I'm going to wear it right now."

Every few seconds, Chris could hear Mom and Blythe laughing as they flipped through pictures. A few moments later, Blythe gasped. "Oh my gosh, Chris. You were so cute!"

"What do you mean, 'were'? I'm still cute."

"Mr. Humble. Mom, where was this picture taken?"

"Oh, how did that one get in there. You weren't even born yet. That's on Martha's Vineyard. Look at your dad's sunglasses. I remember thinking he was so handsome in those. Chris, you're about six in this picture. I'll leave it on the counter for you to look at."

"Thanks."

Mom put her Diet Coke can into the recycling bin. "Kids, I have Bunco tonight, so I'm going up to change. Thanks for coming over and fixing the garbage disposal, sweetie."

"No problem." He sort of meant that. Fixing the disposal wasn't the issue. It was seeing, yet again, all he'd wanted to fix for his mom, for himself, but couldn't. The things that couldn't be fixed with tools.

As soon as Chris heard his mother's bedroom door close upstairs, he pulled himself up from under the sink again, then stood. "Blythe, don't ask Mom for any money for the wedding, okay?"

She turned and looked up. "Adam's parents said they would—"

"No. Dad would never allow that. I'll pay for it." Chris lifted his chin, then nodded. It would wipe out a small chunk of what he'd put aside last year, but now that Blythe's student loan was paid off, his expenses had gone down. And with that 20 percent bonus to compensate, maybe it wouldn't get him too far off track. How much could it cost, anyway? "Your family should be the ones to host your wedding."

"Chris, you're the best!" She ran over to hug him a third time, although this time it was more of a leap into his chest. "Does that mean you'll be coming with me to pick out dresses?"

"No." Shopping. He hated shopping. "That's where I draw the line."

"You're no fun." Blythe walked over to grab the box of photos. "I have to run. I'll call about dinner. Don't forget!"

When the garbage disposal was running again, Chris packed up the tools, but before he returned them to the basement, he stepped over to the photo on the counter. His dad was standing next to the Edgartown Lighthouse, with Chris on his shoulders. He remembered that day, now that he saw the picture. He had gotten a sunburn that made it hard to sleep for a few nights, which Addie Beth thought was hysterical. She called him Lobster Boy for the rest of the vacation. He laughed at the memory, but as he studied the picture, his dad's strong arms and familiar smile, the laughter faded into a throbbing in his chest.

"God can redeem the broken things in our lives." Wasn't that what his pastor had said this morning? But if that was true, why did this still hurt? And why were things still so broken?

Chris put the photo in his back pocket, then took the tools to the basement and cleared his throat. One more look at the Stratton Construction Company sign was all he needed to reorient his focus, invigorate his drive.

As he jogged down the porch steps to his truck, he noticed the old bird feeder he'd built with his dad back in middle school. They'd made it for Mom as a Mother's Day gift. She loved it, loved that her husband and son built it together, and always kept it full of seeds. He walked over to take a closer look at the miniature replica of a dovecote she'd seen in an English garden magazine photo.

Today it was empty.

One more thing he'd fix the next time he came.

...

When Brent and Marshall arrived at the hospital the next morning, Linda had already concocted an excuse to get Marshall out of the room with her for a while, pitiful though it was. Something about a new robotics exhibit they had in the healing garden, which was ridiculous. Of course they didn't have robots in the healing garden. Thankfully, Marshall didn't call her bluff. As they entered the conservatory, Linda looked at him. "How are you?"

"Fine."

"Yeah? Anything you need to talk about?" She tried to sound casual as she strolled past a planter of white flowers and leafy trees.

"Dad ratted me out, huh?"

Linda motioned him to a bench beside the floor-to-ceiling windows. "He didn't rat you out, but he did say he's concerned about you. Frankly, so am I. What is going on?"

Marshall put his right hand under his chin, the left on top of his head, and proceeded to crack his neck—a habit they'd spent years trying to break. "Nothing." He stared at the stone tile between his feet and said nothing else.

"Come on, Marshall, you've always been able to tell me anything. You know that."

He leaned forward and propped his elbows on his legs, and his chin on his clasped hands. "I'm just getting really tired of hearing about Maddox all the time."

"Of course you're hearing about him. He has cancer. People are worried about him."

"I know he has cancer. *I'm* worried about him, too, more than any of them." He jerked upright and turned toward her, eyes blazing. "But they keep saying things like, 'Gee, he's the athletic and strong one. It's weird that he's the one who got sick.' Or 'I never thought it would be Maddox.'"

Marshall rubbed his eyes against his shoulder. "I get that I'm not as athletic as he is, but I really don't need people throwing it in my face all the time that it should be me upstairs instead of him." He spat out the last words, then shoulder-rubbed his eyes again.

"Oh, honey, that's not what they mean. Although, I have to admit, it does sound really insensitive. What they intended to say is that it's hard to believe that someone as young and healthy as Maddox is sick. Period. They don't mean it should have been you."

He stared at the ground a few feet in front of him. "That's what it sounds like they mean."

Linda sighed. "People can be so stupid when they are trying to be helpful in a bad situation." She thought for a moment. "Do you remember when Mamaw died several years ago? People said the craziest things to your father. I know that they were just trying to say something helpful or encouraging, but in times of great stress and grief, we have to allow humans to be human. And a big part of that is knowing that their well-intentioned words will come out really wrong and hurtful sometimes."

"I do remember. Everyone kept saying things about God going out to choose flowers for His garden and selecting Mamaw because she was the best." He rolled his eyes. "I was only ten years old then, but I remember lying awake at night trying to figure out what bad things I could do so

God wouldn't think I was the best in the garden and want me to die."

Linda actually burst out laughing. After a few seconds, Marshall joined her. "I'm glad you weren't overly successful in your new determination to be a bad boy. But that proves my point exactly. You've got to learn to forgive people for being less than perfect in their efforts to be comforting. And you've got to forgive yourself for being the healthy one. This is not your fault. It should not be you up there. Maddox doesn't deserve to be sick, but neither do you. That's just the way things work in this broken world sometimes."

Marshall nodded. "I guess so."

Linda folded her arms across her chest. "Now, provide me with a list of names of the people who have made those comments, and I will put Super Glue on their lips to make certain this doesn't happen again."

Marshall grinned at her. "Thanks, Mom. I'll be okay. I do appreciate the thought, though."

Linda put her arm around his shoulders. "If you change your mind, let me know."

"Will do." He stood then, and the two of them made their way back toward the elevator. Linda promised herself she would be more attentive to Marshall in the days and weeks to come.

CHAPTER 15

La Fête was coming along splendidly. Caroline checked *tent rental* off her to-do list, powered down her computer, then gathered her things.

"Are you going home for the holiday?" Ruth looked up from her computer after making a few adjustments to the Fourth of July social media post she was working on.

"No, my mom is coming out for my birthday in a few weeks. I'll go back when it's frigid and snowing here."

Ruth laughed. "Smart. Maybe I'll join you."

"You'd be welcome." Knowing her mom, Caroline could've invited the whole office to California without hesitation. "All right, I'm done. Enjoy the long weekend!"

It was one of the nicest days in Newport so far, and Caroline was glad she had decided to walk that morning. She even took a small detour and allowed herself some time to peruse the shops on Bellevue before they closed, purchasing a sundress she didn't need but couldn't leave behind. An early birthday present, she convinced herself. Or at least she'd wear it out to dinner when her mom came.

When she got home, she reached for her keys, then pulled the screen back to unlock the front door. Finally, a few days to relax. She'd gone to the blood bank yesterday for the next round of tests, so she could put that out of her mind for a few days at least. She groaned. No doubt this was consuming Linda's entire life, and someone with an ounce of sensitivity would have remembered that. But she wasn't about to pass up a few days off to catch her breath, maybe even spend some time exploring Rhode Island or a day at the beach.

She put the key in the lock when a deep, raspy voice said from behind her, "I've been waiting for you to come home."

Caroline jumped, dropped her bags, and flung herself around, her heart thumping. An elderly gentleman in long khaki pants and a white golf shirt was standing a few feet away. "Can I help you?"

His face looked kind, like a grandfather's, but she fiddled for the safety whistle on her key chain anyway. How ridiculous. It was broad daylight for crying out loud. And one firm push would probably send him toppling over. Definitely no more *Blue Bloods*.

"Are you Caroline Chapman?"

"Yes ..."

"Here, this is yours. Came to my house by mistake." He nodded toward the modest Cape Cod next door, then held a small priority mailbox out to her. "You'd think after coming here for forty-two summers the mailman would know who lives there."

Caroline's body relaxed. She reached out for the box and glanced at the return address on the label. Los Angeles, but no name. "Thank you for bringing it over. I appreciate it."

"You're welcome. Happy Fourth." He turned, then shuffled down the small driveway.

"You too." She put the box under one arm, gathered her bags, and opened the door. She should have invited him in for lemonade or at least asked his name. Next time she'd remember to be more neighborly. It would be nice to have a familiar face around here other than those at work. And the barista at Bellevue Coffee.

Once inside, she plopped everything at the foot of the stairs, then brought the box into the kitchen. With a sparkling water in one hand and a pair of scissors in the other, she severed the tape and pulled back the flaps.

A card lay on top of two old, familiar books she'd read years ago and forgotten about, but when she pulled those out, she found a new and lovely Burberry scarf. It was gorgeous. And so soft. She unfolded it and wrapped it around her neck, even though she wouldn't actually need it for months.

She tore the seal on the card and her lips formed a smile as she pulled it from the envelope. But once she saw the stationery and handwriting, her smile quickly devolved into a gape.

Dear Caroline,

I went back to LA to pack up the last of my things and found the books on a shelf. I hope everything is going well for you in Rhode Island.

With love,
Dillon

The last time she and Dillon had spoken, she expressed her hope that he get kicked by a bull in Texas, preferably in a certain sensitive area. His retort was equally mean … and childlike. Freeze in a snowstorm, if she remembered correctly.

Was this a peace offering? A way to soothe his conscience? And how did he get her address? Her insides warmed, and not just because the scarf was around her neck.

Wait a second. This was the same man who months ago essentially told her his job was more important than she was. Who moved without her, moved on despite her, all to secure his place in his company. The warmth escalated to heat and her chest tightened. Could this actually be a sign of remorse?

Should she call him, thank him, and beg him to reconsider, or throw the scarf away? Well, that would be silly. She should at least get some use out of it.

She grabbed her phone and opted for a simple text, out of courtesy, to start. *Box arrived. Thank you for the books and scarf.*

The phone vibrated, alerting her to his response, and her heart fluttered in kind. *No problem. Hope you like it.*

It had been a long while since she'd seen his name and number on her phone screen, and she couldn't ignore the tug for more. She wanted to ask how he was doing, make sure he was okay.

How are you? She wrote but deleted. *Is Texas*…Delete. *Rhode Island is great, thanks for*…Delete.

A breath filled her cheeks and she held it a moment, then exhaled. It was getting a little too hot for comfort with the scarf around her neck, so she unwound it, folded it, then put it back in the box. What she needed now was some time to relax, not another distraction, no matter how warm and fuzzy it made her feel.

Back to her previously scheduled evening. She took her things upstairs, started the bathwater, then lit a candle, completely content to put it all out of her mind for a few days, lest she come across as desperate for his attention. Besides, it would take a lot more than a scarf to undo what he'd done.

Then again, he did sign the card "with love."

...

"What do you mean the tent isn't available?" Caroline was standing on the lawn at Chateau-sur-Mer with Emily of Soiree Party Rentals, the late-July humidity equally oppressive as the panic building inside. Five seconds ago, Caroline wished she hadn't worn heels since they were sinking into the grass and getting stuck. Now, she couldn't care less about the stupid shoes.

"It's a first-come, first-serve basis. I couldn't hold it for you." Emily shook her head and flipped her wrist out to the side.

"I confirmed it. Three weeks ago. I left a message for you."

Emily looked down at her phone for a few moments, then shook her head again.

Caroline's heart thumped so hard, she could feel it in her cheeks. Beyond a doubt, she had confirmed that tent. "Do you have any others?"

"The only other tent we have available for that night is the mini—it accommodates up to fifty guests."

"That's way too small. Please tell me you at least have the tables, chairs, and linens reserved."

"Yes." Emily nodded, although she had to consult with her phone again before doing so.

"Where am I supposed to get a large enough tent in peak wedding season?" Caroline's armpits started to sweat. The heels of her shoes were now completely underground.

"What about inside?"

"The ballroom will be reserved for dancing, and there isn't another room large enough for dinner."

"Another mansion?"

Why was she arguing with the rental coordinator? "The invitations have gone out. A location change is completely out of the question." And completely unprofessional—a concept Emily had obviously never considered.

"I'll call our sister company on the Cape. They might have one available."

Caroline popped up straight. "Yes. Please, do that." She yanked her heels free, then stepped a few feet away and took out her phone as well.

She sent a text to Ruth. *This is a disaster!*

Ruth's response came only a few seconds later. *12 more tickets so far this morning!* Normally, this would elevate Caroline's spirits immensely, but with no tent, unpredictable weather in late summer, and an airhead for a rental coordinator, La Fête could easily become La Flop. The fewer people to witness it, the better.

She was about to text her thoughts back to Ruth when her phone rang. She recognized the number, contemplated declining the call, but since Emily was still on the phone, she answered.

"Hello?" Her voice was snippy. Why did she always get this call when she was in a bad mood?

"Caroline, hi. It's Sharon White again from Be The Match. I wanted to let you know we have run your blood work and believe you are a suitable donor for Maddox Riley. Now, I will hand all of this over to the transplant team, and they will be in touch with you directly with the next steps if they decide to move forward. Just so you know, they will most likely order more blood samples. You will need to participate in a ninety-minute information session on the donation process, and you will have to undergo a physical exam to make sure you are healthy enough to donate. But they will go through all of the details with you."

Caroline closed her eyes and held her hand up to her other ear. The lawn was full of noisy tourists and the threat of Audrey firing her echoed through her brain. She glanced at Emily, who was sticking out her lips and shaking her head yet again, indicating there wasn't a tent available on the Cape either. Fantastic. "Um, can you call me back in about a month?"

"Ma'am, we do not have a month to wait." Sharon's words were sharp. Jostling even. Of course, this deserved her full attention. It was good news for Maddox. Terrible timing for her, but excellent news for Maddox.

She took what her yoga instructor back in LA called a cleansing breath. "Yes, I'm so sorry."

"You are still willing and able to move forward, correct?" Sharon's tone, again, indicated she wasn't here to play games.

"I am."

"Okay then, the transplant team will be in touch."

Caroline hung up, then pulled her hair back off her face. She forced herself to turn back to Emily. "No tent?" Although she already knew the answer. She let out a sigh that sounded more like a whiny grunt. "If anything changes on that, please let me know. I'll call around and see if I can find anything."

She trudged back to her office and looked at the time— two more hours until she could go home and have a proper freak-out in private. For now, she'd have to compensate with a few dozen more cleansing breaths and whatever gum was left in her purse at work.

Okay, no need to panic. I can find a tent. And the donation? It's not like this was a closed case and surgery was imminent. Another round of testing still needed to be done, and in the end, she might not actually be qualified.

But if so, well, she'd simply have to juggle it all. For Maddox. This mattered to him.

She mattered to him.

She could do it. No problem. She'd planned the Huntington Library annual fundraiser and her wedding at the same time with great success. Well, except for the minor detail of the groom backing out.

As soon as she sat in her desk chair and pulled out her phone to call any and all party rental suppliers in Rhode Island and beyond, Audrey popped her head in.

"I assume you've seen the latest and greatest from Aiden?" She held out a copy of the *Aquidneck Island News*. Her eyes seemed to flicker, but maybe it was just the kelly-green blouse she was wearing that made them pop.

"No, I haven't actually." She took the paper from Audrey. She wanted an iced latte from Bellevue. "Ruth, I thought you were putting a stop to this?"

"The editor said unless anything's inaccurate in Aiden's articles, he'll run them. Apparently, they're getting a lot of attention. Most activity on the digital edition in a long time."

Caroline skimmed the paper until she got to Aiden's column. "Plans for La Fête are in full swing, while the Chadwick announces they are now officially taking wedding reservations for next summer. When asked if he would attend the Preservation Society's annual fundraiser, Chris Stratton remarked, 'I can think of several things I'd rather spend five hundred dollars on, and I'm pretty sure I wouldn't be a welcomed guest anyway.'"

"Well, that part's accurate." Caroline snapped the paper onto her desk.

"I actually think this might be working in our favor." Audrey tapped her chin a few times with her finger. "We've already sold more tickets than last year, and we still have a month to go."

Her body tightened a bit. "I would suggest excellent planning and marketing have contributed to the event's success so far." *So long as I can get another tent...* Caroline opted to leave that detail out and hoped her smile radiated a humble confidence.

"Oh, of course. That too." Audrey turned to leave. "Keep it up, ladies."

As soon as Audrey was out of earshot, Caroline let out a little groan. If only she could get a little more of that confidence.

The humble part, she feared, was well on its way.

CHAPTER 16

Dear Linda,

I got a call today that my second round of testing shows me as a close match. They still want me to do some more blood work and have a physical, but I knew you would want to know.

Best,
Caroline Chapman

Linda dropped her phone and doubled over in the chair. She put both hands behind the back of her head, rocking back and forth. *There is hope. There is hope. There is really hope.* The words ran over and over through her mind.

"Mom, what are you doing? Are you okay?" Maddox turned down the volume of the Red Sox-Orioles game. "Do I need to call the nurse?"

Linda jerked back up, suddenly aware that she had been making something like wheezing sounds, and her son had witnessed the whole episode. She shook her head. "No, sorry about that. I … uh …" She choked a little in her effort to regain her composure. "I'm okay. Sorry I alarmed you." She hiccupped a little giggle.

"Are you laughing?" He tilted his head and stared at her, as if trying to identify this strange woman in his hospital room. "Don't tell me Kristyn is sending around more of those corny email jokes the two of you like so much. I thought you had moved past that phase a couple of years ago."

She cleared her throat and nodded. "You know how we are." *Thank you, Maddox, for providing that excuse.*

"You two are so weird." He rolled his eyes. "It's good to see you laugh again, though. You used to be funny. Before I got sick, I mean."

Funny. Yes, she had almost forgotten. And now that kind of carefree life seemed possible again. At least there was hope. "Funny? Since when did you think that? All I've ever heard was 'embarrassing.'" She quirked her eyebrow at him.

"In a mother, it's more or less the same thing." He grinned his biggest grin. It felt so good to see him teasing again.

"Well, I'm going to work harder at being more embarrassing from now on, okay?"

He shook his head. "Kind of got myself into that one, didn't I?" Maddox picked up the pink plastic cup from the bedside tray, adjusted the bend in the straw, and took a sip of water. He grabbed the remote, but before he pushed the button, he turned back toward her. "You sure you're okay?"

She smiled what had to be the biggest smile of her entire life—and it was completely honest and truthful, no forced act now. "I'm fine, I promise. Maybe I'll just go for a walk and get some fresh air."

"Sounds like a good idea." He watched her as she walked toward the door, but he didn't even wait before she crossed the threshold before he turned the volume back up on the baseball game. Linda was glad he had something to keep him distracted, because she had no intention of coming back to this room until she found Dr. Stern.

It was over an hour later when she returned to the room. Maddox looked over at her. "There you are. I was getting ready to call hospital security and let them know that a hysterical woman was wandering around the hospital premises, likely lost and confused, clearly in the midst of some sort of breakdown. I thought we'd maybe have to go in emergency lockdown mode or something. I was kind of hoping so. Might break up a bit of the monotony."

"I'm sorry to disappoint you by my safe return."

He shrugged. "I'll get over it. Eventually."

She scowled at him. "I'm sure you will." She reached into her purse and pulled out a plastic bag. "Just remember this, young man. If you get me locked out of here, I won't be able to bring contraband to your room." She produced an individual container of vanilla ice cream from the plastic bag and held it up as evidence.

He pressed the button to bring himself to a sitting position and cleared off a spot on his bedside tray. "Good thing I didn't make that call then."

It had been two weeks since his last round of treatment finished, and his appetite was very slow to come back this time. At this point, any kind of calories they could get in him, they were happy about. Plus, the cold of the ice cream would feel good to the new sores in his mouth.

He pulled out the wooden spoon from the top of the cup, then scooped up a small portion. "Thanks, Mom."

"You're welcome."

Things were going to be all right. She could finally bring up a picture in her mind that involved their family back as usual.

She waited until later than evening, when Maddox was engrossed in a Dodgers-Braves game before she pulled out her phone and sent the email she'd been composing in her head all day long.

Dear Caroline,

This news is too wonderful for words! I cannot begin to express the depths of my thankfulness to you, and I wish there was more I could do to show my appreciation. My offer stands to buy you dinner, or lunch, or coffee should you ever want to meet face-to-face, but until you are ready, I will respect your boundaries. You are in my thoughts and prayers, as you have been for the past twenty-eight years.

With love,
Linda

...

Brent awoke in the hospital—although it's hard to wake up when you've never actually been asleep. Honestly, he didn't know how Linda did this night after night, but then again, she'd always been able to sleep through anything—anything except the sounds of her babies' cries. He was glad he had insisted she go home last night and sleep in her own bed. She had mostly refused to do that since Maddox arrived at the hospital, but now that he was recovering from his last round of chemo—and perhaps in for an extended rest before the next round of treatment—she had finally relented.

Maddox was asleep. Aside from the fact that he was a teenager and therefore by nature a late sleeper, it was impossible in this place to get any real rest, with all the blood draws, beeping alarms, and unusual lights and sounds. After several months of this, he must be so exhausted. Brent sat up, thankful to see his son get at least some respite.

He picked up his phone, which had been set to Do Not Disturb overnight and checked to see if he had missed anything. He clicked on the Home button and could not believe his eyes. There were almost a dozen missed calls. From work.

He stepped outside the room to call his coworker back. "Hello, Elliott, I noticed I missed several calls from you last night. Is everything okay?"

"I wouldn't say that, no. In fact, I would say everything is about as not okay as it can be. How fast can you get to Chicago? We've got an all-out SOS with the Game Changers campaign."

"What's happened?"

"Long story short, it seems that Rodney got involved with a woman he met on the road. He broke it off eventually, but not before she got pregnant. She's threatening to go to the press." Rodney Litchfield, a former NBA all-star, was the spearhead of the entire organization. Adored by fans, well-spoken, a man of integrity. Or at least, he had appeared to be.

Brent put his hand to his head, as if by doing so he could keep it from exploding. *No. No. No. What was he thinking?* "Do you know what kind of disaster this will bring on the entire program?"

"I'm pretty sure I do. Anyway, all hands on deck at the offices as soon as you can get here."

"I'll get a flight out today."

Brent paced around the halls, trying his best to convince himself that he didn't all but hate Rodney right now. How could he have been so stupid? This would ruin everything they had been struggling to achieve. *Why? Why?*

It had been so nice to be able to provide his wife a weekend at home, to give her some relief from this burden she had been carrying. Now he was about to dump the entire load squarely back on her shoulders.

CHAPTER 17

She was cutting it close. Caroline had to be at work in less than ten minutes, which didn't really give her enough time to wait in this stagnant line, but Monday morning without Bellevue Coffee was out of the question.

Maybe if she could just get Isaac's attention, he would start making her usual. She cleared her throat louder than necessary and waved in his direction, but it was no use. All she got was a dirty look from the man in front of her.

She shifted her weight from one foot to the other as she waited. Thankfully, her phone buzzed in her pocket, giving her a welcomed distraction.

"Hi, Mom!"

"Hi, sweetie." Mom sounded tired. She must have just woken up since it was a few minutes before six on the West Coast.

Caroline inched toward the cash register. "I'm glad you called. I made reservations at The Mooring for Thursday night, and I booked us each a facial on Sat—"

"Honey, I can't come."

"What?" Caroline's work bag suddenly felt much heavier than it was. "What do you mean?"

"Gram Gram isn't doing too well, actually. She's had a mild stroke but she's stable now. Still, she's going to be in the hospital for at least a few more days."

"Oh no. Do they think she'll be okay?"

"I'm waiting for the doctor to come back in and give me more information. I can call you with an update later."

"Okay." Her breath hitched and it hurt to swallow all of the sudden. "Is there any way Dad can fly out instead?"

"Dad's work schedule is set. You know how that goes." Her heart sank. Over thirty years at the same engineering firm afforded Dad privileges, but he never took advantage of them. Knowing he could be replaced by the hundreds of UCSB engineering graduates each year at a fraction of the salary meant no last-minute time off.

"I know you were looking forward to it, honey. I was, too. When things settle down here, I can rebook my trip. Maybe in the fall?"

"Yeah. I hear it's nice that time of year." Fall, it wasn't so very far away. It would be here before she knew it. She liked apple picking.

"I'm sorry, Caroline." Mom sighed. "I would much rather be with you."

"I know, it's okay. Tell Gram Gram I'm thinking about her and hope she gets better soon. That's the most important thing."

After exchanging "I love yous," Caroline hung up and took another ministep toward the counter. The line hadn't seemed to move at all. Then again, she hadn't really been on the phone that long. Just long enough for all of her birthday balloons to pop.

Finally, she had her skim latte and was walking to her office, although the oomph in her step was gone, and she really didn't care if she made it on time. When she reached her desk, she dumped her bag on the ground, then sunk into her chair.

"Rough morning?" Ruth looked over her shoulder.

"I got some bad news. Anymore RSVPs?"

"Twenty-six!"

This put the head count at over five hundred. Caroline took a sip of her coffee and tried to motivate herself to secure a tent by the end of the day. But the ache inside was too big a distraction at the moment. In fact, her eyes moistened, clouding her vision as she searched local party rental companies on her laptop.

She pulled up a new window and navigated to a potential flight to Santa Barbara. If her mom couldn't come out, then Caroline wanted to be there, especially since Gram Gram wasn't doing well. But with La Fête in less than a month, she couldn't afford the time off.

She hadn't anticipated this when she took the job in Rhode Island—how being so far away would impact her life and those she loved most. That's what planes were for. But it wasn't always as simple as that in real life. Even when it mattered.

Her mind drifted to other options for her birthday. She could keep the dinner reservation and go alone. No, too humiliating.

Takeout? *Meh.*

She could cancel the reservation. This seemed the only logical choice. Maybe she could get a pedicure after work instead. *Yippee…*

She rolled her damp eyes and just wanted to bury her head in her arms on the desk. She felt like a toddler right now, throwing a fit over a dropped ice cream cone. See, this was exactly why millennials had such a bad reputation.

There was one more option. One other person who might be interested in celebrating the occasion. She tapped her fingers on her desk and allowed her semifunctioning brain to cartwheel a few times.

Maybe she was just being ridiculous. Foolish even. She should probably make this decision when she had a more level head.

An image of herself—old, alone, and with several cats—scurried across her imagination. Perhaps it was worth the gamble.

Finally, she let out a deep breath, opened an email, then typed.

Are you interested in getting dinner on Thursday night?

And before she could talk herself out of it, she pressed Send.

...

"Maddox, how are you feeling this morning?" As usual, Dr. Stern came to stand at Maddox's bedside and looked him directly in the eyes. This was something Linda had always appreciated about her—she treated Maddox as a person, not just a bunch of lab numbers.

"Fine." He focused more on the ceiling than the semicircle of doctors standing around him. It seemed to be easiest for him if he didn't fully engage in the present, and they all understood the reasons why. Now that almost three weeks had passed since his last round of chemo, the color was starting to come back to his face and a little bit of the spark was returning to his eyes. Still, he was a long way from feeling fine.

"I come bearing good news this morning."

"Yeah?" This news turned Maddox's attention directly on Dr. Stern. He put his right hand behind his head. "Let's hear it."

Linda jumped from the corner chair where she'd been sitting and came to stand beside the bed. "What? What news?" She held her breath and looked at the team of residents and fellows in the room. All of them were smiling.

Dr. Stern smiled, too, and continued to look at Maddox. "I am pleased to inform you that you are officially in remission."

"Really?" Maddox sat up from his semireclined position. "Does that mean I can go home?"

Dr. Stern touched his shoulder. "Well, possibly for a short time, but not until next week at the earliest."

"But why? You just said I'm cured."

"I did not say cured, what I said is remission."

"Aren't they the same thing?"

"Not exactly. Remission means that there are less than 5 percent blasts in your bone marrow—in other words, no detectable leukemia. Unfortunately, just because it's not detectable, doesn't mean it's not there."

"So basically remission doesn't mean anything?"

"It means a great many things. First of all, it means that you have successfully completed the treatment phase that we call induction. Some patients never achieve this milestone, so the fact that you are here is a victory. However, in the case of your particular kind of leukemia, if we stop treatment right now, the chances of a relapse are high. We have to be aggressive to make certain that this doesn't come back."

"And how do we do that?"

"We move on to the phase we call consolidation. Now we strive to knock out every last leukemia cell in your body to make sure we never have to do this again."

"Well, I'm all for not ever doing this again, so let's get started with that consolidation stuff. Let's finish this."

"That's the spirit." She smiled and released his shoulder. "We're going to give your body a little more time to catch up and heal from the last round of chemo, and if your blood counts stay steady, we may send you home for a couple weeks before we start 'that consolidation stuff.' I have good news in that respect, too."

"What?" he said.

"We believe we have located a suitable bone marrow match for you."

Maddox sat up straight in his bed. "Really? I thought we had given up on that. Who is it? Is it someone I know?"

"Maddox, we never give up on anything that would help you, but you are correct in your understanding that the earlier marrow drives did not give us a suitable donor. As for the donor's identity, the process is anonymous, so unless the person chooses to contact you, it will remain unknown. There are a few more final steps that must occur, but the match is confirmed."

Was Linda just imagining it, or did Dr. Stern intentionally turn her head farther away from her as she said this? She, of course, knew who the donor was. Dr. Stern would not say it out loud, but Linda knew what she was thinking. *It's time to tell your family the truth.*

And maybe she was right. Linda just didn't know how to start.

...

"Hey, Siri, call Dad."

At the sound of Maddox's voice, Linda turned her attention from the residents and fellows filing from the room back toward her son and his phone. He motioned for her to move closer. "I've got it on speaker so we can all talk."

For the most part, they kept their daytime conversations with Brent to texts and emails, because he had never liked to be disturbed at work. Especially now, with the current emergency. News like this, however, warranted an interruption.

The phone rang and rang and then went to voice mail. Maddox touched the red End Call icon on the screen and sighed. "Well, so much for that happy announcement."

"He must be in a meeting. I'm sure he will call us back as soon as he sees the missed call."

"Yeah." Maddox laid his head back on his pillow but kept his phone tight in his hand. "Mom, they found a match. Can you believe that? After all our friends and family didn't fit, after the entire database didn't work out, some random person got tested and is a match. What are the odds of that? Crazy, isn't it?"

At this point, Linda needed to be careful about her responses. When the truth came out about who the donor was, she didn't want Maddox to remember something she had said in this moment and hate her for it. She did nod. "That donor is a true answer to prayer." And every bit of that statement was true.

"For sure." Maddox had already turned his attention to his phone. "When's he going to call? Maybe we could call the office and have him interrupted?"

"He's not in the office, remember? He's in Chicago this week. I think they're meeting at a client's office, but I don't know the number."

"Oh, right." Maddox stared at his phone.

Linda sat on the edge of his bed. "Why don't you send him a text and tell him to call you ASAP. He'll likely see the text pop up on his computer even if he can't answer it."

"Good idea." Maddox sent the text and collapsed against his pillow. "A donor. Mom, can you believe it?"

"Yes, I can believe it. And I am so thankful for it."

"I can't wait to tell my friends about it. They're going to be so excited. Of course, I have to tell Dad first."

"He'll be more excited than your friends."

"Pretty sure you're right about that." He stared down at his phone as if willing it to ring.

What would his friends think when they found out his donor was his half sister, one that neither he nor his father had ever known existed? The timing of this truth would be especially hard for Brent, given what was happening with Game Changers. He had put so much energy into that group, wanting it to be a legacy he left behind someday.

Two years ago his father had been given a lifetime achievement award through the Academy of Sciences for his research in virology, listing him as one of the most influential scientists of the past decade. This award coincided with Brent's fiftieth birthday and the accompanying obligatory midlife crisis. Since then, Brent had become obsessed with, "living a life that mattered," going so far as to consider leaving his job altogether to pursue something he deemed more meaningful.

Legacy—and everything associated with the word—was so important to Brent. Between Game Changers and the stepdaughter he'd never known about, it was all going to be ripped apart now.

Then it occurred to her, she didn't have to tell them. Dr. Stern herself had said the donation was anonymous. If Caroline wasn't interested in any contact with Linda, then why should she say anything?

Maddox called across the room, "Dad's calling. I'll put him on speaker."

"Is everything all right?"

"Dad, everything is so all right it couldn't be any better. You're not going to believe it, but I'm in remission, and they have found a bone marrow match for me, and I get to go home soon."

"Oh, thank You, dear Lord. That is the best news I've heard in ... a really long time. Oh, Maddox, this is the best possible news." He paused one more beat. "Listen, I'm in the middle of something pretty critical here. Let me call you back when I'm done so I can hear all about it."

"Sounds great. Love you, Dad."

"Love you, too, buddy."

Maddox pressed the disconnect. Without looking up, his fingers moved across the screen. "I'm going to text Marshall, and then can I tell my friends?"

"Sure." Linda was so thankful to see her son so happy again. How long had it been since she had seen him this excited about anything? Before the diagnosis of cancer, that much was certain.

As Maddox started a series of phone calls and texts to his friends, Linda returned to her corner seat to give him a little space. She had some calls and texts of her own to make with good news like this.

She picked up her phone and saw the new email: *Are you interested in getting dinner on Thursday night?*

So much for a secret that need never be told. She pulled up her calendar to make a note to herself and when she noticed the date for Thursday it took her aback. August 1. Really?

There was only one answer possible at a time like this. She typed back immediately. *I would love that. We can celebrate your first birthday on the East Coast.*

Her daughter's birthday. The daughter whose marrow donation was going to save her son's life. None of it seemed real.

Chapter 18

"Are you sure you two will be all right for a couple hours?"

Maddox waved his hand toward the door. "Mom, relax. We're fine. Look at all these." He had just returned from a visit to the recreation center and now held two DVDs and a video game. "I've got plenty to keep us occupied and out of trouble. I promise to do what I can to keep Marshall from getting arrested in your absence, but well . . . you know how he is."

"Maddox, I'm serious."

"So am I." He walked over and hit the eject button on the DVD player built into his television set. He pulled out one disc, inserted another, then turned back to her. "Come on. Calm yourself, woman. I'm in remission. Numbers are up, and I'm heading home soon. We might as well enjoy this time before we do the bone marrow transplant and the bad stuff starts all over again. Besides, Marshall's here. He'll fetch me whatever I need."

Marshall looked up from the 3-D model he was building on his computer. "Yeah, right." He tapped a couple of keys. "Don't worry, Mom. We're good. If he begins to show signs of dehydration or starvation while you're gone, I'll press that little button on his control and call for prompt delivery of sustenance."

"And if I should start to puke, he'll clean the mess with his bare hands."

Marshall shuddered. "I wouldn't count on that if I were you." Marshall bordered on germaphobic, so while it was a good thing having him around his immune-compromised brother because he was very conscientious of hand washing and keeping things mostly sterile, bodily fluids were definitely out of his realm.

"Maddox, you haven't puked in over a week. Stop messing with your brother." She turned to Marshall, who was looking a bit green. "And Marshall, in the unlikely event that something like that should happen, then please do press the nurse's call button."

"Have no fear there, Mother dearest, I will press that button and run out of this room on hyperspeed I assure you. Now, go have a fun birthday dinner with your old college friend. What did you say her name was again?"

"Caroline."

"Right. Go have fun with Caroline."

In the current situation, Linda was thankful for teenage sons who were exceptionally uninterested in her life. No one even thought to ask the question, "Why haven't I ever heard of this friend before?"

She made her way out of the hospital and spent the hour-long drive praying. As had been the case since all this began, there was nothing spiritual or eloquent about her prayers. They mostly sounded like, *God, please keep Maddox safe while I'm gone,* and *God, please heal Maddox,* and *God, please help me not to say something stupid during this dinner with my daughter.*

...

Caroline wiped her clammy hands along the sides of her new sundress as she climbed the stairs leading to the restaurant's front door. She'd been saving the blue-and-white-striped ensemble for tonight, although when she'd bought it, she anticipated spending the evening with her mom. Well, her real mom. Well, the woman she called mom. "Hi, reservation for Caroline? I'm meeting someone, but I don't know if she's here yet."

The taller of two women standing behind a hostess table glanced down at a list. "No, she hasn't arrived, but we can seat you and show her to the table once she arrives. Follow me." She offered a smile, grabbed a couple of menus, then turned and led Caroline through The Mooring's dining room.

The flutter inside eased a tad as she followed the hostess to a large patio overlooking the harbor. When she got to the small staircase leading down to it, she had to shield her eyes from the sun that seemed more determined to join in for an appetizer than say good night. It was one of the things that had surprised her about the area—in the summer, it wouldn't get completely dark until after nine.

"Is this okay? I have you written down for a patio table." The hostess stopped at the bottom of the stairs.

"Oh, it's fine. I just wish I had my sunglasses, that's all."

"We can lower those if it starts to bother you." She pointed to the blinds, then an open table at the bottom of the stairs. "Here you go. Your server will be right with you."

Caroline kept her hand up, then used her menu to block the sun. Other than that, the table was perfect—she'd be able to see Linda come in.

She adjusted the seat this way, then that, but she'd just have to deal with the sun for now. Her phone buzzed from inside her purse. She reached in to make sure it wasn't Linda—late or canceling—although she couldn't decide if the latter wouldn't be the worst thing in the world. She hadn't noticed that her hands were so unsteady until she held her phone in her palm.

But it wasn't Linda. It was Dillon, and the unsteadiness in her hand filled her whole body.

Happy birthday, Care Bear.

Care Bear? Her stomach tightened. He wasn't allowed to call her that anymore. She'd let his birthday come and go without a hint she'd even remembered, and she nearly put her phone away without responding. Then again, it was nice of him to acknowledge it. She texted a quick *thanks* back, then laid her phone on the table.

"I was thinking about the Newport Beach Club." A young woman's voice got gradually louder just before the woman herself came down the stairs. "I went to a wedding there in June, but it's really expensive."

"What else is new?" A man followed, although Caroline could only see his bottom half from under her menu.

She couldn't help but giggle to herself. She lifted her menu slightly to catch a glance at the couple, now making their way to a table at the other end of the patio.

Dillon always used to criticize her for paying too much attention to other people at restaurants. But since Dillon wasn't here and the couple couldn't see her from her table anyway, she could look all she wanted. It would be a nice distraction while she waited for Linda.

A server came by to fill Caroline's water glass, but other than that, she was left to watch as the couple settled into their table. The man's back was to Caroline, but the woman was within view. It didn't take long for her to pull out a magazine with sticky-note bookmarks throughout, then start showing pictures to her date.

Of course. *The Knot.* Caroline could spot that magazine from a hundred yards away. How many times had she and

Dillon sat at a table just like that, filtering through photos of centerpieces, bouquets, and cakes? From the looks of things, this gal's fiancé didn't seem to offer much help. He kept shaking his head and scrunching his shoulders.

Poor girl. Well, no doubt it would end better for her than it had for Caroline. Hopefully, it would, anyway.

"Caroline?" A voice snapped her back to her own table, her own dinner, her own reality, and she nearly jumped at the sound.

"Linda." Caroline pronounced her name far louder than she'd intended, as if she needed to convince herself this was really happening. For a couple of seconds all she could do was stare at the older version of the woman from the picture. *Say something, Caroline!*

"I'm sorry I'm late. I—" Linda said just as Caroline began talking.

"Thanks so much for coming—" Caroline stopped as soon as she realized she'd interrupted.

Linda stood for another moment, like she wasn't sure what to do next. As if Caroline knew. Should she get up and hug her? Offer a handshake? Her mouth went dry. Even if she knew what to do, she wouldn't have been able to do it. Her body was as stiff as the taxidermic swordfish above her.

Finally, Linda offered a kind smile and a soft laugh, then sat down. "This is one of my favorite restaurants."

"I haven't been here before, but I've really been wanting to try it." Her voice cracked a tad, so she cleared her throat, then took a sip of water.

"Are you an oyster girl?" Linda opened her menu but didn't read it.

"Honestly, I've never been brave enough to try them, so I don't know."

"Me either. My husband claims they're good here, but I can't confirm it." Linda laughed again, that same soft laugh from earlier. She set her menu back on the table. "I was really happy to get your email. It meant a lot to me that you'd allow me to spend your birthday with you. And I can't tell you how good it feels to get out." She tilted her head back, closed her eyes, and smiled, as if she was soaking up the sun.

"My mom was supposed to come out, but my grandma had to go to the hospital. She had a—" Caroline paused, her thoughts suddenly tripping over themselves. Making this woman feel like a second choice, regardless of any other circumstances, wasn't how she wanted to start off. "Never mind. I really appreciate you coming. I know you have a lot going on."

Several moments of silence passed. Caroline wasn't exactly reading her menu as much as staring at it until it became a blurry jumble. Her heart was pounding. Were they just going to sit here in a swamp of awkwardness all night?

"So, um..." Linda lifted her shoulders. "Why don't you tell me a little about yourself?"

"Oh, okay." She welcomed the chance to ease the strain of silence. "Well, I grew up in Santa Barbara, went to Westmont, then started working for the Reagan Ranch Center as an assistant curator right out of college. I did that for two years, then started working for the Huntington Library in Pasadena as an event coordinator. The more I did it, the more I loved it. Room for creativity, but I like things planned out and organized so it was a good fit. I did that for almost four years before I came here."

"And now you're the director of special events for the Newport Preservation Society?"

"I am. I'm working on the annual fundraiser now, and then we'll move into a new event series in the fall."

Linda sat back and smiled. "Well, I was utterly flabbergasted to see you in the paper, and very proud. Although I have no right to be. Your parents did a great job."

Caroline sat up a little taller. "Thanks."

"Any men in your life?" Linda shook her head. "I'm sorry, too personal?"

Her toes scrunched against the bottom of her wedges. She'd left Dillon, the fact that she'd moved to LA for him, and the tidbit about his mom serving on the board of the Huntington Library and pulling a few strings out of her bio for a reason. "Not the right kind."

"There's plenty of time for that."

Linda smiled and Caroline pretended to do the same. It wasn't that she minded the question as much as the consolation that followed. Plenty of time, right. All of her friends were married, most with kids, and she was supposed to have been among them. If all had gone according to plan, she could have answered with a triumphant, "yes!" and flashed her ring. But no, she was single and stuck with insufficient encouragement, like a bad party favor at someone else's wedding.

Caroline took another sip of water, then glanced around for their server. "So, have you lived in the area awhile?" She clenched her napkin a little tighter. It seemed like a stupid question after the fact, but she couldn't think of another icebreaker.

Linda nodded. "Since Brent and I were married."

Thankfully, the server interrupted to take their drink orders, but once he was gone, Caroline was thrust back into searching for something to say. Linda had mentioned her husband, Brent, twice now. Was this her biological father? Was she even allowed to ask?

Linda leaned over and pulled out her phone. "Here. This is a picture of all of us last summer. Brent, Maddox, and Marshall." She pointed to each of them along the way, then stared at the photo.

Caroline felt a bit disoriented as she looked at this photo of people she'd never seen before, almost like she couldn't catch her balance. "Wait, you have another son?" She had another brother? She left that last question alone, along with several others she pushed to the back burner like, "Why didn't you tell me?" If she wasn't careful, that one might boil over.

"Yes. He's fifteen now, and Maddox recently turned seventeen."

"Hmm." Caroline looked again at this family she was simultaneously a part of but had no business calling her own. First at Maddox, then at Marshall. "Marshall looks like you." Maddox was the spitting image of his dad. Except for the black hair. Neither really resembled her, that Caroline could tell, anyway.

Linda's gaze lingered and Caroline leaned back a bit. She was about to search for the server again or pretend to need the restroom when Linda finally spoke. "You look like Jack." Her voice was barely audible, as if she was thinking aloud instead of making a statement.

"Jack? Who's that?" She scrunched her forehead.

Linda sat back, almost as if she was startled. "Um..." She took a deep breath. "Jack Perry, your dad. I mean, biological father. I didn't notice it as much when I saw your picture, but I see it now. Except for the blonde hair, I have no idea where that comes from." A slight smile formed.

Jack Perry. Caroline had never heard the name before, and up until this moment, she didn't feel the need to know it. But now...now that this information was right there in front of her, she wasn't able to ignore the pull for more.

"Do you keep in touch?" Maybe that was a stupid question, too.

Linda shook her head. "I heard he's living in Chicago, working for one of those big investment firms, but that's all I know. We never really spoke again after I...after you were born."

"He didn't want to be involved." Of course. Caroline leaned against the chair back and crossed her legs.

"He was a year older than me and ready to move on with his life after college. I was not part of that plan. The truth is, Caroline." She rested her arms on the table and clenched her hands together. "He thinks..." She paused for a couple of heartbeats. "Well...he doesn't know you were born. In fact, to be perfectly truthful, no one else here knows about you, either."

...

"I don't know, Elliott. I think maybe it's time to just give the whole thing up." Brent spoke softly into his cell phone so as not to be overheard—although the hospital lobby was all but empty tonight. "I've been trying to do something meaningful for the world, and instead I've made things worse. Not just for us, but for the young men we were hoping to help." His exhaustion, both physical and emotional, made him likely to say something he would regret, so he stopped speaking.

"I get it. This was your pet project, but we're going to salvage this as best we can. As for you, take some time, take care of your family, get a good night's sleep, and we'll talk again tomorrow."

"Yeah." He scrubbed his right hand across his face. "After seeing Rodney and his messed-up family, it makes me appreciate my wife that much more."

"You've got one of the best, no doubt. She must have been happy to hear you were flying home a day early."

"I didn't tell her. Or any of them. I thought it would make a nice surprise."

"Good for you. Well, give her a hug for me, and tell Maddox we're all rooting for him."

"I will. Thanks." He picked up the bag at his feet, which contained little tokens of appreciation for his family, and made his way into the hospital elevator. His mood lifted with each floor. Finally, there was good news for Maddox. That made everything else bearable.

A few minutes later, he pounced into Maddox's room. "Happy remission!"

"Dad! You're here. We weren't expecting you until tomorrow." Maddox swung his legs over the side of the bed and stood to greet him. He grabbed his IV pole and moved over for a hug. "How come you're here now?"

"We wrapped up our business a little earlier than expected, and I was able to switch flights. I started to call you all and let you know but decided a surprise would be better." He removed the Cracker Jacks from his bag and set them on the tray table. "Next time we eat these, it will be at Fenway."

"Sounds right to me. Thanks, Dad. This is awesome."

Marshall had also walked over but stood patiently waiting his turn. Brent hugged him. "Good to see you, buddy."

"You too, Dad."

Brent pulled the lemon drops out of his bag. "From your favorite candy store in Chicago."

"Thanks, Dad." Marshall worked on the seal as Brent reached the remaining item in his bag. A bouquet for Linda.

"Where's my best girl?" He glanced around the room.

Marshall said, "I think you should be aware that they don't allow flowers on this hall. Too many potential contaminants."

"Oh, right. I think I knew that. I'll just show them to your mother, then go put them in the car. Where is she?"

"She went to dinner." Maddox rolled his IV pole back to his bed.

"Dinner? I'll walk down to the cafeteria."

Maddox had already plopped onto his bed and poured himself a handful of Cracker Jacks. "Not the cafeteria. Somewhere outside the city, I think. It was one of her friend's birthdays, and she really wanted Mom to join her for dinner. She said she would stop by the house and pick up a few things while she was down that way."

"Outside of town? Really?" Knowing how hard it was for him to get Linda to drive home on Saturday when he was here to watch Maddox, he couldn't imagine she would leave the city to have dinner. "Which friend?"

"What did she say her name was, Marshall?"

Marshall, who had also resumed his seat, computer in his lap, said, "It was…uh…Caroline. I think she was her college roommate or something."

"You mean Julie, right?" Caroline was a name he had never heard before. Certainly not a name he would associate with her driving such a long way for dinner when her son was in the hospital.

"No, she said Caroline," Marshall said. "Whoever Caroline is, she must be important. Mom was all dressed up and seemed even more uptight than usual."

"Really?"

Before Brent could pursue the line of questioning any further, Maddox pressed the button to unmute the television. "Tied in the bottom of the eighth. Get rid of those flowers and pull up a chair, Dad. You want some Cracker Jacks?"

CHAPTER 19

"What do you mean no one out here knows about me?" The server approached the table with their drinks and a basket of bread, although Caroline hardly even noticed.

"Have you ladies decided what you want to eat?"

After Linda ordered the scallops, Caroline managed to squeak out, "Salmon."

When the server left, Linda took a deep breath and pressed her lips together. "I went to California for the second semester of my junior year—you know, the Gordon and Westmont exchange program. Anyway, I discovered I was pregnant right before going, and my parents thought I stayed in Santa Barbara the following summer for an internship. Jack had graduated and moved on by the time I got back."

"So, Jack never knew you were pregnant?"

"He knew. He just thinks … he just thinks …"

The silence fell thick and heavy for a few seconds, before Linda continued. "I met Brent several years later and never told him."

Caroline attempted to untangle the mess of information she'd been hit with. She wasn't sure where to start or what business it was of hers to even ask. This was Linda's life, her story. But now that their lives were intersecting a second time. and Linda's story was overlapping with Caroline's ... "Who do they think the match is?"

"A random person. Proof of God's provision. Which it is, but not quite in the way they think."

Caroline swallowed hard. A random person? Was that all she was? "Do you plan to tell them?"

"I'm going to wait. I don't think it would be wise to do anything that would cause more disruption right now. But if Maddox—when Maddox—pulls through this and things get back to normal, yes. I want to tell them."

"Oh." She nodded a few times but inside, she was crumbling. "Who do they think you're with right now?"

"My husband is out of town. I told my sons I was going to celebrate a friend's birthday. As teenagers, they are spectacularly uninterested in what their mother is doing." Linda let out a soft laugh.

Caroline forced a smile. So if she wasn't a match, would Linda really care to know her more?

She needed to change the subject. "How's Maddox doing?" It was the first thing that came to mind. It was the main reason they were here right now. Together.

"He's doing pretty well, especially now that you've brought hope for a long-term recovery. Still, the chemo has taken quite a toll on him, physically and emotionally. It's hard to watch your child go through something like this." She stared off into the distance, her eyes unfocused. "I'm sorry. I didn't come here to unload all of this on you. I really didn't. But I do want you to know how much I appreciate what you're doing for me. Us."

"I'm sorry you all have to go through it." It didn't do much to dull the hurt, in her own heart or on Linda's face.

After their entrees arrived, Caroline poked at her salmon while Linda ate her scallops. Her stomach was churning too much to really enjoy it… and that question she'd tossed to the back burner was starting to sizzle.

She took a deep breath. "Linda—" She wasn't entirely convinced she really wanted the answer. But not knowing would eat away at her, and this might be her only opportunity. "Why did you ask my parents to stop sending you pictures of me?"

Her cheeks warmed. Perhaps it was a bit too blunt. "I'm sorry. You don't have to answer that."

Linda set her fork down, sat back a bit, then wiped her lips with her napkin. "No, it's okay. You have the right to know." Her voice was soft again and she kept her eyes down. "At first I liked receiving the pictures. It helped me see that you were doing well and reassured me that I had done the right thing. But as time went by, the pictures of you growing into such a beautiful and happy little girl, well, they made me sad for what I was missing. Eventually, I wanted to reach out again, but then Brent came along, and I was convinced if he knew my secret, he wouldn't marry me. I should have just told him from the beginning. For over two decades, I have regretted that. But at the time, it seemed like the right thing to do." Linda looked up, and this time, Caroline could definitely see tears spilling over her lower lashes.

"I'm sorry, Caroline. I never should have kept this secret for so long. And now… the truth is going to make a mess of everything." An ache filled Caroline's throat. For her own sake, yes, but for Linda's, too. She wanted to put a hand on her shoulder or grab her hand, but nothing felt quite appropriate. Still, she didn't mean to add to the weight of what Linda was already carrying. Only alleviate the weight of what was building in her.

"Well—" Caroline tilted her head to the side. "Probably better anyway. I had a really bad haircut all through middle school, and I'm actually relieved that you never saw it."

Linda stared at her for a moment, then a smile crept over her face. Then a laugh—and not the same soft laugh from earlier—erupted as she tilted her head back. It was several moments before she came up for air. "Thanks." Linda dabbed at her wet eyes and laughed again. "I needed that."

Now Caroline was laughing as well. "Me too, actually."

The conversation took a lighter turn, and Caroline learned more about Maddox and Marshall. As it turned out, they had a few things in common—baseball was Maddox's passion, and he'd once expressed an interest in going to Westmont. And Marshall, well, he just might be able to beat Caroline at a game of chess.

After the server cleared their plates, Linda stood. "I'm just going to run to the restroom." She grabbed her purse from the back of her chair before she turned to leave. "I'll be right back."

Caroline was relieved to have a moment alone, just to regroup and collect herself. She glanced up and noticed the couple in the corner getting their bill already. Hmm, no dessert?

Okay, that's enough staring. She forced her gaze elsewhere and found an oil painting of a fishing village on the wall behind her, under the swordfish. Probably nineteenth century. *Continental* by M. Adrian. Stunning. Oh, who was she kidding? The painting was no more interesting than listening to Ruth talk about her Hummel collection that afternoon. She turned her head back to the couple. The woman was walking away from the table, leaving the man behind to deal with the check.

A few moments later, he stood, returned his wallet to his back pocket, then grabbed his fiancée's sweater she'd left on her chair. *What a gentlema—*

Ohmygosh. Caroline flipped her head back to the oil painting, then put her hand up as if she had an itch on her eyebrow. Okay, there was still a chance he didn't notice her. *Just stay still.*

"Happy birthday to you..." A chorus of servers burst into song and came to stand directly in front of Caroline's table, holding a piece of key lime pie, complete with a lit candle. Caroline's ribs squeezed together, like a boa constrictor, snuffing out every last ounce of self-respect she had. When they finished their round of melodious humiliation, the pie was placed in front of her, and the servers gave themselves a round of applause.

She glanced up at them but kept her head down. "Thank you." She didn't mean it at all.

"Caroline?"

Shoot me now. She turned her head slowly. "Hi, Chris."

"Is it your birthday?" It looked to Caroline as though he was trying to suppress a robust laugh.

She pointed to her pie, blew out the candle, then gave an exaggerated grin. "Yes. I'm finally twenty-one!"

This time he laughed out loud, then looked around her table. "Are you here with anyone?"

"I am. My...um..." What was she? Mom? Recent acquaintance? "Friend just went to the restroom." Friend felt right. It's what Linda had called her when she told her sons where she was going.

Chris nodded and offered a smile. "Happy birthday."

"Yep, thanks." She maintained as much confidence as she could muster as he walked away.

Just after he left, Linda returned. "Oh, I missed it?" She sat back down in her chair.

"Yeah, it's okay." The fewer people to witness that the better.

Linda grabbed Caroline's hand, then gave it a little squeeze. "Happy birthday, Caroline."

After the pie was gone and the check had been paid, Caroline and Linda stood outside the restaurant for a moment. She'd promised to call her parents as soon as it was over, and knew they'd be waiting anxiously for her to do so. Still, she didn't want to rush off.

"I would like to get to know you more, Caroline. At least keep in touch." Linda clenched her purse tight to her chest with one leg crossed in front of the other. Funny, Caroline was standing exactly the same way.

"Yeah, okay. I'll keep you updated as I know more."

"Yes, please do." Linda approached slowly, extended one arm, then wrapped it around Caroline. "And I'd love to get together again."

Caroline returned the hug, more out of obligation than desire at first. Usually she didn't enjoy hugging strangers at all, yet this felt different. Better than she expected. "Yeah, that would be great."

And as she thought about it on the way home, she was pretty sure she actually meant it. But a small, persistent whisper nestled in her heart: did Linda?

...

Brent's phone finally vibrated in his shirt pocket. After several calls had gone unanswered, he was beginning to get worried. He pulled up the text.

Sorry I missed your calls. I'll call back in the morning—I'm really tired and am about to settle in for an early night.

About to settle in for an early night? That could only mean she was in the hospital and on her way to the room. He watched the door, eager to surprise her. Several minutes passed. He opened the door and looked down the hallway.

Nothing.

Then he did something he had never done before. He clicked on the Find My iPhone app, specifically to locate his wife.

It took a minute for the map to load up. When it did, he couldn't believe what he was seeing. Linda was in Newport. That was over an hour from here. Something was wrong. Very wrong.

Given the week he'd just had, his mind went to places it had never gone before. It was ridiculous though. Linda would not cheat on him, would not do that to their family, especially now. *Isn't that what Rodney's wife had thought a few months ago?*

Marshall looked up from his cell. "Cedric's dad is downstairs to pick me up. I didn't think to let him know you are here."

"Oh, right." The fact that Marshall had been spending a week with his friend from Boston hadn't even occurred to Brent. "I hadn't thought about that. Do you want to ride home with me?"

Marshall considered for a moment, then shook his head. "His dad is already here, and my stuff's at his house. I'll stick to the plan and stay there tonight. I'll catch up with you tomorrow for a ride, though. Welcome home, Dad." He threw his laptop in his backpack and made for the door. "See you tomorrow, dweeb." He punched Maddox on the arm, the closest the boys ever got to showing affection.

"Only if you're lucky, dork," Maddox responded.

Brent vaguely registered Marshall leaving the room. *What is going on?*

His current state of agitation dictated that he not confront Linda in front of Maddox. He needed stability and security now, not confrontations between his two main support people. No, Brent would wait for tomorrow.

He sat with Maddox for another hour. If he didn't leave soon, the chances were great for him to encounter Linda. Also, Maddox would not be left alone for long.

"I'll see you tomorrow, sport."

"You're not going to wait for Mom?"

He glanced at his watch and feigned a big yawn. "Nah. I'm really tired after traveling all day. I need to go home and get unpacked."

He gathered his things, then turned to his son. "Do me a favor. Don't tell your mom I was here tonight. I'll show up for breakfast tomorrow and surprise her."

Maddox shook his head and grinned. "You two are so weird."

Brent kissed his son on the forehead and hurried out. When he reached his car, he went first to the passenger side, removed the bouquet, and made quick work of depositing it in the nearest trash can.

Chapter 20

"**I** wouldn't do that if I were you."

Linda stopped, her hand still on the door. "What's wrong?" She hurried to Maddox's bedside, prepared for the worst.

"Nothing's wrong. I just don't think you should go to breakfast right now." He didn't appear ill, but something was off.

"Tell me what's wrong." Linda wasn't hungry, but she needed to get out of the room and go for a walk. She hadn't slept at all last night, tossing and turning and thinking about Caroline, and Maddox, and the right time and way to tell her family about all of it.

"Nothing." He fiddled with the water jug on his bedside tray, refilled his cup, but didn't take a sip. "I just don't think you should go get food right now, that's all. You want to play *Mortal Kombat*? I'll set it on the easiest level."

"I do not, thank you very much." She looked at him, trying to gauge his reaction. Was he hiding some new pain because he wanted to be allowed to go home this weekend? "Maddox, if something is wrong, I need to know and I need to know it now." She picked up the box with the nurse's call button.

"No, Mom, it's nothing like that. It's just that... well, I've heard a rumor that there might be someone surprising you for breakfast this morning. If you go eat now, it will ruin everything."

Linda breathed a sigh of relief. "Oh, thank goodness." She looked at him and grinned. "What time is Kristyn planning to be here?" This kind of thing was so like her friend.

"Um … it's not Kristyn exactly."

"Really? Then who exactly?"

He shook his head. "I can't say. But please act surprised when your mystery date arrives."

Linda laughed. "Cross my heart."

The door opened, and she turned to see who the surprise guest might be. Marshall entered the room. "Good morning, Mom. Did you have fun last night?"

"I had a nice time, thanks." She looked at her son. "Why are you here so early? I thought you had plans to go into the city with Cedric today."

"Changed my mind. I've been with Cedric all week, and I'm ready to get back home." Marshall tossed his duffel bag into the corner of the room, then dropped into the blue chair, arms and legs sprawled in every direction. "Dad said he would take me."

"Yes, but he won't be back in town until late tonight."

Marshall cocked his head to the side, as if staring at an unusual specimen in a museum of oddities. "He got in last night." Marshall looked at Maddox. "What, you didn't know?"

Linda's heart nearly stopped beating. "Your father arrived last night? I wonder why he called you instead of me." Then she remembered the missed call notifications after she left dinner last night. Of course he had tried to tell her. And she had sent him that text about making it an early night.

"You bonehead, it was supposed to be a surprise. He's taking her to breakfast this morning."

"Nobody said anything to me about a surprise. Last I heard, he was planning to stay here and wait until she got back from dinner, and then he was going to give me a ride home this morning."

"Here? Your father came to the hospital while I was out?"

"Isn't that what I've been saying?" Marshall looked completely confused.

"Yes, I guess it is. Sorry. Haven't had my coffee yet." Linda walked over to look out the window into a cloudy, gray morning. Well, there was nothing to do but tell it all now. She was caught.

...

It was all Linda's fault. She was the one who had made every single poor choice along the way, but she wasn't the only one with consequences, and the others were innocent. Her family would be crushed because of the choices she'd made—choices she made to protect them—or maybe to protect herself?

When Brent arrived, he walked through the door neatly dressed, offered a large smile to the room in general, but never quite turned in her direction. "Good morning, family."

Once again, Linda found herself grateful for the general oblivious nature of teenage boys. They both acknowledged their father's greeting, exchanged pleasantries, and seemed not to notice the tension crackling through the air in the room. Finally, Brent turned to Linda. "Let's go for breakfast, shall we?"

He didn't wait for an answer but walked to the door and held it open for her. As they made their way down the hallway, past the nurses' station and to the elevators, neither of them spoke. Brent hit the button for the parking garage instead of the first floor.

Until now, Linda had assumed they were headed to the cafeteria. "Where are we going?"

"Somewhere away from here. I want to be able to talk without being overheard."

She nodded and said no more. They climbed into his car, and he drove toward the Charles River, neither of them speaking. It was as if they both understood that the conversation that followed would need to be said face-to-face, not staring out a windshield in downtown Boston traffic. Brent parked in the lot beside Teddy's, a favorite breakfast place when they were in Boston.

Linda climbed out of the car, and in spite of the restaurant being busy, they were able to get a table beside the floor-to-ceiling windows. Several kayaks and a couple of sailboats dotted the water outside. On a normal day, this view would lend itself to happy conversation and appreciation for their splendid table location. Today was not a normal day.

As they were settling in their seats, a waitress appeared. Blonde. Pretty. She reminded Linda of Caroline. "I'll leave you two to look over your menus, but in the meantime, would you like coffee? Juice?"

"Coffee please," they responded in unison. This did not provoke the usual laughter and comments about how they'd been married so long they even spoke alike.

Brent waited until the waitress left and then said, "So, I was more than a bit surprised to arrive at our son's hospital room to find you out for the evening."

As much as she had planned to come straight out with the truth, Brent's condescension made her angry. "You're the one who's been telling me that I've got to make sure to take care of myself during all this. I don't know why it should surprise you that I actually took your advice."

"What surprises me is that when I took you out for our lobster dinner, we were only a couple blocks from the hospital, and you were a nervous wreck the whole evening and anxious to get back. This time, however, you apparently weren't so concerned, to the point that you felt free to drive all the way to Newport."

"How do you know I was in Newport?"

"I grew concerned when you were gone so long, so I hit Find My iPhone."

"You were spying on me?"

"I was worried about you. The fact that you would even consider my doing that as spying tells me that you're hiding something."

The truth of that statement knocked every bit of fight out of her. She slumped forward in her chair and rubbed her face. "You're right. You're absolutely right." She shook her head and looked up. "It's time I told you the whole truth."

CHAPTER 21

"**D**o you remember me mentioning Jack, the guy I dated my junior year of college?"

Brent's face went pale. "Yes, vaguely."

As Linda recounted the story, the memories came back so strong and so alive that it was as if she were reliving the whole thing. She could still see the envious stares of the other girls as she walked past on Jack's arm. She could remember how lucky she felt that of all the girls, he had chosen her. She could remember the way he looked at her with such love—or that's what she had believed it was. His words certainly backed up that assumption. In the end, his actions proved it all to be false. She relived that last awful scene, could still see the little stone bridge just beside the bench where they had been sitting almost thirty years ago.

"Pregnant? What do you mean pregnant?" Jack's voice game out in a gasp.

Linda grasped his hand tighter but continued to gaze into his blue eyes. "I mean pregnant."

He looked at her for another moment, then pulled his hand from hers and scrubbed both hands across his face. "Oh man." He shook his head, then turned to watch the creek flowing past. The gurgling of the water was the only sound for a long time. Finally, she couldn't take it anymore. "Say something."

"What am I supposed to say?"

"I don't know. Something like, we'll figure this out together. I'll go with you to talk to your parents. I'm going to be here for you as we work through this. Any of those things would be a good place to start."

"Linda, I..." He pulled his hand through his unruly curls. "I can't handle this right now. My parents..." He let several curse words fly, something he never did. "I need to get out of here." He rushed across the bridge and broke into a run.

Late the next afternoon, he had asked her to go for a ride. They pulled up at a nearby park and sat in the car. Across the grass there were picnic tables, all empty now due to the recent cold spell. "I was up all night trying to figure this out," he said, "and then it hit me."

"What?" Linda couldn't imagine what great answer could have possibly hit him, because she certainly hadn't been able to come up with anything, and she had been up all night for several nights.

"Christmas break starts next week, and then you're heading to California for the semester exchange, so what I'm thinking is..." He paused a long time. "It'll still be early. You could take care of it while you're out there. No one here would ever know."

"Take care of it?"

"Don't you see, Linda? It's the only way." The conversation had continued from there, but she heard little of it at the time and could remember none of it now. She did remember, however, the swing set across the way, the squeaking sound of the chains as the empty swings blew back and forth in the wind. Back and forth. *Screech, screech.*

The next few weeks passed in a blur. During Christmas break, her mother had grown concerned, but Linda played it off as just being extra tired. And that was true enough. She was exhausted.

Three weeks later, when she boarded a plane to Santa Barbara, she had more or less convinced herself that Jack was right. This news would destroy her parents. And his. Most especially his, since his father was the pastor of a mega-church near Chicago. She could make an appointment, go in, and just a bit later, this problem would go away.

Linda pulled back from the pain of the past and returned her focus to the present, and the pain on the face of the man she loved, the one who had stood by her for the past twenty-one years. He stared at her with a look somewhere between horror and utter heartbreak. She stared down at her hand as it closed around the white coffee cup on the table in front of her.

"Long story short, I couldn't do it. I made some calls and eventually found a nice family who was seeking to adopt. I wore baggy sweatshirts to class, didn't befriend anyone, and no one at school ever knew I was pregnant. I told my parents I had an internship for the summer, so I was able to stay away until the baby—her name is Caroline—was born, and I had sufficiently recovered. My parents never knew anything."

"And until this moment, neither did your husband."

The waitress arrived with their food. They both turned their heads away from the other, as if they each needed a break. Only in a situation like this, there could be no break. Not really.

...

After the waitress walked away, Brent picked up his fork and stabbed at his hash browns. How was it possible that this conversation was happening, that this—event—had happened and he'd known nothing? He thought about the meetings he'd just come from. Was he really this naive about people? He'd never believed so.

Linda lifted her napkin to her face, the tears leaving translucent spots on the solid white paper. For the first time in his life, he watched her cry and felt no ability to comfort her—or even the desire to do so.

"I am astounded. Not only that this all happened, but that you have never thought to mention it to me before now."

"Of course I've wanted to. For all these years it's been eating me up that you didn't know. I kept thinking I would tell you when the timing was right, and of course it never felt right. And then after so much time had gone by, there was no way to tell you without—well, ruining everything. I couldn't bear the thought of that. So ... I've kept it secret all these years."

"Your parents? You've never told them?"

"No." She shook her head.

"And Jack? What is his part in all of this?"

"Not long after I arrived in California, he sent me some money and a letter saying it was better if we went our separate ways." She choked on those words. It took a few seconds before she continued. "I've not spoken to him since."

"Until last night."

Linda actually gasped. "Is that what you think? Brent, I was not with Jack last night. I was with Caroline."

"Caroline? So all these years when you couldn't think of a way to tell me, you've still thought of a way to sneak out and go see her? Has this been going on since we were first married?"

"No, I've never ... Brent, Caroline is the match. She's the one who is going to save Maddox."

Linda watched her husband's face go white. "You need to tell me everything. Right now."

"For a while I kept in touch with Caroline's new family. Her mother sent me pictures. They were quite wonderful actually. After about a year, I finally asked her not to send me any more, because it was painful to receive them. I haven't been in touch with any of them since then, although I did google Caroline sometimes. I have for years. Not long after Maddox was diagnosed, I discovered she had moved from California to Newport. When we couldn't find a suitable donor, I sent her an email and asked if she would get tested."

"And you did this when?"

"Two months ago."

"Two months? Yet you haven't found a spare moment to mention any of this to me?"

"There was a good chance she wouldn't be a match, and I knew all this would be upsetting to you when you found out."

"Upsetting? You think so?" Brent rarely used sarcasm, so on the rare occasions that he did, it stung that much more.

"I just didn't see a reason to say anything about it until I knew for sure there was a reason to."

"I've got a reason for you. How about honesty? We've been married for twenty-one years, and you've never thought to yourself, 'Hmm, I wonder if I should tell Brent I have a child he's never heard about?'"

"You're carrying so much on your shoulders right now. I didn't want to be the one to add more to it. In fact, even with Caroline being the match, I had not planned to tell you who she was until after. When Maddox was better."

"What made you go to Newport last night?"

"When I first contacted Caroline about getting tested, I had offered to buy her coffee or dinner, but she said she wasn't ready for anything like that. Well, yesterday was her birthday. Her mother was supposed to fly out from California for a long girls' weekend, but her grandmother ended up in the hospital. Caroline is new in Newport, so rather than be alone, she asked me to join her."

Brent leaned back in his seat, put both hands behind his head, and turned his eyes toward the ceiling. "Just when I think my life can't get any more complicated, it does." He shook his head.

Linda waited without speaking. She had told him everything. Now, there was nothing left to do but wait for his response.

"And Jack? You said you haven't spoken to him since that letter. So I'm guessing he thinks..."

Linda turned the full force of her gaze up to Brent. "He is unaware that he has a daughter."

"I see." He nodded and stared at the eggs on his plate, long since gone cold. "And Maddox is unaware that he has a sister, who is also his bone marrow donor. What are we going to do about that?"

"I don't know." A drop of condensation slid the length of Linda's water glass and soaked into the checkered tablecloth. "I know we need to tell him eventually, but I don't think now is the right time."

Brent drummed his fingers on the table, each finger landing with a thud. "Well, history has shown us that you have a problem discerning the right time, hasn't it?"

The finger tapping continued, and Linda heard a word in each strike. *Wrong. Wrong. Wrong. Wrong.* And that was what she had been, so how could she argue with even an imaginary accusation? She turned her attention back to her water glass while the thrumming continued. *Wrong. Wrong. Wrong. Wrong.*

Finally, Brent said, "There are many things to consider about timing in all this. For now, I'll take you back to the hospital and bring Marshall to the house with me. I need some time to think all this through."

Linda nodded. "I'm sorry."

There was nothing more to say.

Chapter 22

It was going to be another scorcher today. No doubt the beach would be jam-packed in just a few hours. A handful of early morning exercisers paced Cliff Walk, the three-mile path that separated Newport's rocky coastline from vast summer "cottages" like The Breakers and what was once the more modest, by comparison, Chadwick Place. But for now, Chris was one of the only ones on Easton's Beach.

He wiped the sweat from his forehead with his shirt and allowed his breathing to steady. Usually at this halfway point on his six-mile run, he'd turn right around and finish up. But today, he gave himself a few minutes to enjoy the peace and quiet of the morning. The waves crashing on the sand, the sun starting to break over the point, the breeze, the solitude—even he needed a reprieve once in a while from the constant sounds of construction. He thought for a second about jumping in the ocean—his athletic shorts were quick-dry material—but did he have enough time? Maybe, if he picked up his pace on the run home.

The email notification buzzed through the song in his earbuds. So much for solitude. He pulled out his phone, fully expecting it to be junk mail, but it wasn't. It was from Blythe.

Forwarding him junk mail, for all intents and purposes, with *PLEASE!* in the subject line. He scanned the digital invitation, his heart rate spiking again.

No. He emailed back without further consideration.

Why not? The text came about five seconds later.

NO. He punched the letters.

Pleeeeeease? You'll miss me when I'm in Hawaii and wish you had said yes.

Chris rolled his eyes. She knew just how to get him, didn't she? *Why can't Adam take you?*

He's on a submarine, remember???

Another text came in, this time from Addie Beth. *Come on, just take her.*

Oh, good grief. What was this, an attack from all sides? Didn't his sisters have anything better to do at six thirty on a Monday morning? *Good morning to you too.*

Addie Beth chimed in again. *Don't tell her I told you this, but you remember when she said she didn't want to go to prom her senior year?*

It had been nearly a decade, but he vaguely remembered Addie Beth freaking out over Blythe not wanting to go to prom. He didn't see what all the fuss was about at the time. He hated that kind of stuff. *Sort of, yeah.*

Addie Beth continued. *She told me a few years later that it was actually because she didn't want Mom to stress about buying her a new dress. Just do it. It would mean the world to her.*

He groaned. He had to admit, when they teamed up his sisters were good. Of course, he'd need to run it by Tom. Not that Tom controlled his personal life—well, that was up for debate—but agreeing to this wouldn't be a completely personal matter.

He wiped his forehead again, then joined the two conversations so he could text both his assailants at once. *I'll think about it.*

He didn't wait for their responses—who knows what else they'd rope him into? Instead, he took out his earbuds, took off his shoes, socks, and shirt, then headed for the ocean.

...

"You two sure have been going out a lot lately. This is not one of those midlife crises, getting all mushy and googly-eyed, old married folks kind of thing, is it?" Maddox crossed his arms and looked at his parents. In spite of his teasing words, his narrowed eyes hinted at something else. Linda suspected the boys had finally picked up on the fact that something was amiss. Thankfully, the news that Maddox would be allowed to come home this afternoon had kept them mostly preoccupied elsewhere.

Brent, too, seemed to sense the note of alarm in Maddox's question. He answered with his best John Wayne impression. "Don't you worry none, pardner. I'll try to keep the public displays of affection with the little lady to a minimum." Brent put his arm around Linda and drew her into a hug. "It's just so hard to resist your beautiful mother, though."

"Dad. Gross!" Both boys made gagging sounds, their suspicions currently allayed.

"Gross, really? Thanks a lot, you two." Linda's pretence of being offended would further throw them off track. Or so she hoped.

"We won't be gone long." Brent pulled Linda toward the door. The second they were outside the room, he withdrew his arm and took a step away from her. Since the conversation three days ago, the only communication between them revolved around today's temporary discharge—date, time, and procedures.

They walked to a little diner just down the street from the hospital and found an empty booth beside the front door. "So, we need to talk through who should be told and when to tell them."

Linda nodded. She waited for him to continue, but he didn't.

Jingle jingle. The bells on the door happily announced the arrival of new patrons. Laughter and carefree chatter followed the foursome to their booth.

Their own table remained silent. After some time, Brent said, "Well?"

She shrugged. "I am not the best judge of proper timing in this case—I believe those were your words. So, I'm waiting to hear from a better judge of the proper timing."

He scrubbed his face with his hands. "There's no easy answer. Nothing seems right."

At least they were in agreement about one thing. Linda waited for him to say more, but he didn't. The waiter poured coffee, they each ordered scrambled eggs and toast, and then fell silent again.

Jingle jingle. Those stupid bells kept trilling their cheerful little chorus. How did the world continue about its daily business at times like this? Her world had shut down, but to everyone around them, nothing had changed. How was this possible?

She finally spoke up. "We need to get Maddox through the transplant first. He needs every ounce of his strength and energy focused on withstanding what's ahead."

Brent took a deep breath, his gaze trained on the navy-blue coffee cup with a white anchor and red rope emblazoned on the front. "You're probably right about that." He leaned back and turned his attention toward the window. The sidewalks were bustling with shopkeepers preparing to open for the day, and more than a few medical personnel on their way to work, their white coats and cheerfully colored scrubs giving them away.

"Here we are, two breakfast specials." The waiter set a plate of eggs and bacon in front of each of them, then a smaller plate with toast, butter, and jam above it. "Is there anything else you need right now?"

"No, thank you," Linda said. He smiled and walked away.

"I've got to be honest." Brent turned toward his plate but made no move to touch his utensils. "This whole thing is a real gut punch. Never in a million years would I have imagined that you were keeping something like this from me. Now I find myself doubting everything in my life I thought I knew."

"I know." Linda's heart was so heavy it hurt to breathe. She had made a huge mistake, at a terrible cost to her husband. All she could do now was try to make it up to him as best she could. "What can I do to help? I won't say 'make things right,' because they will never be completely right again. I get that—but to help start the healing process?"

"This is the kind of thing that I would tell another man, 'You've got to go to couple's counseling and work this thing out,' and I think that we probably do. Of course, with Maddox coming home for the week and then high-dose chemo after that, I just don't see couple's counseling happening in the near future."

There it was. A lifeline. Linda grasped at it with all the desperation of the drowning woman she was. "In the meantime, maybe you should find someone—a counselor or pastor—and get started? We won't be able to go together for a while maybe, but you have such an awful lot to process. The more you work through this before we tell the boys, the better."

He looked up at her. "You're right." The pain on his face was so raw, Linda reached across the table out of instinct. He pulled his hand away before she could touch him.

Brent picked up the pepper shaker and sprinkled his eggs. "Let's get Maddox through the donation before we drop this bomb."

Drop a bomb.

On her son. With cancer.

A bomb that she herself had constructed. Even her bones ached with the grief of it.

Jingle jingle. And the world moved on.

CHAPTER 23

Caroline's life was a game of Whac-A-Mole. Just as soon as one thing was under control, like finally securing a tent, two more crises would pop their heads and beg for attention. The stress of it all was...There was no time for stress. Not when La Fête was just a week and a half away.

As she sat in the waiting room of a Providence physician's office, filling out a new patient medical questionnaire for her final donation clearance, she couldn't help but be grateful for the few moments of quiet, even though her to-do list was mounting back at work. Answering questions about her height, weight, and medical concerns were a cinch compared to figuring out the table assignments.

She flipped the first page of the medical form and started on the second. "Any known family history of the following" it read. She tucked a piece of hair behind her ear as she looked around the room. *Known* family history? Should she just write N/A, as she'd been doing all her adult life? This information seemed a bit more pertinent now than it had in the past.

"Caroline?" A medical assistant stood in the doorway of the waiting room with an iPad tucked in one arm and motioned for Caroline to follow with the other.

She stood, gathered her things, then followed the assistant, Megan, her name tag read, to a scale. Once that was done, she was taken to an exam room where Megan took her blood pressure and temperature. "Please change into that gown, open in the back, and the doctor will be in shortly."

Once Caroline was left alone again, she pulled out the forms, snapped a quick photo, then texted it to Linda. *Anything I should know about?*

She started to change into the gown as she waited, but it didn't take long for Linda to respond. *Diabetes on my side, dad and grandmother, but that's it. I don't know about Jack. Sorry.*

Although she was hoping for something more along the lines of, "perfect health on both sides, going back ten generations," a surprising sense of warmth filled her. She had a family history. Okay, so they knew nothing about her and it was diabetes, not abnormally high IQ or royalty, but still.

Perhaps she should use the information Linda had provided at dinner to look up her bio dad. Maybe he could tell her where her blonde hair came from. "Hi, I'm your biological daughter you know nothing about. Any family history of heart disease?"

On second thought, maybe it wasn't the best route. What if he had no interest in answering her questions? Or even talking to her? It might stir things up that would be better left alone. She finished changing, then settled back down on the exam table and flipped the page on the form. She was filling out the last question when she was interrupted by a soft knock on the door.

A man in his early sixties, Caroline guessed by his mostly gray hair, popped his head in, smiled, then came into the room. "Hi, Caroline, I'm Dr. Whiting. How are you today?" He reached out his hand to shake hers.

"Fine, thanks." A deep breath escaped through her semiconfident smile.

"Fine?" He looked straight at her with his small brown eyes. "You sighed when you said that. Are you fine?"

"Um." She sat up and her shoulders tightened a bit. "A little stressed, I guess?"

He sat on his wheeled stool, then set up his laptop. After a few clicks, he swiveled around to face her. "Stressed?"

"Yeah?"

"Is that a question?" His brows furrowed, but he appeared equally amused and intent.

"Um, I don't know. Yes, I'm a little stressed, but fine." She hoped she sounded more convincing that time.

He glanced at his laptop, then back at her again. "Your vitals are good. Anything going on that's out of the ordinary?"

Where should she start? "I'm just here to see if I'm healthy enough to donate bone marrow."

"Mm-hmm." He nodded. "Family history of any disease?"

"Diabetes, apparently, but that's all I know of. I was adopted." She handed him the medical forms she'd filled out.

"Oh, I see. Well, let's take a look." He stood, washed his hands, then walked over to Caroline. He ran his fingers down her throat, listened to her heartbeat, prodded her abdomen, and checked her reflexes in silence, then sat back down on his stool. "What's going on in your life that stresses you?"

Seriously? She crossed her bare arms, clenched her elbows in front of her, and hunched over. "All the usual stuff, I guess. Work, my family is far away, the marrow donation."

"This is stressing you out?" He clicked at his laptop as he talked.

"The timing of it. It's been creating a work conflict. Of course the surgery itself is making me a little anxious, but I'm sure I'll be fine." She paused. "But it's my biological brother who needs the donation, so it's been a lot to take in."

"I bet. I noticed you don't have a local emergency contact."

"No, not really. I moved recently." Her voice hitched a little. "I, um, don't know many people here." Tears threatened an appearance, so she swallowed hard and blinked a few times. *Pull it together, Caroline.*

"You'll need someone to drive you home after the donation."

She sat up a little straighter, happy to switch to a less emotional subject. "I hadn't really planned that far ahead. I guess I can take an Uber."

Dr. Whiting let out a laugh, but when Caroline didn't respond, he cleared his throat. "Oh, I thought you were joking. Caroline, you need someone you know and trust to get you home. I'll clear you to go ahead with this under two conditions. You find someone besides Uber to drive you home and stay with you."

She laughed along with Dr. Whiting, and for some reason it felt so good to do so, like a release of some sort. "Okay, and…?"

"And you take some time to meet people, get connected, and build a community here. I think that could be influencing your stress level and stress has a huge impact on your immune system. You'll need to be completely healthy for the transplant, and I want the healing process to go smoothly. I want to see you back a week after the donation and then again in six months, okay?"

Caroline agreed, and after getting dressed and making the six-month appointment with the receptionist, she was on the road back to her office. There was more traffic than usual, and the road to Newport was slow, especially once she got back on the island.

As she crossed over the town line from Middletown to Newport, with the busy and bustling Atlantic Ocean on her left and the bird sanctuary on her right, her music was interrupted by a phone call over her car speakers.

"Hello?"

"Caroline, hi. My name is Dr. Bennett. I'm on the transplant team for the marrow donation."

The name didn't mean anything to Caroline. Practically every time she'd gotten a call it was from someone different, a doctor on this team or a representative for that group, with the exception of Sharon from Be The Match. "Okay, hi."

"I have just received your medical clearance from Dr. Whiting."

"Wow, that was fast."

"Unfortunately, we don't have the luxury of the alternative. I am calling to let you know we are a go and need you at Mass General on the 20th."

"Of August? As in next week?" Her voice was much louder than she intended, but she couldn't exactly help it.

"Yes."

Her heart was pounding. Four days before La Fête? She'd need every minute to make sure it would go off without a hitch. But what was she supposed to say, have Maddox hold on just a few more days? Of course not. He needed her, and he needed her now.

If she remembered correctly from the information session, it's advised to take a few days off and rest after the procedure, but not mandatory. Staying hydrated was imperative, but some patients returned to work just two days after ... and she would be one of them. "Yes, of course. I will be there." She took a deep breath, clenched the steering wheel a little tighter, and stepped a little harder on the accelerator. She had to get back to work.

"Okay, either I or another member of our team will be in touch with more details tomorrow. Thank you, Ms. Chapman."

She made it back to her office via speeding and rolling through a stop sign or two, and as soon as she walked in the door, Ruth turned her chair to face her. "Thank goodness, you're back. You'll never guess who just RSV—" She stopped and tipped her head to the side. "Are you okay?"

Caroline dropped her bag, then plopped into her chair. Her stomach was heavy, despite eating nothing since breakfast hours ago, and she had no idea how to form the next sentence. "Ruth." Her voice cracked a little, and she searched for the right words. "I need to ask you a big favor."

CHAPTER 24

Don't throw up. Please don't throw up. Caroline pointed the air vent in Ruth's Camry directly on her face, then took several deep breaths.

"Are you okay?" Ruth looked over at Caroline, then out toward Interstate 95 northbound.

"Just a little warm, that's all." It wasn't all, not by a long shot, but it was all she was willing to discuss right now. Caroline pulled her phone out and again read the text she'd gotten from Linda early that morning.

I'm praying for you today. Thank you again for taking this step to save Maddox! It came with a photo of Maddox in his hospital bed, flashing a thumbs-up, and it had landed like a bomb in her gut. This wasn't a run-through. This was make or break.

"Do you get to meet the person you're donating to?"

The question was simple enough, yet not simple at all, and her heart rate rivaled the beat of the zippy classical tune playing on the radio. Caroline hadn't divulged every detail about the donation to Ruth. And by every detail, she meant anything beyond that she'd been selected to be a bone marrow donor and needed a ride to and from the hospital. Nothing about the who or the why. She just couldn't deal with the inevitable follow-up questions.

"I'm not sure. Not today, anyway. I think sometimes they meet, but it has to be a mutual decision." Hopefully Ruth couldn't detect the unsteadiness in her voice.

"Isn't it strange that someone's going to have your DNA now? I saw an episode of *Elementary* once where some DNA was found at a crime scene, and they thought it was the murderer's. Turns out the actual murderer was a bone marrow recipient, but they thought the donor had committed the crime, because it was his DNA at the scene." Her eyes wide, Ruth looked over at Caroline again.

"Thanks, Ruth. I feel a lot better now." Caroline yanked the seat belt off her chest and readjusted herself on the seat. "If I'm ever accused of murder, I'll be sure to tell them about M—" She caught herself in time. "My bone marrow recipient. Maybe that can be a plot twist at our Clue party."

Ruth laughed and then spent the rest of the drive humming along to the radio.

As soon as they pulled into Mass General's entrance, Caroline's body went a little limp. She spotted the Patient Admittance sign and took another deep breath. "Okay, I think I go in there. I will be able to go home at five, they said."

"I'll be there for you and sending good thoughts your way the whole time!" Ruth gave a thumbs-up and smiled.

Caroline appreciated the sentiment and returned the smile, but now, especially now, she needed so much more than good thoughts. She needed her parents back at home praying for her. She needed Linda praying for her. She needed to be praying herself.

She was pretty sure the last time she prayed, actually prayed, was when she had asked God if He would strike Dillon with lightning. Not enough to kill him, just zap some sense into him. God hadn't answered that one.

She took another deep breath and started walking.

Lord, give me Your peace today. Right now, I need to feel You with me. Help me get through this.

She whispered *Amen* just as she approached the counter. "Hi, I'm Caroline Chapman."

PS, Lord, please, please, please let this work.

...

Day 0. Transplant day.

Linda stood before the number grid on the wall, her fingers tracing that big, beautiful, bright-red zero. Not only was today the beginning of a new hope, but it was the end of days -7, -6, -5, -4, -3, -2, and -1—numbers she had gladly x'd out as the days progressed. Those were days spent blasting Maddox with high enough doses of chemo to kill any remaining cancer cells, wipe out what remained of his bone marrow, and keep him barely alive in the meantime. The process had been brutal. From today, the numbers on the grid moved into the positive range, and hopefully toward recovery.

She made up her bed and folded it back into the wall. *The next time I pull out this bed, Maddox will have new stem cells inside his body.* The thought permeated everything she did that morning.

Upon their return to the hospital last week, Maddox had been moved to the Stem Cell Transplant floor. There was specialized airflow in this unit, so the patients weren't forced to remain inside their negative pressure room twenty-four/seven but could actually walk around the hall when they felt like doing so. Not that Maddox felt like it at this point, but it was encouraging to see several of his neighbors out walking. Every patient on this unit was like Maddox—battling cancer, sicker than most people see in their worst nightmares, and much too young for any of it.

When they'd first arrived here, a package had been waiting in his new room. The envelope attached was blank on the outside except for the purple preprinted heart with the words *Dec My Room* on the flap.

Maddox pulled out the card and read aloud.

I know you said you didn't need a room makeover, but you did say you liked baseball and first base in particular, so I thought this might brighten up your new space a bit.

Janice

He looked at Linda. "Is Janice that one ...?"

"That you were extremely rude to? Yep, that's her."

"Thought so." He had the good grace to at least grimace at the memory before he tore open the wrapping.

A framed photo of Steve Kleen, the first baseman for the Red Sox, airborne in a full dive, ball barely in his glove, stared out at them. Written in the bottom corner was

To Maddox—
Keep up the good fight!
Steve Kleen

"Wicked cool!" He held it closer to the light, as if checking a large bill to see if it was counterfeit. "I think I'm about to write that Janice lady a very long apology note."

"I think that's an excellent idea."

A week later, that photo hung on the wall across from Maddox's bed, directly beside the countdown calendar. A good reminder to reach hard and hang on tight.

The doctors had come in early, double- and triple-checked everything and then gave Maddox premeds. He was pale, but he gave the thumbs-up and said, "Let's do this."

Linda snapped a picture and texted it out to their little core group, along with the message, *Here we go.* She considered it for less than a minute, then sent the picture to Caroline as well.

Just after noon, the first stem cells began flowing through Maddox's central line. Each bag was run over a thirty-minute period, then removed so they could start the next one. And then the next. And then the next.

Two hours later, it was done. Maddox had remained asleep for most of it due to his weakened condition and the medications they had given him. Linda watched, feeling so helpless that she couldn't take this burden from her son, couldn't do one thing to even lighten it.

But she could pray.

Please let this work. Help the stems cells find a new home. Help Maddox's body not to reject them. Please use this to heal my son.

But her son was not the only person affected by today. *Thank You for Caroline. Help her to heal quickly. Help her to always know how very precious she is.*

Late that night she got a text from Caroline. *Hope all is going well there. I'm back home and resting. Uncomfortable but otherwise fine. Please keep me updated on Maddox's condition.*

Linda looked toward her still-sleeping son and whispered, "You've got an amazing big sister. You just don't know it yet."

CHAPTER 25

"No, stop!" Sweat was beading on Caroline's forehead. "I want the bar over there." She pointed to the corner of the tent on Chateau-sur-Mer's lawn. The throbbing pain in her lower back was palpable, like she'd been punched just a few hours ago. But with La Fête tomorrow, she didn't have time to take it easy or get plenty of rest. Two days of that had been all she could afford.

"Caroline, eight chairs at each table, correct?" Emily was directing the deliverymen like a member of the air-traffic control ground crew.

"No, ten." How many times had she said that? She couldn't decide if Emily or the heat and humidity was having more of an effect on her mood, but right now, she needed a break from all of them. She glanced at her phone—2:37. The electrical crew should be here shortly to start installing the chandeliers. After that, she could go home. "The linens are arriving at 10:00 a.m. tomorrow? And the flowers at noon?"

"What linens?" Emily looked at Caroline with wide eyes. "You wanted linens, too?"

"What do you mean, what linens? The ones I ordered, then confirmed—twice." The last of her patience drained from her cheeks and her heart rate soared. Her mouth was dry beyond tolerability and she needed water. Now. She walked over to Emily, faster than was comfortable, but she had no choice.

"I'm just kidding. The linens will be here at ten." Emily giggled at herself.

"Oh my gosh, that's not funny." Caroline stopped, put her hand on her chest, and took a deep breath. Then another. But no matter how many deep breaths she took, she couldn't quite seem to catch it, and soon the tent was spinning. The grass beneath her felt like it was giving way, like she was on a boat over choppy water. She looked around the room for a chair or her water, but before she could get to either, all went black.

"Caroline, are you okay?" Emily was shrieking, but Caroline could barely see her, or much else for that matter.

She blinked a few times and waited a moment for her surroundings to come back into focus as she lay on the grass. "I'm okay. I just need some water." Although she wasn't sure if her words were actually audible or coherent.

Emily ran out of eyesight, then returned with a large bottle of water and held it out to Caroline. The more she drank, the more she came back to life, so it seemed.

"That's better. Thank you." A couple more deep breaths and large sips were enough for Caroline to feel like she could move again. She started to get up, made it to all fours, but then everything seemed to sway again.

"Here, sit on this chair." Emily grabbed Caroline by the arm, then helped her get to a seated position. "Do you want to go home? I can finish up here."

"No!" Her mind was foggy, but she could process enough to know she could not leave Emily in charge of finishing up while she went home to sleep on the couch. Although … sleep on the couch did sound so wonderful.

"Are you sure? I know where you want the lights. It will be fine. Let me call an Uber for you." Emily was kneeling next to the chair, her hands on Caroline's lap. "Really, you should go home."

The tent was still spinning slightly, and her legs felt so heavy, like she could barely move them. If things didn't go right here, that would be the end of her job. But mentally and physically, she had nothing more to give today. "You have the layout I drew?"

Emily nodded with no hint of hesitancy, that Caroline could detect anyway.

"Okay, fine." Hopefully she wouldn't regret those words. "But please call me if you have any questions."

As soon as Caroline made it home, she fell onto her couch and laid her head back on a pillow. Her eyes shut almost immediately, only one coherent thought trickling through her mind as she drifted off. Well, it was more of a plea, really.

Please, God. Please do not let Emily screw this up.

...

Thank the Lord, the Tylenol was starting to kick in. As long as it lasted for the next four hours and the server kept the coffee and water coming, she just might make it through La Fête.

"What can I say, Caroline?" Audrey's black-and-white-striped ball gown swished as she moved toward Caroline, and the lights under the tent made her diamond earrings sparkle like disco balls. "It's a success! Over six hundred people, fantastic cocktails, and the silent auction table is buzzing. Very well done."

Caroline finished greeting the older couple walking into the tent, then turned to Audrey. "Thank you. I'm so glad you're enjoying it." She relished the sense of lightness that filled her and let out a satisfied breath. Of course, the relief was only temporary—the event was just beginning—but still, it was nice to know that it met Audrey's standards. So far, at least.

Audrey took a dainty sip of a hot-pink concoction, then leaned in and rested her hand on Caroline's forearm. "Make sure you enjoy yourself, too."

Caroline flashed her signature charming smile, although she knew the chances of that were slim. She was already exhausted and running on caffeine and adrenaline. But besides that, she was never one of those people who could manage to actually enjoy an event she put together. So much could go wrong and if it did, all twelve hundred eyes would be on her. Obviously, she could never appear tired or stressed. All that would have to remain on the inside, packaged up tight with a poised manner for wrapping paper and said charming smile for a bow. She got the hang of it her second year at the Huntington Library.

"Caroline," a man said from the tent's entrance.

Showtime. She turned to greet the next arrival, but when she looked up, her breath stopped, and her stomach plummeted. "Chris? I'm surprised to see you here. I thought you had better ways to spend your money." How could his RSVP have slipped her radar? Ruth must have known about it. Why didn't she say anything?

"I didn't have a choice." He tilted his head toward the woman at his side, the same lovely brunette from the restaurant a few weeks ago. But lovely wasn't an adequate description. Now she was in a floor-length floral chiffon dress, complete with hair and makeup. Caroline was even more grateful she'd taken the time to have hers done professionally after meeting the florist. If she truly looked the way she felt inside, she wouldn't want to stand anywhere near this lady.

The woman held out her hand. "Hi, I'm Blythe. I take it you two know each other already?"

Caroline nodded. "We're frenemies." When Chris laughed, she couldn't help but notice his dimples. Or how good he looked in a tux. She averted her gaze and hoped he didn't catch it lingering. Or his fiancée, for that matter.

"I've been wanting to come to one of these for years, and since this is really my last chance, I pushed him into it." Blythe's smile grew as she spoke.

"Well." Chris raised an eyebrow. "That, and Tom thought it would be good for PR."

Blythe rolled her eyes. "All work, no fun."

"We're so glad you're here." It wasn't exactly true, but it came off without a hitch. "You know, Chris, what would really be good for PR is if you spent a lot of money at the silent auction on behalf of the Williams Hotel Group."

"Oh really? Even better than dancing with you?"

"In your dreams." It shot out automatically and with a sassy smile, but a millisecond later, Caroline wished she could rewind and edit it out. Or hide for the next four hours.

She was about to apologize to Blythe when the woman started laughing and hit Chris in the stomach with her handbag. "Denied!"

Before Caroline had a chance to respond—if she even knew what to say—another set of guests walked through the tent.

A few hours passed, and Caroline's cheeks were officially worn out from smiling so much. Despite the Dr. Scholl's inserts in her stilettos, her feet were past due for slippers, her lower back was starting to ache again, and she felt like she could sleep for days. Everything was going well and most of the guests were dancing in the ballroom, so she found a lounge chair on one of the house's many patios, far enough from the party that no one should notice.

It felt so good to sit, like she was melting into the chair. She leaned her head back on the cushion but didn't dare rest her eyes, even for a moment. If she did, the ground crew would undoubtedly find her passed out the next morning, and that would definitely not be poised or charming.

Instead, she pulled out her phone. She'd promised her mom an update on the party and her condition but hadn't had the time to provide either before now. But when she looked at the screen, her mom had already tried to call her. Six times.

She pressed the voice mail icon and listened to the first of two messages. *"Hi, Caroline, it's me. Can you give me a call back as soon as you can? Thanks, hon."* Something in her tone gave Caroline the impression she didn't want to chat about the fundraiser or find out what dress she had decided to wear. The black one, but at this point, she couldn't care less.

She sat up a little straighter and called her mom back. After half a ring, she picked up. "Hi, honey."

"Hi, Mom, I called as soon as I got your message. Is everything okay?"

"Caroline, sweetie." She paused. "Gram Gram passed away about an hour ago."

"What?" Caroline put her feet to one side of the chair, as if she might stand but couldn't. "She ... died? How? You told me she was doing okay."

"She seemed to be, but this morning she was having difficulty breathing, so I took her back to the hospital, just to make sure everything was okay. They monitored her for a while, said they'd like her to stay the night but that we could go home in the morning. I didn't want to call and worry you over nothing, especially with the big fundraiser tonight. But then she"—her voice was breaking up—"flatlined and they were not able to resuscitate."

The music coming from inside started to blur, and the chair felt like it was spinning beneath her. *This can't be true. It's the fatigue, the coffee.* She had fallen asleep on the chair and this was all just a bad dream. She did her best to catch her breath, but the hot tears filling her eyes were uncontrollable.

"Are you still there?" Mom brought her mind back to the call.

"I'm here. I just can't believe it." She sniffled and dabbed her bottom eyelids, as if that would help.

"I know. It seems unreal. Do you want Dad to book you a flight home?"

"Yes, I can leave tomorrow." Caroline already knew she didn't have anything going on the next day, but it wouldn't have mattered if she did. She just wanted to be home. To hug her mom and dad. To sleep in her own bed.

"Okay, I'll call you back when it's booked, and we'll see you tomorrow. I love you, honey."

"You too."

Caroline hung up and with every ounce of strength she had, she pulled off her shoes, stood, then ran her fingers along the bottom of her eyes again. Wet mascara covered her fingers, but she managed a quick text to Ruth and Audrey, letting them know what had happened and that she'd be going home for the evening. Thankfully, they both responded with kind words as she walked to her car and promised to make sure the party wrapped up successfully.

"You're leaving early. Are you bored out of your mind, too?" A voice came from over by the stone wall lining the parking lot.

Caroline searched for its owner, hoping, pleading it wasn't—Chris. Of course.

"Bored to tears, I see." The comment came with a warm smile but stung like a cold slap.

Caroline cleared her throat. She wanted to clear her path. "I'm quite exhausted, actually."

"That makes two of us."

"And, as it turns out, I just found out my grandmother passed away." *Does that make two of us?*

"Oh my gosh, I'm so sorry." He took a few steps toward her, then put a hand on her shoulder. "Can I drive you home?"

"No, thank you. I'd hate for Blythe to wonder where you went."

"She's fine. A few of her friends are here."

Caroline stood a little straighter and put her hand out. "Thank you, but no. I'd rather drive myself."

Chris didn't object, just nodded. "Okay. Again, I'm really sorry." He offered the same warm smile as before. This time, it didn't really sting.

She returned the gesture, but as soon as she did, a bright flash came from behind a nearby hedge, stinging her already-burning eyes. She nearly jumped, then flipped her head around to see where and what it came from.

Chris seemed to discover the source before Caroline did and took a few quick steps toward it. "Dude, seriously?" His fist clenched as he spoke.

Still confused, Caroline continued to follow him with her eyes, but as soon as Chris stopped, she could see plainly for herself what was happening. Aiden. Her cheeks burned even more, and her heart sank even further. She didn't know that was possible.

She needed to get home. Now, before she burst into tears right then and there. Despite her bare feet and aching body, she jogged to her car, then held her purse up to the key sensor.

"All right, all right, I'll delete it." Aiden's voice was faint and the last thing she heard before she closed her car door. A wave of relief washed over her. *Thank you, Chris.*

The thought popped in without warning, and she shook her head. Surely, he was only doing it to save his own skin. To save face with Blythe. Keep the Chadwick center stage.

Why in the world would he do it for her?

CHAPTER 26

It seemed as if Newport had experienced a costume change. Even though it was still warm out, shop windows swapped cover-ups for cardigans, herringbone for houndstooth, and there wasn't a stitch of seersucker anywhere. After being in California through Labor Day for Gram Gram's funeral, the contrast between the coasts hit her afresh on her first morning back in Newport.

"Welcome back!" Ruth popped up as soon as Caroline walked into the office and pulled her in for a long hug.

It was a bit more awkward than Caroline was prepared for, but she appreciated the sentiment anyway. "Thank you. And thanks for getting everything taken care of after La Fête. I'm sorry I had to leave so suddenly."

Ruth flicked her hands and shook her head. "No problem. Gloria tallied everything up, and you'll be thrilled to know we brought in over twice as much as we did last year." Her smile accentuated her crow's feet and it looked as though she might actually start jumping up and down.

Caroline couldn't help but laugh, although it was more from relief than excitement. "Are you serious? That's fantastic!"

But the lightness inside only lasted a few moments after sitting down at her desk. She opened her laptop and tried to get her head back in Rhode Island and focus on the job at hand—moving on to fall events—but she couldn't seem to get it together. Despite the two-shot latte she polished off on the way to work, her body seemed to drag with exhaustion. Or maybe something more.

"Oh, by the way, this came for you when you were gone." Ruth picked up a white envelope from her desk, the size of a greeting card, then passed it over to Caroline.

"Thanks." She gave the seal a tug then pulled out a card with a water-colored floral wreath printed on it. *Thinking Of You* the text on the front read in swirly script. She opened the card and read the rest of its preprinted text. *At this time of sorrow, know you are in my thoughts and prayers.*

She looked at the handwritten note. *Dear Caroline, I'm so sorry about your grandmother. I hope happy memories of her will comfort you as you cope with the loss. Warmly, Chris Stratton.*

Her breath hitched. She rubbed the card in between her thumb and forefinger, read the message again, then a lump in her throat started to swell. The same one she'd felt last week at Gram Gram's funeral when her mother spoke. The same one that had nearly choked her as she packed up for Newport again.

Of course, Gram Gram and her parents wanted Caroline to pursue her goals. They'd always been her biggest cheerleaders, were always so encouraging, so giving. And if they had seen La Fête, all of them would have been so proud of her. But now, even the success of the event didn't seem to compensate for the twinge in her heart.

The room was so quiet. Normally, she liked it this way. It helped her focus. But today, she would have preferred the warmth of familiar voices. She folded the card—a kind gesture on Chris's part, she conceded—then carefully put it under a stack of papers, along with, she hoped, the distraction it induced.

She stood and fidgeted with the blinds. She adjusted the height of her chair. She pulled out a fresh pack of gum. Surely that would boost her concentration.

"When you get caught up, let's go over the fall calendar. I have some questions for you." It was as if Ruth knew Caroline needed a little push in the right direction.

"Definitely." She hoped she sounded more enthusiastic than she felt. The events they had planned for the fall were, in a sense, even more important than La Fête. The summer fundraiser was standard—a matter of excellent planning and effective marketing, which they had done. But the fall events—they were entirely her new ideas, and it was her head on the chopping block if they flopped.

Caroline brainstormed an event, highlighting the discrepancy between the plight of women servants at the mansions and the suffrage movement many in high society endorsed, for as long as she could. She looked at her phone, saw it was only three thirty, and let out a groan.

"Ruth, I'm sorry. I'm not going to be of any more use today. I'll come back ready to roll tomorrow."

Her smile was one of disappointment, but it didn't seem unkind either. "You've been through a lot lately. Get some rest."

When Caroline got home, she made a cup of tea, then flipped through the pile of mail on her counter. Mostly junk and a few coupons worth keeping. Couple bills. No sympathy card from Dillon. She grumbled. *What good would that do?*

Come to think of it, she had been expecting to hear from Linda, too—just a quick text even to let her know how Maddox was doing now. *She's probably just busy, keeping 100 percent of her focus on him. Making sure he's taken care of.* Yeah, that was it.

Besides, someone else was on Caroline's mind. She'd thought about reaching out so many times when she was in California. Something about being on the other side of the country, in her childhood home, encouraged by her supportive, if not persuasive, parents made her feel less vulnerable. And something about her grandmother's passing made her less comfortable putting it off. But it never really seemed like the right moment.

Would there ever be a right moment? Probably not for this sort of thing. Perhaps it was as good a time as any.

She picked up her phone, found the company number she'd uncovered in a Google search, then hovered her finger over the call icon. For a moment, she couldn't get it to move, her pounding heart willing her to forget the whole idea. Then she pressed it, navigated her way through the automated directory, and held her breath.

"This is Hadley O'Brien. How can I help you?"

Hang up. Hang up! "I'd like to speak to Mr. Perry, please." Her voice quivered.

"May I ask who's calling?"

She cleared her throat. "My name is Caroline Chapman."

"Are you looking for investment assistance for your portfolio of one million dollars or more?" Her voice sounded a bit robotic, like she was reading from a cue card.

"No, this is a ... personal call. Of an important nature."

"One moment please."

Caroline took another sip of tea as she waited, then another. Soon she'd finished the whole cup.

"I'm sorry, Mr. Perry isn't available. May I take your number?"

Caroline couldn't decide if she was more relieved or discouraged as she gave her number to Hadley. She guessed it would depend on when, or if, Jack returned her call.

And how he reacted when she told him the truth.

...

Linda stood at the wall grid, marker in hand, and put a big X through 19. Only eighty-one more days to go.

The first one hundred days were the most critical for avoiding Graft Versus Host Disease—GVHD as the medical team referred to it. Unlike a heart transplant, where the doctors had to be careful that the patient's body didn't reject the heart, the invader in stem cell transplant was just the opposite. Once the stem cells made a home in the recipient's marrow, there is the possibility that the T cells being produced would see their new host's entire organ system as an invader.

So far, so good. Maddox was currently receiving a transfusion—a constant necessity at this point. Still, his white blood counts were slowly starting to rise.

"Want to walk around the hall when this is done?" Maddox's head was all the way back on the pillow, as if it was too exhausting to even attempt to hold it up. His face was so pale and thin that it hurt to look at him sometimes. Still, he was in there fighting, as evidenced by his determination to go for a walk. He was up for doing anything that might get him out of here faster.

"You bet. Think we'll break a four-minute mile today?"

Maddox snorted. "Pretty sure." A few minutes later, his eyes drifted shut and stayed that way.

As she had done so often, Linda wondered how Caroline was doing. She hesitated to text her because she wasn't sure Caroline wanted much contact. She had asked for updates, however, and today she would get one.

Hello Caroline. I hope you are doing well and are fully back up to speed after the donation. I wanted to let you know that Maddox is slowly improving. Doctors are saying they are hopeful he will be able to be discharged from the hospital early next week. Every time I look at him, I think of you and the selfless decision you made to help him. You are an amazing young woman.

PS—I saw some photos online of the La Fête. It seemed like it went off beautifully.

She pressed Send, then stared at her phone for a long time before she typed in the next message.

Would you like to meet your brother?

She watched the blinking cursor for a long time. Finally, she took a deep breath, let her hand hover above the screen for another second, then reached down and pressed Delete.

CHAPTER 27

After all these months, Linda took pride in her ability to read the doctors in spite of their poker-faced expressions. This being the case, she jumped to her feet when Dr. Levin entered the room. Despite his usual deadpan, there was almost a twinkle in his eyes today. Or, at least that's what she hoped she saw. He walked over to the bed, glanced at the clipboard in his hand, then peered over the top of his half-moon glasses. "Young man, how would you like to go home today?"

"Yes!" Maddox did a fist pump. "Can I leave now?"

"Easy there. We've got some paperwork and discharge instructions to work through yet, but by lunchtime we should have you ready to go. Once you leave, though, you need to promise me to be vigilant. Your immune system is extremely fragile right now, and any infection would be disastrous. It would land you right back here and we start the process over again. Understood?"

Maddox saluted. "Yes, sir. When I see bacteria, I'll run the other way. I promise."

Dr. Levin, who did not have much in the way of a sense of humor, actually laughed. Linda took it as a good sign. "If only it were that easy."

...

Maddox sat in the wheelchair. Although he was wearing a mask—something he would be required to do in public for a long time yet—there was no mistaking the fact that he was smiling. He looked up at the transporter, a cute blonde. "Sarah, you've never let me down before. Now get me out of this place before they change their minds."

Sarah laughed. "You got it." She pushed the chair through the door of his room, "Tell me you're going to miss these little rides we take together."

"Um...Sarah...to be perfectly honest, I will not miss these rides. You, however, are a different subject. You, I will miss. Feel free to come visit me at my house anytime, but I'm telling you now, I'm not planning to come back here ever again."

"Sounds like a fair deal." They all laughed a little, but they all knew there was no truth in Maddox's words. In fact, at the very least, he would be back at least three times a week as an outpatient for the foreseeable future. Still, it felt like an escape and no one was going to argue details. Not today.

As they made their way down the hall, there were several calls of, "Bye, Maddox," "Be well, Maddox," "We'll miss you, Maddox," from nurses and lab technicians and medical residents. Maddox waved at them all. "Don't call me, I'll call you," he said the words over and over.

Brent had the car running, passenger door open, when they reached the exit. He held the door and bowed. "Your chariot awaits."

As soon as they were all inside and Sarah had closed the door behind him, Maddox turned to his father. "It's times like this that I wish you had a sports car. Pedal to the metal, Dad."

Linda couldn't stop smiling. Well, that wasn't technically true. She stopped smiling every thirty seconds or so when she pulled out another antibacterial wipe from the canister and wiped one more surface, "just in case."

"Mom, relax."

"I am relaxed." She wadded up the spent wipe. "Mostly."

"Dad, is she going to be like this once we get home?"

"Probably worse. I can honestly say, that between your mother and Kristyn's work, there are likely surgical suites that are less sterile than our home currently is."

Those words were the closest thing to affection she'd heard from Brent since she'd told him about Caroline. She accepted them for the gift they were.

"Oh boy." Maddox sighed and leaned back against his seat. He sat still for long enough that Linda assumed he had fallen asleep. Then he turned around and reached back to touch her arm. "Thanks, Mom. It'll be so nice to be in my old room again. Thanks for making it ready for me."

"You're welcome." Linda choked back tears. It had all been so worth it. They just needed to keep reminding themselves of that.

...

Maybe HGTV would hire him.

Chris could picture the veins in Tom's neck popping as he found out the new floors in the meeting room cost 30 percent more than estimated and were completed two weeks after the October 1 deadline. He didn't need to picture the resulting phone call; he'd just survived it. Barely.

As soon as his pulse started to steady, his phone rang again.

"How much?" Chris put his finger up to his other ear to block out the noise as he walked into the Chadwick's lobby. Was that the sound of his heart pounding in his ears now or the nail gun securing the new drywall?

"Sixty-five hundred dollars." Blythe's voice sounded hesitant, almost like she was asking a question, not stating a fact.

He nearly doubled over. "For a band? Are you kidding me?" He regretted his tone as the words came out. This was his baby sister, not a sub. But good grief, this extravaganza was starting to take its toll, on his savings and his patience.

"I know it's expensive, but I promise they're worth it. I just need to know soon because they usually book six months in advance, and we're already in the middle of October."

He rubbed his forehead. It wasn't exactly Blythe's fault since he'd never designated a budget, but it felt like things were spiraling out of control. It was as if he could see her hopes beaming and glowing, while his own were fading into a heavy fog.

But Blythe had lost enough. They all had. Delaying things just a bit longer, stretching just a little further, was better than losing more, if he could prevent it. He took a deep breath. "All right, go ahead."

"Eeeee! I'm so excited. Did you put the deposit down for the cake?"

He remembered the five hundred-dollar Venmo payment to The Fancy Farmer bake shop. "Yes, I sent that over last week. You didn't pick the one with raisins in it, did you?"

"Vanilla buttercream. And how about the pictures of the flowers I sent? Which did you like better?"

"Honestly, Blythe." He ran his hand through his hair. "They all looked the same to me. I really want to be helpful, but this isn't my thing. Ask Addie Beth."

"No, she'll take over the whole thing. I need help, not an override."

"Adam? Mom?"

"Adam doesn't care what it looks like, and Aunt Dianne took Mom on a fall foliage cruise. Plus, you're the one paying for it. I think you should have a say. Please? I need some direction."

The idea of Dianne buying their mom's cruise ticket, with money that should have been his mom's in the first place, was enough to make his blood boil. He bit the inside of his cheek and sucked in a sharp inhale. At least she was out having a good time.

Just as he was about to tell Blythe to just pick daisies because they're cheap and no one noticed anyway, a worker approached, motioned for Chris to come into the other room, then mouthed the words, *All done.*

Chris nodded and gave him a thumbs-up. "Blythe, I need to run. Let me look again and I'll call you later, okay?"

He hung up with his sister as he followed Giovanni into the meeting room, then surveyed the herringbone white oak floors. "Nice work, it looks good." He walked over the length of the room, just to ensure they were completely level as promised, when his coffee cup from that morning, along with the weekly paper he'd brought but never had a chance to read, caught his eye. "Oh, sorry. I forgot I left this in here." No wonder he was dragging today. The cup was still full.

He took a sip of the hours-old coffee, not really caring how cold it was. "Where do you want to start next, Giovanni?"

"I'll probably get going on the stairs. We may need to rebuild the whole flight if it's off as much as this room was."

Chris nearly spit out his coffee. "No. We cannot rebuild the entire flight of stairs. We have to make up for the time we lost in here. Just figure it out, please."

Giovanni huffed out of the room, mumbling something about not being a miracle worker, then something else in Italian, leaving Chris alone in the meeting room.

It was suddenly and oddly quiet for a construction site, and Chris took the opportunity to flip through the paper and check out the new Chadwick hotel ad. As expected, it took up half the page and looked great. He'd have to remember to thank their head of marketing for this.

Before he closed the paper, he couldn't help but notice, "According to Aiden," the column that had rapidly been growing in popularity and getting on Chris's nerves in proportion.

With the success of the Newport Preservation Society's summer season behind them, Caroline Chapman digs into fall events and looks ahead to the holiday season. Things aren't looking quite as good for the Chadwick. Reports indicate they are significantly behind schedule and over budget. How will Chris Stratton save his hotel?

He rolled his eyes and tossed the paper into a nearby trash can without finishing the article. "His hotel." *Please.* He was just doing his job. And they were not "significantly" behind schedule. Okay, perhaps a tad over budget. Whatever. He could feel the coffee kicking in and his heart rate escalating again. He needed a sledgehammer. And a wall to demo.

A text from Blythe interrupted his inner fuming. *Did you look at the flowers?*

In the last five minutes? He was dangerously close to typing a text he knew he'd regret later. Instead he let out a sigh. Maybe the queen of event planning could help.

It took a moment for the sarcasm of this thought to dissipate into curiosity. He entertained it for a couple of moments as he walked outside. Maybe it wasn't such a bad idea after all.

He didn't need to look up the number—he still had it stored from the whole debacle months ago—and as soon as he pulled it up, he let impulse take over.

"Newport Preservation Society, how may I direct your call?" The receptionist's voice was slightly more than a whisper.

"Can you connect me to Caroline Chapman?" He walked nowhere in particular, kicking the gravel under his feet as he did.

"Who's calling?"

He contemplated making up a name but decided against it. "Chris Stratton." It was more of a mumble than a statement.

"I don't think she's available."

Come on. He wasn't in the mood for games. Not today. "It's really important. I'll leave a voice mail if she doesn't pick up." He attempted to sound as patient as possible but wasn't quite sure if he'd succeeded or not.

"I'll connect you."

He waited a few moments, just enough time for the reality of what he was doing to kick in. He thought seriously about hanging up, but before he could decide what to do next, he heard, "This is Caroline."

Too late. "Hey, it's Chris." *Keep it casual, Stratton.* "Would you be willing to help me plan a wedding?" *Smooth. Real smooth.*

"No."

He stood upright, his meandering coming to a halt. "What? Please?"

"Why in the world would I help you plan your wedding?"

"My wedding?" He let out a laugh, which sounded more like a nervous chuckle, then cleared his throat. "No, it's for my sister, Blythe. You met her at La Fête, remember? She needs some advice, and I am not the person to give it."

"Oh. That's your sister?"

"Yeah. Wait, you thought she was—?" Now he couldn't even finish the sentence without laughing. "Sorry. Yes, younger sister. Getting married in March."

"I see. Can't she hire a wedding coordinator?"

A wedding coordinator? He'd never thought of that. He didn't even know it was a real job. "I think she just wants someone to help, not plan it for her." This was going nowhere. He'd have to pull out the big guns—the latest gift from Tom, given as a thank-you for his work on the St. Lucia pool. "Listen, I have two tickets to opening night of the World Series. Red Sox versus Dodgers?"

"Is this a bribe?"

"Yes?" *Please work. Please work.*

"Are you offering me tickets to the game or to take me to the game?"

This girl was a real pill. And if he was being honest, he kinda liked that about her. Kept things interesting. He bit his lips together and let a breath out through his nose. "I am offering you one ticket. We can go together or just sit next to each other and pretend we don't know each other."

Caroline laughed. "That will give Aiden plenty to write about. 'Rivals, on and off the field.'" Her voice sounded like a newscaster's.

Chris relaxed and started to smile, but then the sense of heaviness from earlier hit him again. "Listen, my sister deserves a beautiful wedding, and it would mean a lot if you could just give her some guidance."

More silence blared through the phone. He was about to give up, tell her never mind, and apologize for interrupting her day, when she said, "Fine. But you're buying the hot dogs."

CHAPTER 28

"Where are you sneaking off to?" Gloria emerged from the office kitchen just as Caroline was approaching the building's exit.

"I was able to get a ticket to the game tonight." She'd arrived at the office at eight that morning to compensate for her early departure. She had nothing to worry about, but still, she wasn't all that eager to give any more information.

"Oh really? Lucky you. Who are you going with?"

"Someone who owes me one." She hoped her tone was as lighthearted and casual as she'd intended it to be.

"A date?"

"No, it's not a date." Caroline shook her head for emphasis. *Change the subject.* "I emailed you those invoices for the wine festival, and I meant to tell you earlier, Roger Williams the 13th has agreed to fly in and speak at the Religious Freedom Forum." She knew getting the direct descendent of the founder of Rhode Island—a state established on religious liberty—would earn her several points with Gloria.

"How did you track him down?"

"It wasn't difficult. He lives in Santa Barbara and goes to church with my parents." Call it providence.

"Nice work." Gloria nodded. "Have fun tonight. Go Sox!"

Caroline grumbled under her breath. If she heard that phrase one more time … She made it home with just enough time to change out of her work clothes and into jeans and a blue sweater, then freshen her makeup, even though it definitely wasn't a date. Unfortunately, she hadn't brought her foam finger with her to Rhode Island, but she found her Dodgers hat and put it on with a sense of pride. Red Sox Nation could deal with it.

She peeked out her downstairs window at five o'clock, just as Chris's truck, complete with a Williams Hotel Group decal on the passenger door and a Red Sox sticker on the back window, pulled in front of her house. Her heart quickened a little, but it was more from the anticipation of the game than the company. Just because Chris's relationship status was different than she'd assumed didn't mean his place of employment was, or his baseball team loyalties, for that matter.

She grabbed her purse and jacket, then locked up and made her way to his passenger door. Although she was surprised to see how nice Chris's truck was inside, she paused, put one hand on her hip, and grimaced. "I'm not sure I want to get in this truck."

"There's nothing wrong with my truck. One of the perks of working for a hotel tycoon." He patted the steering wheel a few times, then pointed to her hat. "I'm not sure I want you in it. Remind me why I invited you?"

"You gave me a ticket because I'm helping your sister, remember? And if I recall, yesterday you said it was dumb for us to drive separately." She buckled her seat belt, then noticed the seat warmer had been turned on for her.

"Oh, yeah. Speaking of which, are you available next Saturday? Blythe wants to look at some venues so she can order the invitations. I figure if you come, she can ask you for whatever she wants help with, and I can stop being the middleman."

"Sure." If she was being honest with herself, she was rather looking forward to helping out. Per Dr. Whiting's instructions, she needed to start making connections, and Blythe seemed like someone who was fun to be around, even if she was Chris's sister. At least it would give her something to do on Saturday beyond drive around and discover new towns by herself.

"Great. Bellevue Coffee at ten?"

"No problem." She pulled out her phone to set a reminder.

The Bristol Ferry Lighthouse blinked its welcome from the other side of the Mount Hope Bridge as they left Aquidneck Island. Caroline grabbed a pack of gum from her purse, offered a piece to Chris, then chewed through two pieces herself. "So." She started up a conversation with the first thing that came to mind. The only thing that came to mind, really. "How are things coming at the hotel?"

Chris let out a little laugh. "Do you care?"

"Well, I'd hate to hear about an electrical fire or a failed inspection." She gave a coy smile.

"I bet you would. With old buildings there are always surprises and setbacks, but thankfully, no fires or failed inspections."

"Yet."

"We have security cameras. Don't get any ideas." He slid her a glance, his eyes narrowed, but his lips held a hint of a smirk.

She put her hand on her chest and let out a mock gasp. "I wouldn't dream of it."

After an hour, Caroline was well acquainted with all the hotels Chris had worked on in his nearly eleven years with Tom and how Chris had worked his way up in the company. The drive went by quickly, and soon he pulled into the parking lot of a T-Station. Caroline had yet to experience Boston's public transportation system, and as she followed him through a sea of people, she was glad she had an escort who knew where he was going. The subway's map alone was enough to make her brain hurt.

As soon as they made it into Fenway Park, the glares came with full force. "Go back to LA," a man hollered as he walked by. Caroline turned around to see who it was but couldn't distinguish the culprit among the deluge of scowls.

"Boooo!" A young boy, maybe seven or eight, thrust a thumbs-down in her face, sparking an uproar of laughter from his father and others nearby.

Her body tensed and she wanted to stick her tongue out at him but refrained. No, she wouldn't stoop to their level. "Such a charming group of fans."

"What did you expect?" Chris turned back with a smile. Judging by the look on his face, Caroline was almost certain he was enjoying this as much as she wasn't.

She did her best not to give anyone else the satisfaction of getting under her skin. She kept her head straight and followed Chris, although she wasn't exactly paying attention to where they were going so much as hoping she didn't get separated and left alone in this pack of wolves. Soon, they stopped three rows behind the Red Sox dugout on the first base side.

"Are you serious? These seats are amazing!" They were so close, she could see each individual blade of grass as she sat down.

"Another perk of working for a hotel tycoon."

"Gaining the world and losing your soul?"

Chris chuckled. "Means to an end. I'm hoping to leave within a year." He stopped and looked up, the smile gone. "Don't let that get out, please. Tom is big on loyalty, and if he found out I was planning to leave, I'd be out of a job sooner than I can afford."

Caroline ran her fingers across her lips like she was fastening a zipper. "What is it you plan to do?"

"Start my own construction company."

"Really? That's ambitious." She couldn't help being intrigued, although she wasn't quite sure why she cared. Perhaps because Chris's secret was so unexpected.

"Well, more like buy one from my uncle."

"I'd assumed you were living the dream, but that's awesome."

"Thanks. I appreciate you saying that." He smiled.

"Why not work for your uncle now, if you're planning to buy his company later?"

He scowled. "I'd rather work for the Preservation Society."

"Oh. And starting your own?"

"Aren't you the inquisitive one." He stopped and looked as though he was considering his words carefully. "His company is pretty big and very well established. I don't think there would be much hope for a start-up trying to compete with it. Look, it's a long story."

"It's a long game."

Chris laughed, although Caroline got the impression it wasn't necessarily because he was amused, and he sat back in his chair. It seemed he was about to continue when the announcer diverted their attention to the field. First the teams were introduced, then the national anthem's singer.

"Just do me a favor." Chris leaned his head over but kept his eyes toward the field. "Don't let Blythe get too carried away. I want her to have a nice wedding, but let's just say I had no idea how much it was going to cost."

"You're paying for it?"

Chris nodded as he took off his Red Sox cap, then stood.

Hmm, Tin Man does have a heart. Suddenly, she felt a little flutter in her own. Caroline took off her hat and stood as well, and both remained silent while Cody Johnson sang "The Star-Spangled Banner."

As soon as it was over, the two of them sat down. "Too bad the Chadwick won't be done in time." Caroline nudged her elbow into Chris's side. "What about the other hotels? The one on Nantucket?"

"You're hilarious. Trust me, I've had the same thoughts, but she wants Newport because it's where she met Adam, and it has to be March because he's being deployed to Honolulu. But they are going to the hotel in St. Lucia for their honeymoon. At least that's free."

"It's incredibly generous of you. You two must be close."

"She missed out on a lot growing up, and I guess I always felt bad about it. Our dad died of a heart attack when I was nineteen, she was only thirteen." He shrugged, and Caroline felt a small ache nestle inside. "Our older sister helped a lot, too, but she lives in South Carolina now and has four kids of her own. Anyway—" He slapped his hands on his thighs. "I owe you a hot dog, if I remember correctly." He turned in his seat, then nodded toward a vendor making his way down their aisle. "Perfect timing."

Caroline didn't press for more. She looked around Fenway Park and had to admit, although she didn't quite want to, the Green Monster, the comradery, the tradition, was all quite exciting. The stadium was smaller than she'd expected, but still, the history was awe inspiring. As a baseball fan, she could allow herself to appreciate it and not compromise her dignity.

With the Dodgers up four to one, the boisterous crowd had subdued slightly, including the man behind her who made his objection to her cheering for the enemy quite obvious, until the middle of the 8th inning when a familiar tune came over the stadium's speakers. Her head popped up and before she knew it, she was standing with the rest of the crowd.

"I love this song!" She had to yell over all the noise. Everyone, including Caroline, was singing in unison to Neil Diamond's "Sweet Caroline."

"I had them play it just for you."

Her body went slightly numb, and her mouth hung open for a second. "Are you serious?"

Chris started laughing and shook his head. "No, they play it at every game. It's sort of a thing here. I got you, though."

"Oh." She started laughing, too, and her cheeks warmed. "Well, maybe the Red Sox aren't so bad."

"Is there hope for a conversion?"

"Absolutely not." The song ended so Caroline returned to her seat. "That was fun, though."

The Red Sox took the field for the top of the ninth. What Caroline really needed now was a bathroom, but she didn't want to miss the last of the Dodgers' at bats either. One out later, the Red Sox opted for a pitching change. Maybe now was a good time to make a break for it.

"Hey, you." The man sitting behind her tapped her shoulder.

Now what? Caroline turned to face him but noticed he wasn't looking at her, he was looking toward the Jumbotron and pointing.

Caroline looked up as well, but it took her a couple moments to understand what she was staring at. As soon as she did, her heart started to pound.

She and Chris sat inside a heart graphic, with the words *Kiss Cam* stamped across the bottom. There was no denying it—the Red Sox and Dodgers hats side by side and the bright-red faces definitely belonged to them.

"Oh," was all she could squeak out. She could barely hear the thunder of the crowd over her thrashing pulse, and she couldn't seem to move beyond her jaw dropping.

"Uh, well, what should we do? We can't disappoint the fans." She heard Chris's voice but didn't dare look at him.

"Um..." Why didn't she just go to the bathroom when she had the chance?

Without further warning, he reached up and pulled off her Dodgers hat, then replaced it with his own Red Sox hat, inducing another round of cheers from the crowd.

"Hey!" A nervous laugh surfaced, but it didn't have time to mature. Before she could say anything else, Chris leaned in and planted a kiss right on her lips. *Oh my gosh*, she nearly peed her pants.

Again, the crowd erupted, and in direct proportion to Caroline's discomposure. He pulled back, then smiled and shrugged. "When in Fenway..."

"I can't believe that just happened." The words fell out of her mouth. She could barely think straight, never mind process what had just transpired. She pulled his hat off her head and thrust it at his chest.

He winced, then leaned back in his seat and laughed a little. "I'm sorry if that was awkward."

"*If?*" But she couldn't help laughing now either as she shook her head. Truthfully, she was shaking all over.

"If I hadn't, we would have been booed out of the stadium."

She pointed to the field, hoping he couldn't see the unsteadiness in her hand. "And miss the opportunity to see the Dodgers take game one? Not a chance."

Caroline tried to relax but couldn't. The adrenaline rushing through her was just too much. She spent the last two outs of the game wondering if she just wanted it to end so she could go home.

Or if she never wanted to leave.

...

On the way home, Caroline's heart was still pounding. She kept fidgeting, adjusting in her seat, anything to get comfortable. Her phone chimed, then chimed again. Thankful for the distraction, she reached into her purse and grabbed her phone. But the gratitude only lasted until she saw who it was from. Dillon. She angled the screen away from Chris as she read.

Saw you on ESPN's game highlights. Wow. Not sure if I'm more impressed you were able to go to the World Series or that you've managed to move on so quickly.

Caroline let out a half groan, half grumble and her shoulders tightened.

"What's the matter?" Chris looked over.

"Apparently, that little stunt landed us on ESPN."

"Seriously?" He started to laugh but sounded more uneasy than amused. "Oh boy."

She nodded and hummed in affirmation, although she wasn't sure it was audible. She was too caught up in trying to decide how to respond to Dillon's text.

He's just a friend, Dillon, she typed but then deleted.

What gave him the right to care how she spent her time and with whom? The tightness in her shoulders sunk in deeper now and landed somewhere between her heart and her resolve. It's not like this was anything more than a game.

A joke. All in good fun. When in Fenway… right? Caroline knew that. But Dillon didn't need to know.

Great game, huh? She wrote it with a satisfied smile, and this time she hit Send.

"Oh no." Chris cut through the silence.

"What?" She looked over at him but as soon as she did, she knew exactly what he was thinking.

As if on cue, they said in unison, "Aiden!"

CHAPTER 29

"What do you mean, you're not coming?" Blythe set her cup down on the corner table inside Bellevue Coffee, then leaned back in her chair with crossed arms. "Adam's coming."

"I mean, I'm not coming. I'm sorry, but I'm not going over to their house. I don't care if it is Thanksgiving." The napkin Chris gripped in his hand was starting to shred. He wasn't sure if he was more annoyed that his mom and sister had accepted Jim and Dianne's invitation or that they actually expected him to go. Was he the only one who remembered what had happened, or just the only one who cared?

"Chris, this has to end at some point. I'm obviously inviting them to the wedding."

"It will end when he apologizes for what he did." Which would be never, probably. *So be it.*

Blythe's posture seemed to soften a bit. "I know it was hard for you, but I really think Uncle Jim was trying to help. Don't you think it's time to let it go?"

His neck tensed. He couldn't believe what he was hearing. Let it go? Like it was that easy? He'd tried to go that route, tried to forgive, but Jim had taken too much. And Thanksgiving dinner at his big house on the golf course wasn't enough to compensate.

"You were thirteen. You have no idea what you're talking about." His tone was sharp, and Blythe's face reflected it. He took a deep breath and was about to apologize when her gaze turned upward. Chris looked up as well, then instantly wished he could start this entire morning over again, starting with that text from the electrician.

"Hi." Caroline stood a few feet from their table, fidgeting with her keys. "I hope I'm not interrupting."

"Not at all. Thank you so much for coming." Blythe smiled. She pulled out the chair next to hers, then patted it a few times.

"Of course. Chris told me you could use some help with your wedding?" Caroline glanced up at him quickly but didn't exactly return his smile. *Great.* He was hoping things wouldn't be awkward this morning. From what he could tell, ESPN only ran the clip from the game once. God knows he'd replayed it in his head a few times. Her enthusiasm, her spark...and anyone who was that pretty and actually wanted to sit through all nine innings of a baseball game was worth getting to know better.

Okay, so maybe he'd replayed it a few hundred times. He really should've called her, or at least sent a text yesterday or something. She probably hated him now.

Caroline tucked her hair behind her ear and rotated her body toward Blythe. Away from him. "So, what have you picked so far?"

"The cake, the band, and my dress. I've put a deposit down for the caterer and the florist, but I haven't picked anything specific yet. Here's a picture of the dress."

Caroline nodded, then leaned to look at Blythe's phone. "Gorgeous! And now you want to pick the venue? I think that's a good next step. What did you have in mind?"

Wedding chitchat was a bit more than he could take right now. The line had died down since he and Blythe arrived twenty minutes earlier, so Chris took the opportunity to get a refill on his coffee. He walked over to the register. "Large coffee, black. And do you know what she usually gets?" He pointed toward their table. "The blonde one."

"Caroline?" Isaac, so his name tag said, smiled, his man bun bobbling on top of his head. "Yeah, she's a skim latte."

Chris nodded, then pulled out his debit card, inserted the chip, and waited for the purchase to complete. *Tip amount?* The iPad flashed the options on the screen. *Here's a tip, Isaac: get a haircut.*

A few moments later, Chris returned to the table and set Caroline's coffee in front of her before he sat down. She leaned back, looked at the coffee, then at him. "Thank you." This time her smile seemed a bit bigger, and warmer, but maybe he was imagining it.

Blythe interjected before he could read any further into it. "Chris, she said Rosecliff has a winter rate and it's available on the ninth. We're going to check it out. Do you want to come?"

There was more he wanted to say to Caroline, but not in front of Blythe. Besides, days like this he needed a construction site, not a ballroom. "I need to go over to the hotel and check on some problem the electricians ran into in the attic yesterday." He waited until Caroline's eyes met his. His pulse quickened, but maybe it was just the second cup of coffee. "I'll see you later though."

Caroline seemed to pause before she nodded. "Okay."

"Blythe, I'm going to Mom's next weekend to paint her garage doors. I'll talk to her about Thanksgiving when I see her." He leaned down, then gave her a quick hug. "Have fun. Don't go crazy."

As he walked out into the parking lot, he pulled out his phone and texted Addie Beth. *What are you doing for Thanksgiving?* He hadn't seen his nieces and nephews in a while. Maybe a trip down there was in order. It would be warmer than here, too.

She responded just as he made it to the Chadwick. *Going to Mark's parents' house in Asheville. You?*

He sighed, then took another sip of his coffee. *No plans yet.* Great.

As soon as Chris climbed the stairs into the attic, he searched for what the text from the electricians described as something he "needed to see." Everything looked good so far. Not quite as much progress as he was hoping for but nothing out of— Ah. His gaze landed on a wooden box, about the size of a shoe box in the corner of the attic. Maybe this was it? He walked over carefully, making sure he didn't hit his head or trip over a wire then leaned over and opened the lid.

Several black-and-white photos of what Chris assumed was the Chadwick family were inside, and a pipe. That was random, kinda funny. He looked at the photos for a few moments, then back in the box. He saw an envelope sealed with one of those old wax things you stamped when it's still hot. He turned it over, but it was blank.

Should he open it? He remembered finding a stash of money once, in a secret compartment of a man's closet on the Cape when he'd first started working for Tom. Chris's boss at the time, the man whose job Chris now had, told him that anything left on a property after the sale went through belonged to the buyer. Apparently that was enough to justify taking the cash, although Chris never really respected him after that.

So technically, this all belonged to Tom, and as Tom's project manager, he saw no problem in opening it. He pulled his thumb through the envelope and found a single sheet of paper with a handwritten note on it. He glanced at the signature quickly—J. Chadwick. *No way, how cool.* He glanced at the date at the top—February 23, 1945. He thought about putting the pipe in his mouth for dramatic effect but decided against it, then started reading the letter.

But as he did, his teeth clenched and his heart thrashed. *You've got to be kidding me.* Without intending it, a swear word fell from his mouth, maybe two. He wasn't sure. Usually he was good at keeping those in, ever since the time he accidently slipped in front of his dad back in high school and spent the next eight Saturdays cleaning the bathrooms at Stratton Construction Company's office.

By the time he got to the end, he could barely see straight. He folded the letter and put it back into the envelope, then the envelope in his back pocket. His hands felt numb as he did. In fact, his whole body did, except for the burning in his chest. For a moment, he thought he might actually punch a wall. With every ounce of self-control he had, he took a couple deep breaths and forced himself to calm down enough to get out of the attic.

Well, at least now he didn't give two hoots about finding a place to spend Thanksgiving.

Soon he may need to focus on finding a new place to work.

...

"Oh my gosh, it's beautiful!" Blythe's eyes seemed to light up as soon as she and Caroline walked into the Rosecliff ballroom.

Caroline nodded. "I've heard the weather here in March is still gloomy, so you'll want to make the inside as nice as possible. The heart-shaped grand staircase, trompe-l'oeil ceiling, and those perfume chandeliers definitely provide a stunning backdrop. Actually, there was a construction mishap here back in the early 1900s. Mrs. Oelrich was giving orders to the carpenters when a tack fell from the scaffolding and landed right in her eye."

"Be sure to tell Chris that story. He never wears the gear he's supposed to. But this place is stunning. And the price, I can't believe it."

Me either. There was no winter rate, but she'd figure that one out later. "It's the largest ballroom in Newport."

"The size is perfect. We're expecting about 160 people, and I can put Chris over there." She pointed to the far end of the ballroom on the right. "And Uncle Jim way over there." Her other arm extended to the left as her giggle echoed through the room.

Caroline was quiet for a moment, but soon her curiosity bubbled to the surface. "Blythe, what happened between them?"

"According to who? Honestly,"—she shook her head—"I don't know the whole story. I know that before my dad died, we were all really close. Jim and my dad were brothers. He and his wife didn't have any kids, so they were like our second parents. But after? Jim bought my dad's company from my mom, and Chris and Jim have not spoken more than five words to each other since. We don't really talk about it much, because it always gets so personal. All I know is Chris will not be happy until he buys it back."

Caroline nodded, then opted to lighten the mood. "Well, we can definitely arrange the seating chart accordingly. We want fireworks, but not that kind."

Blythe gasped. "I can have fireworks?" Her smile looked like it would jump right off her face.

"I meant metaphorical fireworks." Caroline couldn't help but laugh.

"Oh, of course." Blythe laughed, too, and her cheeks reddened. "Okay, let's reserve this. Now do you have time to help with the invitations?"

The request struck an unexpected chord. Caroline couldn't control the memory of her and her mom looking at wedding invitations together. It had been over a year now, but it rushed into her mind as if it had just happened. The excitement. The giddiness. The thud. It all came back.

She forced herself to push it all aside and offered a smile. "Sure, let's do it."

CHAPTER 30

Brent's teeth chattered. "I sure am glad we have a nice, warm house."

"Yep, me too." Maddox tossed the baseball up and then caught it. Up and down. Up and down. He stopped long enough to vigorously rub his hands together, then resumed the process.

Brent motioned toward the back door. "You know, we could go sit inside."

Maddox shook his head without ever looking at him. "Can't do it, Dad. If Mom is insisting on sitting outside in the cold to hand out Halloween candy, then I'm going to sit outside in the cold to toss my baseball. It only seems fair."

After a month at home, Maddox was slowly regaining his strength—and his strong will. Brent applauded all of it, at least for the time being. And Maddox did speak truth. Linda had set up shop at the bottom of the front porch steps. There was no way she would allow several dozen random kids with their random germs anywhere near their front door.

"Your mom would prefer that you were inside where it's warm."

"She's a girl. Of course she would." He blew into his hands. "But what kind of men would we be if we let her sit out there and take one for the team, and it didn't cost us anything? Besides, I think a couple of the guys are coming over for a while."

What kind of men would they be indeed? It was a question Brent had been asking of himself a lot lately. Something he was slowly working through with the help of Dr. Medved, the Christian family therapist he had been seeing. In particular, Dr. Medved's common question, "This 'life that matters,' is that more a big picture, I want to make an impact on the community because of what they see me do, or is it a nitty-gritty I want to dig deep and love the people around me, in spite of excruciating circumstances that are unfair?"

Of course, the answer was both, especially the second, but Brent had trouble seeing a way past all this. First, the Rodney Litchfield debacle, which had undone a year's worth of ministry and a lifetime's worth of influence. Game Changers would never fully recover, regardless of how hard they tried. Brent had finally acknowledged it was out of his control and made uneasy peace with it. But now this. How could Linda have kept something like this from him for all these years? All the people he'd looked to as role models were proving false.

Good thing you've never fallen short.

The thought smacked him for a moment. Yes, of course he had made mistakes. But not in big ways like this. Never.

Define "big"?

The thud of baseball against brick pulled him back to the present. Maddox jumped up to retrieve the rolling ball before it reached the edge of the patio.

"I thought your friends were going to some sort of haunted house tonight."

"I think most of them are. Keaton said it's lame. Parker agreed. So they said they might drop by."

Brent knew Keaton and Parker well enough to know that tonight's visit was less about a lame event and more about supporting Maddox. This was no "drop by." Those two were friends of the truest sort, and Brent was thankful for them.

This also further explained Maddox's insistence on sitting outside. One of the doctor-imposed rules upon Maddox's return home was no guests inside the house. Immediate family only, with the exception of the home-care nurse and the tutor. Maddox's friends could drop by. They just had to sit outside to talk and stay at least three feet apart. So far this had worked well, although when winter hit, it was bound to become problematic.

"We're here. Start the party." Keaton had half a Hershey's bar hanging from his mouth and was already in the process of unwrapping a Reese's peanut butter cup. "Your mom hands out the good candy. I've always liked that about her."

Parker, who was stuffing his mouth full of M&Ms, nodded his agreement. "Sure does." His mouth was so full, Brent could only guess at the exact words spoken.

The boys settled into chairs and finished their candy. No one said much, and then Brent realized the presence of a parent was likely hampering the free flow of conversation. "I'm going to check on things out front."

"Sounds good, Mr. R."

Brent hadn't even made it around the corner yet when he heard the hum of teenage boy chatter behind him. *Bingo*.

At the front of the house, Linda was entrenched behind a card table, a bowl of candy centered in the middle. She wore mittens and a beanie, as well as her winter coat and a blanket wrapped around her legs. At times like this, he remembered why, and just how much, he loved her. He really did want to forgive and forget everything, but it was so much harder than it sounded in theory.

"You know, you could just leave the candy on this table and the kids could get it themselves. There's no reason to sit out here and freeze."

"Of course there's a reason. Hospitality for one thing. And probably more important is to keep the teenagers from grabbing the entire bowl."

He gestured toward the backyard. "Keaton and Parker helped prove that point."

"Exactly. And they're like family, so for them it's fine." Linda leaned forward. "Oh, look at these beautiful princesses. Would you ladies like some candy to eat before you return to your castle?"

The older girl, probably eight, and dressed in a tiara and white gloves said, "Yes, please." Her younger sister, Elsa from *Frozen* if Brent knew his characters, toddled up. "Twick or tweet."

Linda held out the bowl. "Choose the one you'd like."

"Thank you. Marla, tell her thank you."

"Fank you."

The two girls made their way back toward the sidewalk, the big sister carefully guiding the smaller one down the driveway. "What darling girls. It's nice to have a break from superheroes and mummies, I must say. This neighborhood is overrun with boys."

"So is our house."

"Yes, it is." Linda laughed, but it struck Brent that all these years when Linda had been raising sons, she had a daughter on the other side of the country. He tried to picture her with a little girl, surrounded by pink and frills and tea parties. And where would he fit into that picture? Would he have played dress up and fairy princess like other fathers of girls he knew?

The thought hit on a pain Brent wasn't quite prepared to deal with, so he said, "I'm going back around to make sure the big boys are staying out of mischief."

"Probably a good idea, as there are so many ways they could get into trouble in our backyard." Linda quirked her eyebrow. Her sense of irony was another thing he had always liked about her. It was good to be reminded of these things.

As Brent rounded the corner, he could hear Maddox's voice raised with excitement. "Really?"

"Really. Look, here's the story."

Parker held out his phone, which Maddox didn't touch. Instead he leaned forward for a closer look. "That is crazy. Wow. What are the odds? I wonder…" Maddox noticed Brent then. "Hey, Dad, guess what? There's a story about how Steve Kleen donated bone marrow a couple months ago to a kid with leukemia. What if I got his bone marrow? Maybe that's how Janice got the signed picture of him. Wouldn't that be the coolest thing ever?" Maddox shook his head and leaned back against the chair. "Me, with Steve Kleen's DNA. I bet my batting average will go up this spring."

Maddox knew on an intellectual level there would be no baseball this spring. The doctors had long ago told him this. Emotionally he wasn't quite ready to accept that, yet. With this new thought, that he might share DNA with the American League MVP, things would be even harder.

Later that night, after everyone was back inside, except for Marshall, who was doing a scary movie marathon at a friend's house, Brent and Linda sprayed and wiped down every possible germ-harboring surface. Brent made two cups of chamomile tea, then sat beside Linda on the couch.

After a minute, he reached over and took her hand. It was the first time he'd done so since learning about Caroline. "We've got to tell Maddox the truth about his donor."

CHAPTER 31

"**O**ne thousand dollars for Rosecliff for the Stratton-Dingledine wedding, huh? Please tell me that's a deposit."

Busted. Caroline was just finishing up an email to Roger Williams when she heard Gloria's voice in her office. Ruth had already gone home for the evening, and up until now, Caroline was enjoying the quiet. "Friends and family discount?"

"We don't do that. And no one with the last name Stratton is a friend."

"Military discount?" She simpered.

"We don't do that either. Does it have anything to do with this?" Gloria held up a copy of the *Aquidneck Island News*. A photo of Chris and Caroline's now infamous kiss at the Red Sox game took up over half of "According to Aiden's" allotted space.

Fabulous. Caroline's stomach did a somersault as she attempted to suppress a sigh. "I've already told you we were just playing along for the crowd. And that is nothing more than a gossip column."

Gloria's eyes narrowed and her lips scrunched to the side. "Gossip, huh? For once, I wish it were true. In fact, if it is, I'll happily forget about the five-thousand-dollar hit on the rental fee. I'd pay double to see that project fail."

"What do you mean, fail?"

"You haven't read it?" Gloria took her glasses from on top of her head and slid them onto her face. She cleared her throat, held up the paper, and read the subtitle aloud. "One delay after another at the Chadwick. Is Chris distracted? Unmotivated? Or even switching sides?"

Caroline rolled her eyes. "I'm sure he's exaggerating. And who reads that nonsense anyway?" Perhaps this explained the silence since they'd last met a couple weeks ago with Blythe. Not the article—it just came out today—but maybe things were going south at the hotel and it was taking up all Chris's time. There was that electrical issue ...

Then again, maybe he wasn't busy, just disinterested. Maybe he actually was just playing along for the crowd or feeling like Caroline really was too much of a distraction. She wasn't even sure if it mattered to her why he wasn't calling. It was better for both of them and she knew it.

"I don't have a problem with you distracting him. I just hope he's not distracting you."

"I'm not distracted." She sat up a little straighter. "I'll figure out a way to compensate for the rental fee, okay?"

Gloria pushed a hip out to the side, then placed a hand on it. "If you say so."

Out of the corner of her eye, Caroline noticed her phone screen light up, alerting her of an incoming call. She didn't recognize the number, but it could be the Old North Church's pastor getting back to her about the Religious Freedom Forum. Plus, it was a welcome excuse to stop this conversation with Gloria, even if it was spam. She held up her phone. "I'm sorry, Gloria. I better take this."

She nodded, then slipped out.

Phew. She pressed Accept, then held the phone up to her ear. "This is Caroline."

"Hi, Caroline, this is Jack Perry calling. I've just received a message that you called back in September?"

Panic stampeded through her body. "Jack Perry?" She blurted out his name, then after realizing what she did, she took a deep breath and tried to compose herself. Her voice quivered. "Oh, yes, I did. I, um, I'm sorry. I wasn't expecting to hear back from you."

It had been over two months. She'd figured since he hadn't called back by now, he never would.

"You'll have to forgive me. My assistant just returned from maternity leave this week, and the temp who took your first message put it in the wrong place. We just found it this morning, so I hope I didn't inconvenience you too much."

Caroline stood, then walked over to her office door. Her legs felt like wet noodles. After a quick look into the hall and seeing no one, she closed the door. "No, that's okay. I understand." She hoped her voice was loud enough for Jack and quiet enough for the thin walls. Truthfully, she had little control over her voice at this point.

"Is there something I can do for you?"

Do for me? Yes, be very patient. "Well, um, not really do for me, but I do have some information you might be interested in."

"Sure, go ahead."

She opened her mouth, but the words didn't emerge. She swallowed what felt like a golf ball, then tried to think of how to start. Information for you... *consumer discretionary sectors tend to be volatile...*

No. Come on. What was that little speech she'd prepared when she called him? She couldn't remember. She paced her office. Finally, she managed to speak. "Does the name Linda Riley mean anything to you? I suppose you knew her as Linda Newton."

There was a brief pause before he spoke. "If you're calling about her son, I saw the article in Gordon's alumni newsletter. I was sorry to hear about it and hope everything works out for her." His tone was assertive but not unkind.

"Oh. Um, well no. I'm not exactly calling about her son." The neck of her sweater was a tad too tight, so she gave it a yank. She walked over to her window, then cranked it open, but the frigid night air bit her nose instead of providing the relief she was looking for.

"Then what can I help you with, Ms. Chapman?"

He's losing interest. Think. Get to the point. "I'm calling about Linda's daughter. Me, actually. I was Maddox's bone marrow donor."

"Great. I'm glad they found a match." He didn't exactly exude enthusiasm.

Caroline clenched her lips together. "Mm-hmm."

"And?"

Caroline returned to her chair and let out a deep breath. *Here we go.* "And, well, according to Linda, I'm—" She stopped. Her palms were sweating, and she ran her free hand up and down her pant leg. *Come on, you can do this,* "— your daughter, too."

This time, there was a long pause. Caroline thought the call might have failed, but after another moment, Jack spoke. "I'm sorry, but that's impossible."

Caroline looked at the floor, the wall, out the window. It wasn't impossible, assuming Linda's story was legit. He just needed more information. Facts about her life ping-ponged around her brain, and her heart continued to do the same against her ribs. "I'm twenty-nine. I was born in

Santa Barbara while Linda was on an exchange program with Westmont her junior year. Adopted. I understand you weren't aware I was born. But I was, and I thought y-you"— she stammered. What? Would like to know? Probably not— "should know." Her mouth was dry.

"And I think you should know Linda's mistaken." His tone was still assertive. No longer kind.

"I think she's telling the truth. Anyway, it wouldn't be difficult to confirm." This wasn't working. She was getting nowhere. She couldn't think of anything else to say. There was nothing left to say that would make him suddenly believe and, what? Invite her over for dinner? To meet his family? Her cheeks got hot despite the cold air flooding in through the window. She shouldn't have called.

"What do you want from me, Ms. Chapman? Even if it were true, what do you expect me to do?"

She slouched over and placed her elbows on her lap, but it didn't ease the nausea that was building. It was a fair question, really, but it stung nonetheless. Anything she'd allowed herself to expect evaporated now. "I thought you should know, that's all. I'm not expecting anything."

"Good." His voice punched through the phone. "That I can do. Do not contact me again."

The call went dead.

Quiet had never been so stunning.

She started to wonder, did his daughter tiptoe downstairs on quiet mornings and find him reading a devotional at the kitchen table? Did he call her his Coffee Girl because she sat quietly on his lap as he drank his early morning cup? Did she interrupt his quiet Saturday, and did he drop whatever he was doing to take her out? Shopping? To lunch? To a quiet bookstore? Did he sit up quietly worrying about her when she was out past her curfew?

She looked down at her phone again, and although her vision was blurred by tears, she typed in a text message, then pressed Send. A few seconds later, the chime of his reply broke through the quiet.

I love you, too, Coffee Girl.

CHAPTER 32

Saturday morning started like any other day, but it wasn't any other day, and Brent knew it. So did Linda. Their family had experienced far too many of these not-any-other-day kind of days in the past few months. He prayed this would be the last.

As he shredded the cheese for the omelettes, his mind went over the things he needed to say and the issues he should bypass. He wanted to help his boys understand this all in the right light. But what did "right" look like in this particular case?

Marshall padded into the kitchen, his light-brown hair standing out in every direction. "Morning, Mom. Morning, Dad." He pulled a glass out of the cupboard and stuck it under the waterspout in the refrigerator. "Gary wants me to come over after breakfast. He's working on building a new chess tutoring app and needs some help."

"You can't." Linda's answer came so fast, Marshall had not even finished speaking. He looked at her, face scrunched, totally confused. It was more than understandable. Saturday had always been a day where the boys were more or less free to do their own things—assuming their grades were good and their chores were done, neither of which had ever been a problem for Marshall.

"What? Why?" He turned his attention to Brent, waiting for him to remind Mom of the Saturday rules.

Brent was thankful for the extra few seconds to process before Marshall turned to him. "It's not that you can't." He cut a sideways glance at Linda. "What your mom means is, not right away. We need to have a family meeting with you and your brother after breakfast."

Marshall studied him, obviously trying to gauge the situation. "O—kaaay. Is something wrong? Did one of Maddox's tests come back bad?"

"No, nothing like that. We just need to have a family talk."

"I can go to Gary's afterward, though, right?"

The news might be so upsetting that the half-hour meeting would affect more than just the morning's schedule. Brent didn't want Marshall to promise to be somewhere and then have to explain why he'd changed his mind.

"Why don't you tell him this morning is busy, but maybe this afternoon?" Linda did not look at Marshall as she spoke, instead she kept her gaze firmly locked on the bowl of eggs she was currently whisking with milk.

Eyes narrowed, Marshall leaned against the counter. "Well, how long is the family meeting going to take?"

Brent needed to shut this down now. "Marshall, tell him you'll give him a call this afternoon, and that's all I'm going to say about it."

Marshall's mouth dropped open. He took a breath, clearly thinking about arguing, then closed it again. Brent rarely played the "because I said so" card. Marshall was astute enough to know that something must be wrong, but he was old enough that he did not accept this as a satisfactory answer. "All right then." He mumbled something that sounded like "ridiculous" as he stomped from the kitchen.

Half an hour later the family sat eating their omelettes in total silence. Marshall was too annoyed to attempt any banter, Maddox was too tired, and Brent and Linda were too nervous. Maddox ate through about one-third of his omelette, then stood and picked up his plate.

"Maddox, you need to eat more. Your body needs the protein to help the new bone marrow settle in."

"I know, Mom. I've eaten as much as I can. I'll drink a protein shake later. Keaton and Parker are planning to come over and hang out for a little while."

At this pronouncement, Marshall narrowed his eyes toward his mother. He didn't have to worry, because Brent acted quickly. "Sorry, bud, but we've got some family business to take care of this morning. Tell them they can maybe come over this afternoon."

"What kind of business?" He looked over his shoulder as he continued to rinse his plate.

Marshall leaned back in his chair, folded his arms across his chest, and made something of a huffing sound. Brent saw the challenge for what it was and said, "Just tell your friends you'll call them later. We'll discuss it when everyone is done eating."

"I'm finished." Marshall stood and picked up his plate. Normally he would have eaten an entire omelette and perhaps a second. Today, with scarcely more than half eaten, he chose information over food and moved toward the sink.

Brent looked at Linda and shrugged. Neither of them had taken more than a few bites. Marshall was right. Best to get this over with. He also stood and picked up his plate. "Let's adjourn to the den, shall we? Your mom and I have some things to tell you."

...

Linda followed the boys into the den where they each slumped into their favorite ends of the worn leather sofa. So normal. But not for long. While this was not the life-or-death declaration they'd made about Maddox a few months ago, today's meeting would directly affect the way the boys thought about her now, and for the rest of their lives.

She perched on the edge of her favorite wing-backed chair and waited while Brent settled onto the ottoman. He cleared his throat. "Boys, there are some things we need to tell you—"

"No, there are some things *I* need to tell you." She looked at Brent. "I appreciate your willingness to carry some of this, but it's all on me, so I should be the one to say it."

At this point, Marshall had come upright and was leaning forward. Only Maddox remained in a relaxed posture, seemingly unaware of the tension in the room. "Geez, Mom. What, did you rob a bank or something?"

Linda tried to smile. She stared down at her hands, palms pressed together, then back up at her son. "No, nothing like that." She looked from Marshall's worried face, to Maddox's thin and pale one, then took a deep breath. "Back when I was in college..."

She had relived so much of the story in the past few months, that this time she was able to tell it in a concise, coherent way without losing control. She only got choked up after she reached the part about having given up a daughter for adoption some twenty-nine years ago. "We've raised you both to be men of honor, and it must be hard for you to hear that your mother doesn't always live up to what she preaches, but I want you to know the full truth. And I'm sorry I've kept it from you, and your father, for so long."

Marshall, always the deeper thinker, had listened to the entire story, eyes narrowed, clearly processing a hundred miles an hour. He leaned fully back and stared at the ceiling. "Wow, just wow."

The room remained silent for a couple of minutes. Linda gave the boys time to take in what they'd heard. There was so much for them to process.

Finally, Maddox spoke. "So, we have a sister?"

"A half sister, yes."

"That we've never heard about?"

"That's right." Linda nodded, glanced toward Brent, who sat watching the boys, a grim look on his face. Linda continued. "Her name is Caroline. She grew up in California, but she recently moved to Newport. She's twenty-nine years old, and she's a total sweetheart."

"Caroline?" Marshall was rubbing his chin, something he often did when in deep thought. "Isn't that the name of the friend you went to dinner with a while back? For her birthday?"

"That's right. The friend I went to dinner with was actually your half sister."

Marshall tilted his head. "So, have you always been in touch with her? Why haven't you told us about this before?"

"No, I've only reconnected with her recently, since she moved to Newport. And I didn't mention it that night because there were enough things upsetting in both your lives, and I didn't see a reason to add to it."

"So...she got in touch with you when she moved nearby?" Marshall clearly saw these new items as pieces of a puzzle that must be constructed into a picture that made sense. He would keep asking questions until he reached a satisfactory conclusion.

"No. She didn't get in touch with me." Again she looked toward Brent, who reached over and took her hand. That gesture gave her the strength to continue. "I actually initiated the contact. I sent her an email back in June."

"June?" Marshall mulled that over for a few seconds. "Maddox was really sick in June. Why would you have—?" Marshall paused for just a heartbeat and then his eyes widened. "That's why you contacted her, right?"

Linda nodded. "That's right. I asked her if she would consider getting tested to see if she was a potential match."

"So you're saying…?"

Again, Linda nodded. "Yes. Caroline was Maddox's donor."

"Wow. Just wow." Marshall said it again, and this time he leaned across the couch and gave his brother a shove. "I guess this means your batting average won't be improving after all."

Maddox grinned. "I guess not." He looked at his father for several seconds, then turned his attention back to Linda. "So it was my sister who donated bone marrow for me?"

"Yes."

Maddox sat quietly, his head bobbing up and down slowly as he thought all this through. After a long time, he looked Linda directly in the eye. "When can I meet her?"

...

It couldn't be ignored. It couldn't be shrugged off. And it couldn't come at a worse time.

Caroline had woken up that morning on the tired side, feeling a little stiff and run-down but went about checking things off her weekend to-do list anyway. Now, as she finished cleaning her bathroom, she wished she'd spent her Saturday relaxing instead. Chills overtook her, body aches consumed her, and her head felt like it might explode.

Ugh. She was definitely getting a cold.

The upcoming weeks had been thoughtfully planned out in her calendar so she could get all the NPS holiday events squared away and still take a couple days off when her parents came for Thanksgiving. Getting a cold was not on her agenda. One sick day, and Gloria would probably accuse her of getting distracted again. She rolled her eyes at the notion.

After a hot shower, she wrapped herself in a blanket, then went downstairs in search of noodle soup. Her mom used to make it for her when she was sick, and Caroline was in the habit of keeping it on hand.

As she pulled the soup packet from the box, the chime of a text message blared into her throbbing head. She'd put that on Do Not Disturb mode, ASAP.

She shuffled over then grabbed her phone charging on the kitchen counter. Wait, was this real, or was this a fever induced hallucination? She blinked a few times, pulled her blanket up a little tighter, then read the text from Linda.

I just told the boys the entire story. They are both excited to have a sister! Maddox in particular would like to meet you. Would you be interested in coming over sometime? (Maddox can't go out in public places at this point.)

Her mouth hung open. The boys knew. Linda had told them about her. Made her a part of their reality. She was no longer an only child and they were no longer just two brothers. They were connected, by DNA, yes, but more now. By a common knowledge of something once hidden and a tug toward something new. Exciting, even—that's what Linda had said. A future of shared experiences they would've otherwise never had.

Unless, of course, they thought she was a weirdo and never wanted to see her again. She shook her head. They were teenage boys. Weird was their MO.

I would really like to meet them, too. Unfortunately, I've just come down with a cold. I assume I can't be around Maddox until I'm completely healthy. Should we plan on something in a couple weeks, just to be safe?

The reply came a minute later. *I'm sorry you're sick. Would you like to join us for Thanksgiving? You're on the top of our list of things we're thankful for this year!*

Caroline's heart fluttered a bit. *Thanks so much for the invitation, but my parents are flying out. Might be a little overwhelming for M & M for the first meeting? How about the first Saturday in December?*

Perfect. As the day gets closer we can figure out the time that works best. I look forward to introducing you to the rest of your family.

Caroline responded with a thumbs-up, then returned to preparing her soup. In just a few weeks, she'd actually be meeting her brothers. Real siblings. Family. She closed her eyes and tried to focus her memory on the picture Linda had shown her at dinner last summer, to remind her of what they looked like before all of this had happened.

It had been several months though, and nothing striking came to mind. She stirred her soup and watched the noodles swirl around the pot, then sink back down to the bottom. Nothing striking, except for ...

She picked up her phone and reread Linda's texts. Linda had "told the boys ..." They are "both excited ..." Both means two. But there was another in that photo. One Linda had mentioned several times at dinner but didn't exactly mention now. Brent.

Her mouth went dry and her heart hitched. Of course Brent was thankful Maddox had found a donor. But was he excited that his sons had a sister?

She wasn't quite sure she wanted to find out.

CHAPTER 33

Chris's heart jackhammered against his chest. It was the same feeling he had over a month ago when he first laid eyes on the electricians' discovery in the attic at the hotel. But this time, as he reviewed the photocopy in his pseudo office at Tom's guesthouse, there wasn't a trace of hope that it might not be authentic. He'd just gotten off the phone with a top expert confirming it was. Chris rubbed his hand over his chin. He hadn't shaved in days, as if that mattered right now.

He picked up his phone again and pressed Tom's name in his contacts. Then hung up. No, he wasn't ready for that. Chris paced across the living room, then stared out the window that looked out over the gray ocean. The sky was gray, too, and the wintry mix of snow and rain concealed the Beavertail Lighthouse across the water.

He put his hands in the front pocket of the Boston College Lacrosse hoodie he'd had on all day. The one he had since he was seventeen, sent by the school when he accepted their scholarship. It was practically in tatters now, but that's what gave it character.

He took a deep breath, then dialed again. Tom was in Hawaii until after Thanksgiving. Hopefully he would be relaxed and in a good mood. It was only 10:00 a.m. there with the time change, so not too much could have spoiled his day, yet.

The phone rang several times before Tom answered. "Chris, tell me you have good news." He didn't exactly sound relaxed.

For a second, Chris thought about lying or just saying he called to wish him a happy Thanksgiving. He ran his hand through his hair and inhaled. "I wish. I just heard back and it's authentic. The question remains if it has any legal implications, but it's authentic."

A string of expletives stormed into Chris's ear, and he was pretty sure he heard Tom slam his hand on something. "Please. Remind me why you didn't just rip it up as soon as you found it."

A part of him wished he had. Chris had no problem admitting it. But if anyone ever found out... Chances were slim but still. "I didn't think it was worth the risk to your company. Or reputation." Or his own sense of integrity, knowing he would regret not handling something like this on the up-and-up. "If it ever got out or if another copy is somehow found, you can say you did your due diligence."

Tom grumbled. "Get it over to Murray's office pronto. He's in Paris. Probably won't be able to get to it until January, but we still need to get it over there to cover our bases."

"Will do."

"Who else knows about this?"

Chris racked his brain but came up empty. "No one."

"You're sure the electricians didn't open it?"

"It was sealed."

"How about your little girlfriend?" Tom's sarcasm was on the heavy side, and it landed with a thud in Chris's gut.

Normally Chris would go the "I don't know who you're talking about" route, then reassure Tom he was concentrating on his work, but it didn't seem like the time. Chris knew exactly who Tom was referring to, even if they hadn't seen each other in a month. And she might have been occupying his thoughts more than he'd care to admit to Tom. But good grief, Chris was thirty-two years old. He didn't need to explain his relationships. He was allowed to have a life. *Okay, focus. Back to the call.* "No. She doesn't know."

"Keep it that way. Forty years in business, at least I can say I've learned to never hand the enemy more ammunition."

The twinge in his gut grew, and before he could filter his thoughts, he spoke. "I don't think she's like that."

"Chris, I've got two ex-wives I didn't think were 'like that.' I haven't said anything about that relationship or the ridiculous news articles, because I trust you. Your personal life is your business."

Since when? Chris scrunched his eyebrows together. Good thing this wasn't a video chat. "Thank you."

"But this is not your personal life. This is work. Your job."

Chris cleared his throat. It was dry and he could use a glass of water. Or whiskey. "I understand."

"Good. How are things otherwise?"

The tension in his chest eased a smidge. At least they were talking about something else now. "The bathroom tile the interior designer picked is on back order, but the plumbing is on track, so once the tile comes, it can go right in. The electricians need to step it up on the second floor, but it's not exactly their fault since we had to rewire the entire place. Even the stuff that went in back in the nineties. I'll go back over in the morning and help them put in a full day before Thanksgiving."

"Fine. Let me know as soon as Murray gets back to you. I can't imagine it's legally binding, but we should get a plan of action in place either way."

And by "we" Tom meant "you." Chris rolled his eyes. Definitely glad this wasn't a video chat. "I'm on it."

After hanging up, Chris grabbed a glass of water from the kitchen. He hadn't noticed how little food was around, so he'd better hit the grocery store tomorrow. Wonderful. After this past month of keeping the Chadwick on track, keeping Tom from blowing a gasket, and trying to keep his own sanity while his mom nagged about Thanksgiving, the last thing Chris needed was a busy supermarket the day before Thanksgiving and a snowstorm. Whatever, that was the least of his worries.

He picked up a half-used legal pad from the coffee table, flipped to a blank page, then started to think. Nothing. He took a swig of water, then wrote *Possible Solutions* at the top. Still nothing. Hmm, maybe Caroline was on to something. Perhaps that "electrical fire" wasn't the worst idea.

His mind drifted to Caroline. Of course he'd wanted to call her, kept meaning to, but one thing after another came up and here he was, neck deep in awkward silence. Awkward for him at least. There was always the possibility that's how Caroline wanted it. Heck, she could have picked up a phone, too, if she wanted to talk, right? His sisters would have smacked him for that one.

At this point, maybe it was better to leave well enough alone, especially in light of all that was going on. At least wait until this mess was cleaned up if he didn't want Tom looking over his shoulder every five minutes.

He returned his focus to his legal pad and wrote *accidental electrical fire* at the top. An hour later, it was still his best option.

...

When Chris woke the following morning, yesterday's wintery mix had turned to full snow and had already left a heavy blanket on the Williams's lawn. Normally they didn't get hit until after Thanksgiving and normally Aquidneck Island didn't get hit as hard. But according to his weather app, this wasn't a normal storm, and it was starting to move in hours before they'd expected.

Just perfect. He couldn't possibly make the electricians stay all day. He made himself a pot of coffee, put on some of his warmer work clothes, then went over to the Chadwick where he helped the electricians put in a few solid hours.

Around noon, he looked out the window and decided he'd better get to Stop & Shop before it really started coming down. Even though all he wanted to do was go home, take a shower, and watch football on the couch. He pressed the remote start button on his keys, grabbed his coat, then told the electricians to go home as well and have a nice Thanksgiving.

The parking lot was jam-packed, and it took several minutes for a spot to open up. As he was walking through the slushy mix of salt and snow, he noticed a car sliding toward him. He took a few quick steps to the side.

Except, it didn't stop.

He took a few more steps toward the sidewalk and the car swerved. He was pretty sure it was about to hit something, if not him, when it finally came to a stop only a few inches from a parked car.

Geez, lady. His heart was racing. *Run me over, why don't you?*

He glared into the driver's window and was about to voice those very thoughts, when he noticed streaks of blonde hair underneath a black baseball cap, and a familiar face that made his pulse quicken even more.

He walked over, knocked on her window, then waited for Caroline to roll it down. "I don't think killing me is the right way to express your feelings." He laughed, but as she turned to face him, he realized she was crying. Her nose was red, and mascara was smeared under her eyes. "What's the matter?"

Her bottom lip quivered, then she finally just seemed to burst. "I hate snow!" She put her face in her hands.

"What happened?"

"My parents were supposed to fly in tonight, but their connection was canceled. They can't get another flight to Providence until Saturday, so they're going home. I literally just bought all this food for Thanksgiving dinner when they called." She pointed toward the back of her car. "And my feet are soaking wet. And I can't drive in this."

Chris gave her car a quick once-over. "Well, for one thing, you need new tires." All that did was trigger another bomb of despair. *Nice work, Stratton.* He let out a sigh. "Are you going home?"

"I'm trying to," she said between large sniffles.

There was no way she could drive like this, for everyone's safety. "Come on. I'll get you back." He opened her door and motioned for her to get out.

She stared up at him. Her pink cheeks and swollen eyes made her look like a lost puppy. "Really? What about your truck?"

"I can come back for it."

"Okay." She sniffled again and wiped her nose on the sleeve of her jacket. "Thank you."

He wasn't sure, but it looked like the same jacket from the Red Sox game, when it was at least twenty-five degrees warmer than it was right now. She got out of the car and he confirmed it was indeed the same jacket, and her running shoes. "Are these the warmest clothes you have?"

"I have a scarf, too, but I didn't think I'd need it."

Good grief, no wonder. He was tempted to reach out and wrap her up, Lord knew he wanted to, but he took off his coat and put it on her instead. "You need a warmer coat."

"Yes, thank you. I realize that now. This stuff isn't exactly like it looks in Hallmark movies." She flung her bare hands up into the snow, then trudged around the car to the passenger side.

Chris pulled out of the store parking lot and glanced over at Caroline. She was sitting with her arms crossed and droopy eyes. "I take it this is your first time in the snow."

"I've been on ski trips to Mammoth, but it's not the same. I've never had to drive in it."

"Yeah, I guess it makes a difference when you grow up with it." His dad had taught him to drive in the snow. Chris remembered braking too fast the first time and swerving in the slush.

She turned to face him. "What the heck is a nor'easter anyway?"

Chris couldn't help but chuckle. "I think it's a wind pattern or weather system over the ocean. I'm not sure really, but this is the result."

"Lovely." She turned her torso back toward the windshield for the remainder of the short ride.

Chris pulled into her driveway, turned off the engine, then popped the trunk. It seemed like half the grocery store was inside. "Wow, you weren't kidding. This is a ton of food."

She took her keys from him and grabbed a case of sparkling water. "You can have it. I'm not going to bother cooking a Thanksgiving dinner for myself, and most of it was for my parents' visit."

"I'm not going to take it." He grabbed two armloads, then followed Caroline to her front door. He set the bags on the kitchen counter, then went back outside for two more bundles. As he watched Caroline unloading the groceries when he returned to the kitchen, he got an idea. He didn't bother taking the time to assess if it was a good one. He already knew the answer. "What if I come over and help you cook it? Shame to miss out on Thanksgiving dinner."

She peered at him, a box of Cheerios in her hand. "You can cook?"

Ummm. "No, I meant offer moral support while you cook and then eat it with you."

"Men." She rolled her mascara-smeared raccoon eyes and put the Cheerios in a cabinet. "You don't have plans?"

"I think it's supposed to snow all night, so I'll probably be stuck here anyway." He took advantage of the fact that she had no idea his truck could barrel through anything and the highways would be plowed even if it was still snowing tomorrow. It sounded better than the truth.

"Okay, I guess. But I have to warn you. My mom is the real cook and my dad usually barbecues the turkey. So I'm not promising anything."

I'm not coming for the food. Thankfully he managed to keep that one in. "Barbecue a turkey? Hmm, I can give that a whirl. What time?"

"I'm not going anywhere, so it doesn't really matter to me. How about we aim to eat at three o'clock? The turkey will take a couple hours."

"Sounds good."

He unloaded the rest of her groceries, then walked back to his truck. It was cold out and the snow was really coming down now, but he didn't really care. In fact, he felt rather warm.

CHAPTER 34

No, no! Oh, come on. What had she done wrong? Despite sitting in a warm oven for the past two hours, the dough Caroline had made that morning from her mom's home-made roll recipe hadn't budged. It was supposed to rise and be double the size by now. Maybe it was a sign. Maybe this entire day would be a disaster. Maybe it was confirmation that time with Chris was a complete waste, and in the end, she'd get tossed aside like this useless pile of dough.

Or maybe next time she should just buy the tube of Pillsbury.

Okay, don't panic. It was only ten thirty. She could still cancel on Chris and ... what, go to Linda's house? Probably not the most hospitable or courteous thing to do. Besides, there was no way she was getting anywhere near her car until things cleared up. Why had she accepted Chris's offer to come over anyway? Hopefully he wasn't expecting any-thing actually edible.

She rinsed the bowl and decided to try again, and this time, she'd be a little more careful. Which was exactly how she needed to be with Chris today.

For one thing, she wasn't quite sure what he wanted. Could he really just be trying to distract her like Gloria had said? No matter how much Gloria's accusation irked her,

Caroline had allowed him—although without his knowl-edge—to short NPS five thousand dollars.

Truthfully, she wasn't so sure what she wanted from him either, but the one thing she absolutely did not want to com-promise was her job. Maybe it would be better if her cook-ing proved a disappointment.

A while later, she was about to check on her second batch of dough, when she heard a noise outside—a slosh-ing, scraping sound—and it seemed to be getting louder.

She walked over to the window, then pulled the curtain back to discover Chris shoveling her driveway. Oh, that was nice, especially since she didn't own a shovel or have any desire to do that herself. She opened her front door but remained inside. "You don't have to do that." *But please don't stop.*

"You won't be able to drive anywhere if I don't." Chris looked up but continued shoveling.

That's probably not the worst thing in the world. "Okay, well the door's open when you're done." She returned to the oven and glanced at the timer—four minutes left—then turned on the oven light so she could take a peek. Phew, this time the dough was rising like it was supposed to.

A few moments later, the front door opened. "Smells good." Chris took off his coat. "Feeling better today?" Now he was standing next to her with his arms extended for a hug.

Her heart hitched and her body hesitated in kind, but soon she leaned in and allowed him to wrap his arms around her. "Um, yes. Thank you. Still a bit disappointed my parents couldn't come." His dark-green wool sweater was soft against her cheek and he smelled crisp and clean, too. She pulled away. *Don't go there.*

"I have to admit, I'm kinda pumped about grilling a turkey. How do I do it?"

Caroline let out a deep breath, hopefully without Chris noticing, then pointed to the stack of recipes on her counter. "Instructions are in there and the grill is on the deck. Good luck."

He spent a few moments reading over the recipe, then put his coat back on and opened the sliding back door. The frigid air that seeped in actually felt nice to Caroline. It was starting to get warm in here, what with her fireplace going and all. Or maybe it wasn't just the fire.

No. Focus, Caroline.

She found a pack of gum in her cupboard and pulled out a piece, chewed it, spit it out thirty seconds later, then grabbed a fresh one.

Chris returned a few minutes later and started working in silence. He took the turkey from the brine bag, put it in the roasting pan, then washed his hands at the kitchen sink while Caroline took the dough from the bowl. She was about to ask how work was going, and maybe even use that as a way to reaffirm her commitment to her job, when he interrupted her little mental pep talk.

"How long has this faucet been loose?" He pointed to the wobbly, cold knob.

"Just a few days. I'll call my landlord tomorrow."

"Hmm." He rinsed his hands, jiggled the handle a few more times, then carried the turkey out to the grill. A bit later, he walked back into the house, but instead of returning to the kitchen, he went out the front door. Soon, he returned with a wrench, or at least Caroline thought it was a wrench. She was as unfamiliar with the world of tools as she was with that of snow.

"What are you doing?"

Chris removed a roll of paper towels, dish soap, and dish-washing detergent from the cabinet under her sink. "Fixing your faucet."

She faltered. "Why?"

"Why? Because it's broken." He was under her sink now and his voice was a tad muffled.

"That's nice of you. Thanks."

"Sure."

"Is that a habit of yours? Fixing things that are broken?"

A laugh echoed from within the cabinet. "I guess so. Occupational hazard."

Caroline pulled a bag of corn from the freezer, then tried to get started on the creamed corn recipe, but she couldn't seem to focus. Her heart started to beat a little faster as she glanced at Chris. *Speaking of occupational hazards...* She was about to say those very words, when again, Chris interrupted her thoughts.

"Oh, that reminds me. I've been meaning to ask you something." He scooted out from the cabinet, then started to put Caroline's things back in. "Did you ever meet up with that woman? The one who was asking about a bone marrow donation?"

Caroline stared at the corn recipe and a flush of heat enveloped her. She was trying to think of how to answer when Chris cut in. "I'm just asking because I wanted to say I'm sorry if you felt like I was pushing you into it. I, uh, know that kind of thing can be ... easier said than done."

"Oh. Thank you." The stiffness in her upper body eased a tad.

"So? Whatever happened to her son?" He was leaning against her sink, arms crossed casually in front of him.

She drew in another breath and stood a little taller now. "I ended up being his donor and he's recovering. Actually, the surgery was four days before La Fête."

"Are you serious? That's really cool." He smiled at her but then it disappeared. "Wait, four days before La Fête? But you looked amaz—" He stopped. "You looked totally normal."

"Thanks. Coming from you, I'll take that as a compliment."

"But how did his mom know? If you hadn't been tested yet? You said she had reason to believe you could donate and wanted to meet you."

She thought about making something up. Not because this was a secret, but because it was a more intimate road than she was planning to travel, with this traveling companion, anyway.

Chris's warm brown eyes drew her in, like gravity, and she was struggling to withstand it. The pull for relief, for finally talking about this with someone other than her parents, for revealing this deeper part of who she was—it was all becoming too much.

She took another breath, then released it, along with whatever was holding her back. "That woman? Linda. She reached out to me because I'm her biological daughter and it was my half brother Maddox who needed the donation. I was adopted." She let the words dangle in the heaviness of the moment.

Chris didn't flinch, though, just kept listening, so she kept talking. "I hadn't met her before she contacted me. I still haven't met Maddox yet, but I'm going over to their house next week to meet him and my other half brother, Marshall."

"Lucky."

She tilted her head to one shoulder and squinted. "Lucky?"

"Yeah. I always wanted brothers. I mean, Adam's great, and my brother-in-law's a nice guy, but they don't live close by. For a guy stuck with two sisters, two long-lost brothers would have been a dream come true."

"Well, from what I can gather online, I have three sisters, too, but—" A new heaviness filled her. Now this was territory she hadn't wanted to breach.

"But what?"

"I, um, don't think I'll be getting to know them anytime soon. My bio dad isn't interested in meeting me. Or hearing from me at all." Her voice caught in her throat, but she managed to swallow the hurt that was threatening an egregious game of peekaboo.

"You're kidding, that's terrible. I'm so sorry." He walked over, pulled her in, and wrapped his arms around her, but this time, he rested his chin on top of her head and held her for a few moments.

She didn't want to leave his embrace, although she probably should. "Thanks. It's not the end of the world. I'll be fine. I guess I just let my expectations get the better of me. I thought he'd actually be interested in knowing he had another daughter and maybe even want to meet me." A tear or two puddled over onto Chris's sweater. She pulled away and wiped it with her sleeve. "I'm sorry."

"It's okay." His smile was kind and comforting. His eyes still soft and tender.

Caroline took another deep breath. Her mind teetered between regret for saying so much and relief for finally doing so. It felt good, but she also knew she'd let Chris in further than she wanted to that morning. She'd created a space for him, whether she intended to or not, and now what?

"Well, I'm getting hungry. Can you cut some potatoes?" It sounded abrupt. Not appropriate for the moment, but she couldn't allow their closeness to linger either, even if she wanted it to.

The two of them worked side by side preparing the rest of the meal, and thankfully the conversation didn't diverge from lighthearted topics, like when Chris put dye he'd taken from the high school science lab into his sisters' shampoo.

After dinner, Chris added more wood to the fireplace, then they sat on the couch eating the apple crisp right out of the pan.

"This is good. We make a good team." Chris spoke with a full mouth and pointed to the crisp with his fork.

"Yeah, we do." Caroline took another bite. "Too bad we're mortal enemies." She giggled at her own joke, but then a flood of awkwardness seemed to fill the room, or at least her heart. Now this whole thing just felt weird.

Chris let out a small laugh, too, then stopped and looked right at her. Silence hovered over the sound of the crackling fireplace until he finally spoke. "Yeah, too bad." His gaze lingered a few more moments, and Caroline thought she recognized the look in his eyes. It was the same flicker from the Red Sox game. Just before he had kissed her. Her heart started to beat a little faster and she swallowed the few crumbs of crisp that were in her mouth.

But then it was gone. Chris blinked, smiled, and took another bite. "Family recipe?"

"My grandma's, actually."

"You miss her?"

She nodded and chewed. "It's hard to lose people you love, but I don't have to tell you that." She stopped, her face getting hot. "I'm sorry. Gosh, I didn't mean for the conversation to get so serious today."

"It's okay." He leaned back a bit. "It is hard. You don't realize everything they added to your life until it's not there anymore."

"Exactly." She poked an apple. "But this tastes just as good as hers, and I bet you're just as good at fixing a sink as your dad was, so at least we have that."

"I hope I can at least manage to tighten a loose faucet as well as he did." He stretched his arms above his head. "Well, I'm stuffed and it's getting late. I should probably go."

Caroline ignored an unwelcome twinge of disappointment and nodded. The warmth of the moment zapped. "Yeah, it is. And I think it's supposed to snow again."

Chris stood, apple crisp pan in hand, then stepped into the kitchen. He placed the pan on the counter, then put on his coat by the front door. "Thanks for having me over. It was a nice day."

"It was. Thanks for coming."

He offered another hug, just one arm this time, and then, without another word, let himself out and pulled the door shut behind him.

Caroline let out a sigh. Her house felt empty and suddenly cold now, or maybe that's just how she felt inside. She headed into the kitchen and put plastic wrap over the remainder of the crisp.

She was about to start loading the dishwasher, but she heard a knock on the door. It was faint enough to have been a block of snow falling from the roof and hitting the ground. She set the silverware back into the sink, walked over to the door, and opened it just enough to peek outside.

"Hi." Chris stood on her front step, his hands stuffed in his jacket pockets.

"Hi." When he didn't say anything else, she opened the door a bit wider and continued. "Did you forget something?"

"Sort of. Um…" He pointed upward. "One of your outside lights is burned out. Do you have any extra bulbs?"

"Oh." This time, Caroline couldn't ignore the thud of disappointment, or the anger that followed for allowing herself to be disappointed. Again. "I think so. Let me go check." She went down to the basement, grabbed two that looked familiar, then walked back upstairs. "I think it's one of these."

He took both and went back outside. A few moments later, he returned and placed the old bulb and the unused one back on the small cabinet by her front door. "There. All fixed."

Well, at least she knew who to call if her oven went out. "Thanks."

"Sure. And thanks for having me over." Again, he just stood there.

"You said that already."

"Right, I did. Okay, well I should go." He pointed toward the door over his shoulder with his thumb.

"You've said that already, too."

Chris nodded. "Yes, well—" He exhaled, then walked toward her and stopped about a foot away. "I guess there's one thing I haven't said."

Caroline stood a little straighter, her stomach somersaulting.

He took a final step toward her, then slid a hand around the back of her neck. He leaned in and, in a soft voice, spoke with his cheek touching hers, causing her skin to tingle and her breath to quicken. "I'm glad you almost ran me over." He gazed into her eyes, the flicker simmering, then kissed her lips. Soft in the beginning but then with more gusto.

At first, Caroline's muscles tightened up, but then she relaxed and set her hands on his chest, then up over his shoulders. What she'd hoped to avoid this morning she now wanted to continue. And it did, for several gleeful moments.

When Chris pulled back, Caroline stared at him with a small smile. "Break my heart and I *will* run you over." It sort of just popped out. Her tone was light and playful, but in all seriousness, she couldn't handle one more hit right now.

Chris laughed and gave the side of her shoulder a squeeze. "Good night." He turned toward the door, then paused and looked back. "Would you want me to drive you over to meet your brothers?"

Yes. "I think I'll be fine. Unless it's snowing, then you can drive me."

"Deal." He gave her one more quick kiss, then opened the front door.

Caroline waved and watched him drive away before she locked up. She could still smell his cologne in the air. She leaned her back against the door and pressed her lips together, her body still tingling.

And her head was still nagging—this was not a good idea.

But her heart? Well, maybe she was thankful for snowstorms.

CHAPTER 35

Linda tore through the house in a frenzy. The knot in her stomach grew tighter with each passing moment, no matter how quickly her hands worked.

Maddox sat in the recliner, covered in a blanket. "Whoa, Mom. You need to relax. I haven't seen you this worked up since the first week I came home from the hospital."

"I haven't been this worked up since then." Linda barely glanced at him as she wiped down the coffee table. Again.

"I don't know what you're so freaked out about. Dr. Stern said it was okay to make this one exception to the no-visitors rule."

"It's more than just having a visitor in the house. I want her to … like it here." She looked around and went to plump a pillow on the sofa. "And of course it makes me nervous to have someone else and their germs in the house. And not just someone else, but two someone elses."

"Mom, it's no big deal. Relax already."

"Hmmph. Easy for you to say." Linda adjusted the candles on the mantel one inch to the left.

"If extra germs stress you out so much, why didn't you just tell her not to bring her boyfriend?"

"He's not her boyfriend, just a friend." She moved the candles back to their original position.

Maddox snorted. "Yeah right. That's what they all say."

Linda scowled at him. "In answer to your question, he is coming with her because she is not used to driving in the snow and apparently is terrified of doing so."

"Oh man, this is the worst. I find out that I have a sister, and before I even meet her I realize she's a wimp."

"She is not a wimp. She grew up in Southern California, remember? They don't have snow there."

"Well, she lives here now. It's time for her to toughen up and deal with it."

Brent, who had been walking through the house attacking the door handles with antibacterial wipes, entered the room in time to hear most of the conversation. "Don't start trash-talking before you've even met her. She let them stick needles in her hip bone to save the life of some punk seventeen-year-old she's never met. I'd call that pretty darn brave." He wadded up a used wipe and tossed it at his son.

Maddox reached out, but it fell well short of him. "Yeah. Or just plain stupid."

"Maddox Riley!" While it was nice to see him in a playful mood again, some things a mother could not tolerate. She fixed him with her most serious, mother-like gaze. "And you, young man, will be polite and charming to both Caroline and her friend. Is that understood?"

"Yes, *mon capitan*." Maddox offered a mock salute.

"It better be, or there will be a court-martial, which could result in walking the plank." Linda grinned at him, then picked up the wad and started toward the stairs to check the beef stew, which smelled amazing, if she did say so herself.

Marshall came through the front door, his cheeks bright red. "Driveway is shoveled, front walk and porch are salted and cleared."

"Good job, little brother. Now bring me something to drink, would you?" Maddox called from his spot on the recliner.

Marshall glared down into the den. "I can't wait until you're back to full speed again, because I am going to pulverize you."

"That's enough of that," Linda said, then called down to Maddox, "And you, get up and fetch your own drink. Just because we don't want you scrubbing germ-covered surfaces, doesn't mean you shouldn't be pitching in."

Ding dong.

Showtime. Today felt even more important than their last meeting. Linda really wanted everyone to like Caroline. She really wanted Caroline to like everyone.

When Linda reached out to open the door, her hands were shaking. She took a deep breath, pulled it open, and found Caroline and a young man, who basically personified the tall, dark, and handsome cliché. The two of them made a striking couple, even if they were just friends. They both smiled, each looking a little hesitant. Linda knew just how they felt.

"Come in, come in." She gave Caroline a little hug and then extended her hand toward the young man. "I'm Linda."

"Chris. Nice to meet you." He shook her hand but continued to study her. "You look familiar to me."

As she returned his gaze, she also felt a flicker of recognition. "Yes. I agree. Did you grow up around here?"

"Well, I—" He stopped midsentence and took a step back. "Wait, I know where I've seen you. At the Preservation Society. You were there ... asking for Caroline, right?"

"Wait. What?" Caroline's expression was nothing short of bewildered.

Chris said, "It was a weekend. I was there dropping off that old chandelier. Remember that dilapidated old thing you loved so much? Ick!" He shook his head vigorously as if to expunge the memory. "But that was you, right? On the sidewalk?"

"That was me." Linda's face burned as she turned toward Caroline. "I hadn't heard back from you yet, and I was so desperate that I went searching. It didn't take me long to realize it was a ridiculous idea. Coincidentally, I got your email right in the middle of all that."

Caroline glanced from Chris to Linda. "Oh. That's a weird coincidence, isn't it?" She looked as if she might bolt.

Linda reached out and touched her arm. "I promise, that was my one and only foray into potential stalking."

Caroline kind of laughed. "Good to know."

"Give me your coats and I'll hang them up. And then, I hate to impose, but could I have you both wash your hands? It's something everyone has to do when they enter the house these days."

"Of course." They both answered at once.

Before taking off her coat, Caroline held out a bottle-sized gift bag. "Oh, and I brought you something. It's from my hometown."

"You didn't have to do that." Linda took the bag and pulled out the bottle of *il Fustino* rosemary-infused olive oil. "Thank you so much. This looks amazing."

Caroline smiled. "I hope you like it. It's delicious on all sorts of salads." She handed over her coat. "Where is the closest hand-washing station?"

"Right this way." Linda escorted Caroline and Chris into the kitchen, showed them the motion-activated soap dispenser, then gave them each a paper towel to dry their hands. "If you'll follow me, I'll introduce you to the rest of the family."

Linda led the two of them down the three stairs into the sunken family den. As soon as they entered, the three Riley men got to their feet. Brent, who was closest, offered his hand. "I'm Brent, nice to meet you."

Then Marshall approached and did the same. "And this is Maddox." Linda motioned toward him.

Chris extended his hand briefly but then jerked it back. "Sorry, I forgot."

Maddox waved dismissively. "No worries. Everyone does that. Nice to meet you, Chris." He nodded at Chris, then repeated the gesture toward Caroline. "Sis." The way he automatically called Caroline Sis warmed Linda's heart. "Thanks for—" Maddox stopped midsentence, mouth hanging open, and stared at Caroline and then Chris. "You're the couple from the kiss cam!"

Caroline's eyes went wide as her face flushed crimson. Chris, however, burst out laughing. "Yes, we are." He put his arm around Caroline's shoulder as if to confirm this.

"Oh my gosh! I can't believe it! I can't wait to tell Keaton and Parker. They are going to die."

Caroline stood frozen in place, looking as if she might pass out. Linda made eyes toward her son, trying to telepathically relay the message to stop this train of conversation. Maddox was, as usual, oblivious. "Maddox, maybe we should—"

"This is the best day ever! I meet my sister, and I find out that not only did she save my life, but she is the world-famous World Series kiss-cam girl. This is so awesome!" He doubled over, hooting with joy.

"Maddox." Linda needed to stop this now. "You are being rude."

He straightened and wiped his eyes. "Sorry about that."

Chris was clearly enjoying the moment. "What are you sorry about? That she had to kiss me, or that her beloved Dodgers got trounced for the remaining games of the series?"

Maddox laughed. "Actually, I'm not sorry about either of those things. Especially the fact that the Dodgers got their tails handed to them."

"Maddox!" This alarming turn in the conversation needed to stop now.

Chris, however, didn't seem to think so. He was yucking up this moment for all it was worth. "Maddox, you and I are going to get along just fine."

Caroline rolled her eyes. "I hate to break up this little bromance, but FYI, Maddox. You now have Dodgers' fan DNA in your blood. Ha!"

Chris and Maddox stared at each other in mock horror. Chris said, "The two of us better stick together."

Maddox nodded. "I think that's a good idea."

...

By the end of the evening, Red Sox Nation was fully bonded and having a great old time. Caroline and Brent had begun in polite conversation and proceeded from there, and Marshall made quick work of defeating Chris, Caroline, and then Brent in a game of chess.

Caroline came upstairs and was helping Linda load the dishwasher—in spite of her protests. "Go spend time with your brothers."

"For now, I'd rather spend time with you."

Don't cry, don't cry. "I'm so happy that you came here tonight. It's been great to see you with the boys. And Brent."

Caroline placed a plate in the slot. "Brent told me that I have your forehead."

"My forehead?" Linda cringed. What would cause Brent to make such a weird statement?

"Yes, when I was playing chess with Marshall and trying to escape the embarrassing fate that Chris suffered, Brent came over and said, 'Look at that, Marshall. She has that same little dimple above her left eyebrow that your mother has when she's concentrating really hard.'" Caroline rubbed her left eyebrow. "Personally, I had no idea there was a dimple above my left eyebrow when I'm concentrating."

"I didn't know about mine, either." Linda made a mental note to check that out in the mirror later. So odd, the things Brent knew about her that she didn't know about herself.

Caroline smiled. "Yes, he said he had always found that *adorable*, which of course I thought was *adorable*, but Marshall did not find our conversation *adorable*. In fact, he demanded that we change the subject immediately. I had hoped this would distract him enough to throw him off his game, but it didn't stop him from taking out my queen on the very next move."

"Yeah, he's a hard one to throw off track in the midst of a match."

"So I gathered." Caroline nodded. "It's nice to be here with them. All of you. Do you mind if I ask—how is Brent taking all this?"

"He's working through it. He's never been upset with or about you, just upset with me for neglecting to tell him about you. Or any of it."

"He seems like a wonderful man. Much more so than my biological father."

Linda looked to Caroline then. "Have you googled him or something?"

"I did, yes. And then ... I called him."

"What did Jack say?"

"I left a message for him, and it was a long time before he called me back. When he did and I told him who I was, he said that you were mistaken about him being my father. He asked me what I wanted from him, and when I said nothing, he said, 'Good, don't ever call me again' and hung up."

Linda dropped the glass she was holding. Thankfully it broke in three large chunks instead of tiny slivers everywhere. She picked up the remains and dumped them into the recycle bin. "Hung up?"

Caroline tried to smile, but there was no mistaking the glint of moisture in her eyes. "I mean, I guess I can't blame him. I called him out of the blue. Still ..."

"Still, is right. I can't believe he would do that. To be so cold and insensitive." Linda picked up some silverware and threw it into the tray with enough force to jar the dishwasher door.

Caroline reached out and grasped her arm. "It's okay, really it is. I've found you. And Maddox. And Marshall. And Brent. That's more than enough for me."

Linda drew her into a hug. "It means so much to me that you feel that way." First thing Monday morning, she would be on the phone.

Jack Perry could think again if he thought he could talk to her daughter that way.

CHAPTER 36

Linda closed her eyes and forced her memories back to the conversation with Caroline. The pain on her daughter's face had been so obvious that it physically hurt to recall it. But this was what she needed to remember as she placed this call. She hit Send on her cell phone, taking deep breaths, her palms sweating at the thought of the confrontation ahead.

The call was answered before the second ring. Linda took another deep breath. "Jack Perry, please."

"This is Joanna, Mr. Perry's assistant. May I help you?"

"No, you may not. I need to speak to Jack Perry. Now." Linda's own words stunned her. She had never spoken like this. Then again, she was never this angry.

"I'm sorry, Mr. Perry is in a meeting this morning. What did you say your name was?"

"Linda Riley."

"Well, Ms. Riley, Mr. Perry is a very busy man. I would be happy to take a message, or if you want to make an appointment to speak with him about future investment opportunities, I can transfer you back to the reception desk." The arrogance in her tone further irritated Linda and gave her the fuel she needed to keep pressing.

"No, I do not wish to speak to him about investment opportunities. I need to speak to him about something urgent and personal, and I need to do so immediately."

"I'm sorry, as I said—"

"Joanna, here's what I want you to do. You say that Mr. Perry is in a meeting. I will assume you are telling the truth. I want you to write a note on a piece of paper and go stick it in front of his face. Tell him Linda Newton is on the phone, and if he will not speak to me now, I will call later at home. And if I can't find the number to make that work, I will call the *Chicago Tribune* and see if they would be willing to give me information in exchange for information that I have."

"Ms. Riley, I really—"

"Do it now." Linda hung up. She was shaking. She was not a confronter. In fact, she was something of a doormat, and for the most part, she didn't mind that too much. Peace and harmony were two of the things she valued most—as evidenced by the secret she'd kept for so many years. But when she heard about the way Jack had treated Caroline— Well, if there was one thing that would bring Linda into a confrontation, it was actually three things. Her kids. No one messed with her kids. And Caroline was her kid.

But what was she supposed to do now? She pulled out her computer but knew before she even searched that Jack likely didn't have a landline, and even if he did, it would be unlisted. This proved to be true.

The threat to go to *The Tribune* was made in anger, but in no way was something she would actually consider. Jack's father was still a very influential pastor in the Chicago area. Regardless of what his son had done, almost thirty years ago, she would not be the one to bring out a story that could ruin an entire lifetime of ministry. Jack's father likely didn't know any of this, as her own parents hadn't.

Just as she was beginning to acknowledge to herself that this was something she couldn't change, her phone rang.

She saw the area code and pressed the green call icon and jerked the phone to her ear. "Yes?"

"Hello, Linda." Jack's voice sounded so much like she remembered, it caused actual pain to hear it.

"Hello, Jack." She gathered her thoughts, waiting to see if he would take the lead in the conversation.

He didn't.

"Jack, I found out that Caroline reached out to you a few weeks back. While I understand that you might have been disconcerted to hear from her, the fact that you told her you were not her father was inexcusable. Not only did you treat her as a liar and an outcast, you were, by those words, implying that there was someone else in my life who could have been responsible. You and I both know that was not true."

He sighed. "What was I supposed to do? Some girl I've never heard of calls me and claims to be my daughter. To my knowledge no such daughter existed, so what did you expect? Me to immediately invite her home for Christmas?"

"Maybe not. But you crossed the line, and not by inches, by miles."

"You're right. It's just that, the whole thing caught me completely off guard. I had no idea...I mean, I thought...Why didn't you ever tell me?"

"I think your letter and the money told me how much you wanted to know about what happened with me and our child, don't you?"

"You make it sound so crass. I was doing everything I could think of. That money was to help you."

"To help me?"

"Yes, to ...take care of you and your problem."

"And by *my* problem, you mean *our* daughter, is that correct?"

"Linda, I—" He groaned. "I was young and stupid. I handled that whole situation poorly, but it's all I could think of at the time."

"Yes, but now that you're older, why are you still acting stupid? How could you treat your daughter that way? I understand why you might not want to tell your family everything—in fact, I just recently told mine, so I understand that one better than you might think. But to treat her so abysmally...to hang up on her..."

"You're right. I'm a better man than that. I promise you I will give this a little thought and find a way to work this out. I will make it up to her."

"Good. Thank you."

Linda was just getting ready to hang up when he said, "Linda?"

"Yes?"

"How's your son?"

The question, the tenderness in his voice threw her off-kilter. "He's doing okay. He's at home, recovering from the bone marrow transplant. His future looks good."

"I'm glad to hear that." He paused for a moment. "Well, good-bye, Linda. I wish you all well."

She took a breath to respond but he'd hung up. The ball was in his court now. She hoped he would follow through on his word and make things right with Caroline.

CHAPTER 37

"I still can't believe you don't like clam chowder." Chris held the door of The Black Pearl restaurant open for Caroline after lunch on Saturday.

"Wicked disgusting, as the Rhodies say." Her body shuddered at the memory of the bite Chris had made her take. The New England staple just wasn't her thing.

"That's blasphemy right there. I thought for sure it was just because you'd never had the good stuff."

Caroline shook her head with a grimace. "Nope. Gross."

"Must be a West Coast thing. Had I known that about you..."

"Hey." She put her hands into her gloves, then the pockets of the winter coat she'd purchased a couple weeks ago. She had to admit, having proper attire made quite a difference as she walked up Bannister's Wharf now.

Even still, the bitter mid-December wind made the idea of perusing the wharf's shops and art galleries less enticing than heading back to a warm house. "I think it's time for a movie and a fire. And cookie dough."

"Yes!" His eyes brightened. "Now you're speaking my language. I don't have the ingredients for cookie dough, do you?"

"I keep a supply handy."

A few minutes later, Chris parked his truck in front of her house. As Caroline was fiddling for her keys in her purse, the mailman pulled up.

"Are you Caroline Chapman?"

"I am."

"Certified mail for you. I need your signature."

Holding the electronic pen was a bit awkward in her puffy gloves, but she managed to scribble something along the screen, then took the letter-sized envelope from him. "Thank you."

The first thing Caroline did when she got in the house was crank up the heat. After removing her coat, hat, and gloves, she picked up the envelope again and tore the seal. Her mouth fell open as she read the contents.

"What is it?"

"A letter. From my bio dad. Well, his lawyer actually. Requesting a DNA test." Her heart upped its tempo. This was quite a change from the last time. Well, the only time they'd spoken. "Maybe Linda talked to him?" She must have. How else would he get her address? "That's good, right?" A faint spark seemed to light inside. Why would he want this unless he was interested in knowing more about her?

"Sure." He nodded a few times but didn't exactly look like he believed himself.

"What do you mean?"

He tilted his head back and scrunched his mouth to the side. "Why go through a lawyer unless you're trying to protect yourself? Why not just call you? If I had a daughter, or thought I had a daughter, that's what I would do."

"Even if you had another family who didn't know about her?"

He seemed to consider her question, then said, "Yeah."

"Well, that's because you're...you. There could be lots of reasons. He probably just wants to make sure it's official. Or maybe he's really busy and it was easier to have someone else send this." She raised the letter a tad.

"Okay."

"You don't think so?"

He put his hands on her shoulders. "I hope so."

Caroline set the letter onto the counter, then took the chocolate chips from her cupboard. "It's not like I expect a relationship or anything. I think it would be nice to meet him once."

"Then go for it. It's your call."

"Well, it will have to wait till I get back from California." She pulled out a couple of bowls, then the hand mixer. "Which reminds me, I was thinking about your company, and I know someone who can do a really nice website, when you're ready for that. He did some amazing stuff for us at the Huntington Library, and I think you'd like him. He's got a good eye, but he's not one of those artsy-fartsy types, as you call them."

"Oh, that's cool. Truthfully, I hadn't really thought of that. But it probably would be a good idea to freshen that up. Jim's not exactly the most tech savvy."

"Definitely. A new logo, and I think it should be on Instagram. Before and after photos, design tips, community involvement. I don't know, I'll keep brainstorming."

"Thanks. You're like a little ball of inspiration."

"You're welcome. I'll check in with the web designer when I'm out there." She pulled the eggs from the fridge. "What are you doing for Christmas?"

"I'm flying down to South Carolina on Christmas Eve, and then I'll stay a few days, spend some time with my older sister's family. Blythe and Adam are going to be here next weekend. Will you still be around?"

"I leave Sunday."

"Want to come to dinner Saturday night?"

"That depends." She cracked an egg in the bowl, then pushed a playful glare his way. "Will I be ridiculed for my hatred of clam chowder?"

"Probably."

"Hmm, I'll think about it." She pointed a spatula at him. "Now are you going to help me with this cookie dough or not?"

...

Caroline sat in her parents' living room by the Christmas tree as she worked on a thousand-piece puzzle of Santa and his bag of toys with her dad. She was still in her pajamas and robe even though it was nearly noon, and her mom was making lunch in the kitchen. One of the many benefits of being home.

"I'm out of coffee. Do you need a refill, too?" Dad stood and reached for her mug, which she handed him without looking. She was too busy finding the last piece of a teddy bear's foot. "Be right back. Finish that gingerbread house for me, why don't you?"

"Caroline?" her mom called from near the front door.

"Yeah?"

"Can you come here please?"

She really didn't want to get up and lose her momentum. Then again, she had been sitting here for three hours, and it was probably time for a stretch. And a shower, especially since they were going to a three thirty Christmas Eve church service. She walked to the door and pushed a piece of hair out of her face. "What is it?"

"That box came for you." Mom pointed toward a package on the floor. "And there's someone here to see you." She raised her eyebrows as she spoke and tilted her head toward their front porch.

Caroline tightened her bathrobe, opened the door, then popped her head outside. At first she didn't see anyone, so she walked out a little farther and peeked around. Then she spotted him, sitting on an Adirondack chair on the front lawn. The Ghost of Christmas Past.

Her breath caught in her throat. "Dillon. What are you doing here?" Unannounced. Again, she smoothed her hair back. Nothing like looking hideous when your ex showed up. She started to feel a little nauseous.

"Hey, Merry Christmas." He stood and walked toward her, then reached out for a hug. He was exactly the same, perfect in his casual but put together Rag & Bone shirt and dark gray jeans.

"Merry Christmas." She paused at first, then returned his hug. The familiarity of this, of him, soon drew her in, and before she realized it, her head rested on the same spot it always had, just under the top of his shoulder.

She pulled away as soon as it registered, then sat on the other of the two chairs. The sun was bright and warm, but she didn't mind. Sitting outside this time of year was a welcomed luxury, despite the company. Or maybe because of the company. Her heart was flip-flopping and wouldn't sit still.

"I should have called." He pointed to her bathrobe. "But I didn't think you'd let me come if I did."

"Probably not." Whether or not that was actually true wasn't the point. For one thing, she didn't know. But more importantly, she didn't want him to detect any trace of weakness on her part. "Why did you?"

He leaned his elbows on his knees and kept his face toward the ground. "To let you know Texas isn't working out and I'm moving back to LA."

"Oh." She struggled to collect her thoughts. "What brought this on?"

"For one thing, the company is going in a different direction, and I don't think it's a good fit for me after all. But I also found myself missing my old life. With you."

Caroline widened her eyes. "Wow, I'm stunned. But you do remember that my life is in Rhode Island now, right?"

He nodded. "Would you consider coming back?"

"I really like my job and ... I've met some nice people."

"Mr. Kiss Cam?"

She shifted in her chair. "Not just him."

"But we have friends here. Our life is here. I'm sure my mom can get your old job back, or you can start your own business if you want."

Dillon's words seemed to come off with ease, but they landed with a slice and red anger started to ooze. "I asked you to do something similar for me, and you called off our wedding because of it."

His body tensed and he leaned against the back of the chair. "I didn't come here to argue, Caroline. I was stressed and I didn't know what else to do. I'm sorry."

She sat back and took a deep breath, then another. The sun hitting her cheeks soothed her and the edge of the moment softened a bit. No, it wasn't a perfect apology, not quite what she'd envisioned all those months ago, but then again, he was here. Wanting her.

"I do miss it here." She allowed the words to come as they willed. "I miss a lot of things, including you and the way things were."

Dillon gave her hand a squeeze.

"But it's been eight months. A lot has happened since then, and I don't know if I can just pick up where we left off, even if I did move back."

He let go of her hand. "Will you at least think about it?"

"I signed a contract for a year, so I at least need to stay until May. I'd be interested in renewing it. Would you ever consider going there?"

He shrugged. "I think the most logical thing is for us both to come back here, but I'll make you a deal—I'll think about it if you will."

They'd had four years together. The least she could do was think things over despite what he'd done, right? "Okay. I will. Think about it."

He smiled, stood, and offered a hand to help Caroline out of her chair. He reached out for another hug and this time he kissed her cheek as well. "Thanks. And thanks for seeing me and hearing me out."

"Sure. Are you going back to LA now?"

"Yeah, I've got a family thing tonight, so I should get on the road. But I'll call you later this week? Maybe we can spend New Year's Eve together? Zach and Emma are having people over."

Tempted as she was, she'd already agreed to spend the evening with old college friends. "Maybe, I'll let you know. Merry Christmas, Dillon."

"You too."

He pulled out of the driveway. It seemed too soon to say good-bye again, but maybe it was better, before she got sucked all the way in and agreed to something she'd regret later. She turned back toward the house and could see Mom peering out the living room window.

"Spying on me?" Caroline crossed her arms when she got back into the house. "I am twenty-nine years old."

"I still care about you, no matter how old you are."

"Tell that guy to go fly a kite," Dad called from the kitchen.

Caroline never really understood what that phrase meant, but it was one of her dad's favorites for moments like this. It made her smile, despite the weight that had just been thrust on her.

"Well, what did he want?" Mom stood a few feet away with a "tell me the truth" expression on her face.

"To let me know things aren't working in Texas and he's moving back." She couldn't believe she was saying those words. Or that those words had just come from Dillon's mouth. "And to see if I'd be interested in doing the same ... with him."

"And? Are you?"

"I don't know. Aren't I supposed to forgive?"

"Forgiveness is one thing. Jumping back into a relationship is another. What about Newport?"

Caroline didn't answer at first. She felt like she was sixteen again, getting lectured about her weekend plans. "I told him I'd think about it. I need to get in the shower."

She grabbed the package by the front door, then walked to her bedroom. As soon as she looked at the return label, her heart plunged into a cocktail of dread and excitement, with a hearty twist of guilt. From C. Stratton, along with a Newport address.

She found a pair of scissors, then sat on her bed but was unable to open it. A half hour ago, she would have done so eagerly. But now, well, now things were different, and she sort of felt like she was invading someone else's privacy.

When she finally ran the blade down the tape and peeled back the flaps, she found a six-pack of her favorite gum, a Red Sox T-shirt, and a gift card to Bellevue Coffee inside. She couldn't help but laugh. Before she left, she'd mailed a Dodgers T-shirt, a box of See's candy, and a gift card to his favorite chowder spot to him at his sister's house. But when she pulled them all out, she discovered another box wrapped in Christmas paper. She held it for a few seconds, then slowly tore the paper off. This box had the Christofle logo on it. *Yikes.* Whatever this was, she had a sinking feeling it was a lot nicer than she deserved right now.

She opened the box, then the pouch inside and pulled out a silver picture frame with *Sweet Caroline* engraved on the bottom. Inside the frame was a newspaper clipping—the photo from Aiden's column of the two of them on the kiss cam at Fenway.

That same cocktail now ran through every vein in her body. The scissors on her bed may have well just slit her down the middle as well. She simultaneously wished she could relive that moment at the game and that it had never happened. That she could fall back into place with Dillon and see where things went with Chris.

Was it possible to live two lives? To be two people at once? To maintain two story lines? At least until she knew which one would work out. Almost everything she'd wanted from Dillon she'd gotten today. But why wasn't it enough to settle things in her heart?

She sat on the bed and looked at the frame for a few more moments, then placed it back into its box for now. Santa and his bag of toys was no longer the only puzzle in her life, but today, she'd focus on the one where all the pieces would eventually come together.

CHAPTER 38

"Happy New Year!" Brent and Linda jumped up, blew horns, and whirled around a circle in a sort of hug. Their sons both stared at them as if they were crazy. Linda pointed to the two party horns still resting on the coffee table. "Your turn, boys. Come on. It's time to celebrate."

"No way. That is so embarrassing," Maddox said.

"Exactly," Marshall agreed.

"Come on," Brent said. "None of your friends are here. There's no one to be embarrassed in front of but us, and we don't count."

The boys looked at each other and rolled their eyes in perfect synchronization. Maddox held up his hand, pointed upward, and made little hand circles. "Happy New Year. Woo, woo."

Linda scowled at him. "There's no reason to be sarcastic."

"Mom, there's always a reason to be sarcastic." He grinned at her, then leaned forward, picked up his horn, and blew it loud. "Come on, Marshall, let's act like our parents."

Marshall too picked up his horn and blew it. Then the two boys made a game of trying to out volume the other. By now Linda was regretting her earlier insistence that the boys join in.

Finally, they stopped, but not before her ears were ringing. Eyebrow quirked, Maddox turned toward her. "Better?"

"Much." She laughed and ruffled his hair. And he did have hair again. Slowly but surely it had been growing in, a little curly so far. Maddox had been relieved when it came back in black, as he had been afraid that due to Caroline's DNA he might become a blond.

"Fellas, while the four of us are all together, I have a question I'd like to throw out at you. I want complete honesty with your answers."

All three of them looked alarmed. They all remembered what happened the last time Linda presented complete honesty.

"With a new year starting, I've been thinking over some things, and realizing how I want to move forward in perhaps a different way. As you all know, Caroline and her very existence were secret until Maddox became ill. Since that time, her true identity is still a secret to everyone but our immediate family and hers, a few medical people, and our very closest friends. I've been doing a lot of thinking and praying about it. How would the three of you feel if I were to go more public with the information? Say, share it with the women at church?

"If any of you don't want me to, then I won't, because I know that this truth is embarrassing. But somehow I just feel like it's time I quit pretending to be someone I'm not."

Maddox spoke up immediately. "I wish you would tell it, then I could tell my friends, too. I think it's pretty cool that I have a half sister, and it's really cool that she's the one who gave me bone marrow. And it's even more cool that she and her boyfriend made the ESPN highlight reel."

Marshall shrugged. "All right with me."

Linda looked to Brent, then. "What about you? Would this being public affect your job?"

He thought for a moment. "Even if it did, I would be the world's worst hypocrite if I hid the truth to make myself look better."

That statement wasn't meant as a barb, but the accurate description of what she'd been doing all these years cut deep. It also gave more confirmation that what she wanted to do was the right thing. "I'll talk with the head of women's ministries at the church this week. They've asked me to speak at the monthly women's brunch at the beginning of March. Of course, they are expecting me to speak about Maddox's cancer journey. I want to warn her that there will be a bit more on the plate."

Everyone looked around at each other, but no one said anything for a while. Finally, Marshall said, "Well, now that we're done with the serious stuff, can we get back to watching *New Year's Rockin' Eve*?"

"Sure thing," Brent said.

Just a bit later, as he and Linda made their way up the stairs, leaving the boys still playing a video game, Brent put his arm around her shoulders. "I'm not going to lie, I'm still struggling with all this."

"I know you are." What Linda wouldn't have given to go back and do things differently. "And I'm so sorry."

"I googled him."

This abrupt change in subject made her pause. "Googled who?"

"Jack Perry."

Linda tripped on the top stair, but Brent's grip prevented a face-plant on the upstairs landing. "Why?"

"I wanted to understand what kind of man he is." He took a deep breath and nodded, as if acknowledging something he didn't want to. "Looks like he's super successful. Involved in a lot of charities. Making his mark on the world."

There it was. He had compared what he could see on the outside and found himself wanting.

Linda put her hands on each side of his face. "He left his terrified twenty-one-year-old girlfriend alone and pregnant without a backward glance. Never once did he check to see if I was okay. His 'mark on the world,' as you call it, may look good on the outside, but he'll never come close to the kind of man you are. Your legacy is not because of some image you project. It's because of who you truly are."

He stared into her eyes, as if trying to see if she meant what she said. Finally he nodded. "Thanks." He took a step down the hallway but turned toward her. "I think it's important that you know, I'm proud of you."

"Of me? For what?"

"For your courage. Starting with that terrified twenty-one-year-old and ending right here with this fifty-year-old about to lay it all on the line. Those choices come with a cost."

"Yeah, well, you failed to mention the disastrous choices on each side of those."

He drew her in and kissed the top of her head. "I didn't say you were perfect." He released her and opened the door to their room. "That's why you have me."

...

Caroline had been back from California for three weeks now, but Chris still hadn't seen her. Every time he reached out, she was either jet-lagged, unpacking, or getting caught up at work and it was taking longer than she'd expected. Or perhaps there was more going on. Maybe she was having second thoughts? Had he completely misinterpreted her enthusiasm for his goals as a desire to be part of his life? A heaviness landed on his chest.

He'd give it another shot and text as soon as he carried this load of insulation up to the attic. But when he got there, a call interrupted his intentions. "Chris Stratton," he answered. The high today was twenty-nine degrees, and it probably wasn't much warmer in this attic, but he was still sweating and used his sleeve to wipe his forehead.

"Hi, Chris. Daniel Murray here. How are you?"

His pulse quickened even more than it had from jogging up the stairs. *That will depend on what you have to say now, won't it?* He kept his question in and responded in a more socially acceptable way. "Good, thanks. Have you had a chance to look at the letter I sent over?"

"Yes, and I have good news for you. There's nothing binding about it. I've even dug into cases dating back to the 1940s and found nothing that would lead me to believe otherwise."

"Oh, that's great. I'm relieved to hear it." He felt like a bag of cement had been lifted off his shoulders.

"I can imagine."

"Do you think it would've had any effect on the court case last year?"

"Not in my opinion. Yes, it demonstrates Chadwick's desire to donate his home to NPS, but that's not enough. This isn't a legal document. There was nothing to prevent the outcome that transpired. If I were you, I'd proceed as if you'd never found it."

A smile crept across his face. "Will do. Thanks for calling."

The next person he should call was Tom, but his eagerness to see Caroline, especially now that this ordeal was off his plate, prompted him to pull up a text to her instead. *Hey, are you free any night this week? Would love to see you.* He pressed Send, then returned the phone to his back pocket.

An hour later, she still hadn't responded.

...

Caroline read the text message again as she sat in her office. She'd run out of all the acceptable excuses she could think of, and if she said she wasn't feeling well, he'd just show up at her house with soup. It wasn't that she didn't want to see him. But seeing him, spending time with him—the way he made her feel like she was an open book he actually enjoyed reading would make it impossible for her to think objectively about everything going on in her life.

Still, it wasn't fair to him, so she finally opened his text and typed, *I'm free tonight. Want to grab dinner?* She could manage a simple meal, as long as things remained casual and light.

It didn't take him long to respond. *Sounds great. I'm at the hotel now and I need to take a shower. Mind swinging by my place and I can drive us from there?*

Caroline glanced out her office window. The roads were well plowed and there was no snow in the forecast. *Sure, I'll be there a little after 5.* A second later, he replied with a thumbs-up emoji and the address.

She wrapped up for the day, then powered down her computer. Thankfully she managed to get to her car without Gloria stopping her and prying into her personal life. A few minutes later, she pulled through the gate at Tom Williams's Newport home, then followed the drive to the guesthouse in the back. Good heavens, the backyard was the size of Rhode Island. She chuckled at her joke as she parked her car next to Chris's truck.

The thirty seconds it took for Chris to answer the door felt like an eternity. It was dark out and even with her new winter coat, she was freezing. That was ten points in the move-back-to-LA column.

"Hi, stranger." Chris held the door open. He was wearing jeans, a white undershirt that left little to the imagination, and a broad smile. And his dark-brown hair was still wet. Hmmm, twenty points for stay in Rhode Island.

"Hi. How are you?" She stepped inside the guesthouse, unable to ignore how warm it felt. And how good Chris smelled.

"Better now that you're back." He kissed her without hesitation, and Caroline did her best to hide hers. "I want to hear all about your trip at dinner."

She tried to keep her gaze off of him as much as she could without seeming awkward. "This place is lovely. Do you think you'll miss the perks of working for Tom when you leave?"

"Blythe's wedding keeps pushing that date back, but no, I don't think so. Well, maybe the truck." He winked. "I'm lucky to have this job, don't get me wrong, but I don't think I'll regret leaving."

"That's good. Maybe we shouldn't talk about it in here, though. Might be wiretapped." She increased her volume. "Chris Stratton is such a great contractor. It's a good thing he doesn't have any worthy goals and is so content working for Tom. He deserves a raise!"

"You crack me up. And thanks." He grabbed her hand and pulled her in for another kiss. "Hey, I need two minutes. Decide where you want to go to dinner, and I'll be right back." He disappeared down a hallway, so Caroline took the opportunity to look around the house.

There was a family room with a large window, although it was too dark to see outside now, and a small den off to the side that seemed to be Chris's makeshift office. She took a few steps in and allowed herself to snoop around a bit, get a behind-the-scenes glimpse of Chris Stratton. There was a picture frame on his desk with a photo of a boy, maybe five or six years old, sitting on a man's shoulders. Chris and his dad, she guessed, on a beach next to a lighthouse.

She picked it up and examined it more closely. She didn't recognize the lighthouse from any she'd seen on her earlier weekend excursions, but she did recognize Chris's unmistakable smile and an identical one on his dad's face. It made her smile, too.

She put it down, and her gaze fell on a stack of papers under a leather baseball paperweight. She would have never taken the liberty of looking through these, except the paper on top was signed by none other than John Chadwick. The former owner of the future hotel. *Where in the world did Chris get this?* She picked it up and read.

To Whom It May Concern,

I hereby declare that all my personal effects and financial assets should be given to my wife upon my death. In the event I outlive her, all should be passed on and divided equally among my children. However, Chadwick Place is to be donated to the Newport Preservation Society.

Sincerely,
J. Chadwick

Caroline couldn't move. She read the letter again, then a third time, and still she couldn't believe what she was reading. Or that Chris had it sitting on his desk. Her throat went dry.

"You ready?" Chris's footsteps got louder and soon he was standing in front of her.

She held up the letter, her hand was shaking. "When...? How did you get this?" Her voice was shaking, too.

He narrowed his eyes and squared his shoulders, then crossed his arms over his navy-blue, half-zip sweater. "I found it in the attic at the hotel in October, why?"

"Why? Don't you think we would have been interested in seeing it? You've had it for over three months, and you hid it?"

Chris pulled his head back slightly, his eyebrows scrunched together. "I didn't hide it. I had it analyzed for authenticity and then sent to an attorney, despite Tom telling me to trash it. I just heard back today, actually, and it's not a legally binding document, so it doesn't change anything." He didn't sound angry, just determined.

"Of course it does." She looked at the letter again. "It's proof that he wanted his house donated, not turned into a hotel. We're talking about a man's wishes for his property. You can't just ignore that."

"We can, since he didn't take the trouble of making it official. Even if we had found it before Tom purchased the house, Chadwick's kids had the right to sell it to whoever they wanted."

"Why didn't you tell me about it?"

He shrugged, his tone a little softer this time. "I thought it would complicate things for us."

"Complicate things for us or complicate your job?" She hadn't really intended to say that, but as soon as she did, it seemed like a legitimate question.

"That's not fair."

"Isn't it?"

"No, it's not." He uncrossed his arms and put a hand on his chest, his tone more forceful now. "I complicated my job by sharing it with Tom in the first place. By encouraging him to follow through and make sure everything was done on the up-and-up. Which it was." He took a breath. "And I complicate my job every minute I spend with you because if Tom finds out we're...whatever we're doing—I don't even know anymore because you haven't seemed interested in seeing me since you got back from California—every delay or problem at the hotel will be second-guessed." He paused again. "But some things are worth the risk."

Caroline's thoughts froze for a few seconds. The chill from standing outside was long gone now. "Audrey Brooks needs to see this."

He shook his head and shrugged a shoulder. "Fine, go ahead, show it to her. All it's going to do is make things harder. For me, yes. But for the two of us. Or maybe that's irrelevant now."

She pressed her lips together. "What would you have done if it was legally binding?"

"I don't know. I'm sorry, but I hadn't figured that one out yet. I'm walking a tight line here. And really, what would NPS do with a construction site, anyway? They can't afford to finish it."

"It should have never been a construction site in the first place." She folded the letter and put it in her coat pocket. "I have to go." She grabbed her purse by the front door, then walked to her car.

"Come on, Caroline." Chris followed her out despite not having shoes on. "Can't we at least talk about it? Inside?"

"No, I just want to go home." Her heart was pounding as she entered her car.

As soon as she got back to her house, she sent Audrey an email requesting to meet with her as soon as possible.

CHAPTER 39

Caroline sat in thick silence and tried to distract herself. An entire shelf of books devoted to the Vanderbilt family in Audrey's office captured her attention until her boss finally spoke.

"This is incredible." She placed the letter on her desk, then clasped her hands together. "Chris Stratton found it in the attic? I knew we should have insisted on a thorough inspection."

"He claims it's not a legally binding document, but I thought you should see it anyway."

"I'm glad you brought it to my attention. I'll send it to our attorneys and we'll get a second opinion. Truthfully, we can't afford another legal battle over that place." Audrey shook her head. "Our only play would be public opinion. If it is legally binding, I think we should take it to the papers and put pressure on Tom Williams that way. His ego may be our biggest weapon. I thought for sure he'd cave last go-round with all the negative press his company was getting. In the end he held out, but I'm not so sure he'd do it again."

"And if it's not?"

Audrey leaned her head to the side. "I don't know. Let's see what the attorneys say." She offered a kind smile.

Caroline returned it, if only to hide her uneasiness. She had no problem risking Tom Williams's ego. If all she'd heard about him was true, that man could use a reality check. But the collateral damage ... She was interested in the truth, in honoring a man's wishes, in preservation. Not sabotage, even though she was still upset Chris had kept it from her. From all of them. For being so ready to disregard it.

Then again, she wasn't exactly up-front with him, either. Would she have even mentioned the fact that she was considering a move home had they gone to dinner that night?

She rubbed her lips together. "Could we afford to finish restoring it? You know, if we actually got it?"

"Hmm. I hadn't thought of that. Well, maybe a few fundraising events could get us there. We'll cross that bridge later. While I have you here, there's something else I wanted to talk to you about."

Caroline's heart started to beat a little faster. She was in no mood to discuss the five-thousand-dollar discount she'd given Chris, especially now. Undoubtedly, Gloria had told Audrey long ago, and truthfully, Caroline was surprised it had taken Audrey this long to bring it up.

"Sure, what can I do for you?" Her voice squeaked a tad.

"You can sign a three-year contract." Audrey's smile was bigger now. "I know your current contract isn't up until May, but the board and I agree, you're doing a fantastic job. Not only are your events very well run, they really seem to connect with people. Our donations are up because of it, and we don't want to lose you."

Caroline let out the breath she'd been holding, and her shoulders relaxed. After the wave of relief came a monsoon of excitement. "That's fantastic!" A tingle ran through her whole body, like a soda can had been shaken inside her. But without warning Dillon came to mind, and the buzz fizzled a bit. "I'll definitely consider it."

"It comes with a 20 percent increase in pay, by the way."

"Wow. Um, thank you."

"You deserve it. You're a valuable asset to us, I hope you know that." Audrey tapped her desk with both hands then stood and let Caroline out of her office.

She walked up to her own office, pulled out her phone, then the calculator app. A 20 percent increase in pay, plus the modest but growing savings she had … She just might be able to buy a condo. Maybe even a small house if she went out to Middletown—something she wouldn't be able to do in California for many years, even with the pay increase.

California. Dillon. With shifty fingers, she pressed the Text icon, then his name and told him the news. She was about to add something about how excited she was but stopped. He'd want facts, not feelings.

A few moments later, he replied. *I got a really good offer from Browne and Harrison last week. I'd like to take it. My mom said no problem about your job @ Huntington. Makes the most sense?*

Her stomach dropped. She couldn't exactly object—it did make sense, in her head, as it had over four years ago—so why did she want to throw her phone out the window? She plunked it facedown on her desk instead, then pulled out a pack of gum. After chomping two pieces she directed her attention to something more manageable: the spring events calendar.

Out of the corner of her eye, she saw the Stratton-Dingledine wedding on March 9. She'd originally told Chris she'd be his date, but given everything that was going on, that wasn't going to happen. She groaned and tossed a gum wrapper into the trash can.

Despite Blythe's protests that her help was gift enough, Caroline still wanted to get them one. She pulled out her credit card, perused the registry, then settled on two place settings of their dishes. After writing the gift message offering her best wishes, there was one thing left to do. Not because she wanted to, but because it would be better ... for everyone.

She navigated to the RSVP link, scrolled down, then hit decline.

...

"Good morning, everyone." Linda looked nervously around the room at the fifty or so women assembled for the monthly ladies' brunch.

"Eleven months ago, as most of you know, my family started on a journey we'd never planned to take. My son Maddox was diagnosed with a rare form of juvenile leukemia.

"Most of you also know that he is currently on the road to what the doctors believe will be a long and full recovery. I am so thankful to each and every one of you for the prayers you have offered, the meals you have provided, and the love you have showered on our family.

"There is, however, a large part of the story that very few of you know. I kept it secret because I didn't want to hurt the people I love, but to be perfectly honest, the truth was originally covered up because of my pride. I didn't want anyone to know that I had made a mistake. The kind of mistake people would talk about."

The women shifted in their seats, leaning forward, waiting for the big reveal. "The bone marrow donor for Maddox was no random match ..." And so she began, telling the story to its end. Almost uniformly stunned expressions stared back at her, with the occasional sideways glances between women that said, "We've got to talk about this later." Linda had known that would be part of the consequences of today.

She did not allow herself to dwell on that thought. "You want to know the truth? One of the things that led me to my original decision to 'fix' the problem? There were a couple of women in my parents' church who were quite fluent in the language of gossip. I could just imagine them whispering about me, and my mother, under the guise of 'praying' for us. I couldn't bear the thought of that.

"I know hearing this story makes some of you think less of me, maybe it makes all of you feel that way. And I understand it. But I have come to realize through all this that the biggest mistakes I've made in my life revolved around pride and pretending to be a better person than I am. By acting that way, I have become one of those very people who keep other people—like the scared young woman I was—from being honest and asking for help.

"I'm here now to declare that I am done with that. This is me. The real me. The one who sends out emails full of optimism and faith when inside I'm scared to death and full of doubt. And I am here to tell you ladies that I am done with that kind of pretense.

"In my perfect world, Christian women would circle around others who have fallen or who are having a hard time and say, 'I am here for you, I will pray for you, and you will not be excluded because you have fallen short.' The kind of women who stand together and hold each other up. That's the kind of woman I pray for the strength to be."

Linda started to walk away, then turned back. "Thank you for allowing me to share my story."

As she made her way back to her table, silence roared throughout the room. Just ten more steps and she could sit down. Just ten more minutes and she could be out of here and on her way back to the safety of home. Had she made the wrong decision in sharing this? Would it further damage her family?

She collapsed into her seat, wishing the ground would open up and swallow her. Then it started. A single person, clapping slow, was joined by a second and then a third. Then the women began to rise to their feet. In the end, the entire room gave her a standing ovation.

Kristyn, who was sitting beside her, leaned down and hugged her. "You were amazing."

"Thank You, God." Linda whispered the words as tears filled her eyes. And finally, after all these years, the first flickers of grace, of accepting the forgiveness she knew she'd long since received through her prayers descended, and she experienced something new in this situation—complete peace. There would be backlash, but now, in the beginning of living in the truth, this show of support was all she could ask for.

Over the course of the next week, Linda's mailbox and in-box were filled with notes of encouragement and thankfulness for her sharing. Several also expressed relief, because they had held her up as so impossibly perfect, it had made her unapproachable—something that devastated her to realize. How many ways had her act of pride kept her from being the person she was supposed to be?

She also heard the rumblings of a small amount of behind-the-scenes gossip. People were human, and it was bound to happen. That didn't matter. She wasn't responsible for other people. She was responsible for her own actions, and she had taken the path she felt called to travel.

CHAPTER 40

I t had taken about twelve seconds for Caroline to get a text from Blythe after submitting her RSVP all those weeks ago. *You're not coming to my wedding?!?!?! You HAVE to!*

With reluctance, Caroline gave in. *Okay, I'll come and make sure everything runs smoothly.*

But today, as Caroline stared at this week's edition of "According to Aiden" for the thousandth time, she was convinced going to the wedding tonight was a terrible idea. Audrey had assured her that she didn't send Aiden Chadwick's letter—they hadn't heard back from their attorneys yet. Caroline hadn't done it, that much she knew full well. And yet there it was, under a headline reading "Profit over Preservation."

If it wasn't for a call from the florist's delivery team asking where everything was supposed to go, she would have just stayed home. Instead, she found herself in a cocktail dress, driving over to Rosecliff to make sure things were set up properly.

For the next two hours, Caroline directed the florist, pointed the band in the right direction, set up the cake, and assisted the caterers. Before she knew it, guests were starting to arrive from the church.

The wedding party was introduced, including a saucy redhead who seemed more than content to hang on Chris's arm and, of course, Blythe and Adam, who couldn't possibly look more adorable. Or happy.

Everything was going smoothly behind the scenes, so as soon as dinner finished and dancing began, Caroline decided it would be fine, if not wise, for her to go. She grabbed her wrap and her purse and meandered through the maze of tables and guests to Blythe.

"Ahhhh!" Blythe lit up when she saw Caroline, then gave her a big hug. "You are amazing. This is amazing. Chris? Where's Chris?" She looked around. Caroline's stomach dropped when she saw he was close by, swinging the flower girl—one of his nieces, probably—from side to side. She thought she'd managed to avoid him. "Chris." Blythe pointed at Caroline. "She's amazing."

Caroline turned toward Blythe without making eye contact with Chris. "I'm really glad you're enjoying it. It did turn out beautifully."

"Thanks to you."

Caroline smiled. "Enjoy the rest of the evening and the honeymoon! Keep in touch when you get to Hawaii, okay?" She gave the side of Blythe's arm a squeeze, then turned to leave. She grabbed her car keys from her purse as she escaped through the side door to the parking lot.

"You think you can just sneak off like that?" A voice echoed through the cold night air.

She clenched her wrap and swirled around. When she saw Chris a few feet away, her knees locked and her heart jumped. "I didn't think the host would want me to stay."

He raised his eyebrows. "Maybe. Did you send that letter in?"

"No, I didn't. Audrey didn't either. We don't know how it got there."

He nodded but stayed silent.

"Listen, I'm really sorry if things are more difficult for you now. That wasn't my intention. I hope you know that. But even if nothing changes with the hotel, that letter proves what Chadwick wanted. Chris, you're building something I don't believe in." She swallowed hard. "And you kept it from me."

He widened his stance and crossed his arms. "Even if I agreed with you, that Chadwick Place should have been donated, what am I supposed to do about it? I have a job to do." His shoulders lowered a bit. "Or at least I hope I do. I'm not so sure at the moment."

His words caught her off guard, and she really didn't know what to say, at first. "You're right. You need to do what's best for you."

"What does that mean? What do you expect from me, Caroline?"

The cold was starting to take its toll, and she was shivering now. "I think it's better to face the fact that we can't be together. Like you said, it was difficult from the start, but now this... We can't pretend like this isn't happening. I can't."

He shifted his weight to one side and put a hand in his pocket. "We were doomed from the beginning, is that what you mean? And there's no moving forward?"

"It's not just that." The words hung in the air for a moment. She hadn't intended to say them but couldn't suck them back in either. Perhaps now would be her only chance, anyway. "I'm considering going back to LA. I haven't made up my mind yet, but I miss it there." An ache formed inside. "And I don't want to get in the way of what you feel you have to do, especially if I end up leaving."

"I see." His face remained expressionless.

"I'm sorry, I didn't mean to do this here. Now. At your sister's wedding. I think you should go back inside and enjoy the evening. And I think I should just go home."

Chris pressed his lips together and nodded a few times. "Yeah, I think you're right. I, uh, I'll go back in. Have a good night."

"You too." She offered a smile and watched him turn back toward the door. She was freezing and just wanted to go home, put on her pajamas, and go to bed.

And when she woke up, she wanted everything to be different.

...

It had been several days since Blythe's wedding and no word from Chris. It was better not to expect it—she'd essentially told him not to, but still. Things hadn't ended the way she would have liked, and a call from him would give her the chance to apologize once more. But would that actually make a difference? Probably not. Better to let him focus on his job, just as she should be doing right now.

Caroline was about to return to work after lunch when a knock sounded on her door. She put her purse down, opened it, and discovered a mailman holding out an envelope and keypad.

"Certified mail for Caroline Chapman."

"That's me." She signed for it, thanked him, then brought the package inside.

She recognized the return address. It was the same as the last time she'd received an envelope like this. Perhaps she should leave it for after work? She'd already been gone longer than she'd intended, but the building curiosity nudged her on the detour. She took off her coat, tore back the tab on the envelope, and pulled out its contents.

Yep, it was from Jack Perry's attorney again, but this time, the packet was thicker. Without even reading it, she could safely conclude that the DNA sample she'd provided back in January proved what she already knew. Maybe he wanted to meet her now. Or at least have a real conversation on the phone?

She took the cover letter from the paper clip and started reading, but as she did, the delusion tumbled from her lungs and a sting resonated in its wake. It wasn't an invitation to meet. It wasn't even an expression of well-wishes. Chris was right; Jack was only going through a lawyer to protect himself.

She sat on one of the kitchen stools, her shoulders slumped over. The pull to get back to work vanished. Now a new game of tug-of-war descended. She'd never been offered so much. And the weight of insignificance had never been so heavy. Both sides of the rope enticed her heart, yanked her back and forth—vying for her attention, convincing her of their truth.

She skimmed the letter again, found her phone, then texted her mom.

I'm worth $250,000! She didn't quite feel like she was in an exclamation point sort of mood, but she sent the message anyway.

The call came a few moments later. "I'm driving so I can't text back. What do you mean you're worth $250,000?"

Caroline crossed her legs and leaned her arms on the counter. "I just got a letter in the mail. I was offered a 'generous settlement of $250,000'—" She reached for the letter, just to make sure she got it right. "If I agree to 'never contact Jack Perry again, to never contact any of his family members including, but not limited to, his wife, children, or parents, and never to bribe, coerce, or manipulate any of them in any way for future gain, financial or otherwise' etcetera, etcetera. I have to sign a few forms, send them back, then the money will be deposited into an 'account of my choosing.'"

"Oh my. A quarter million dollars? Really? He must have a ton of money."

"Yep. What should I do?"

"Golly, I don't know. Were you planning on contacting him again?"

"No." Definitely not.

"His wife or children?"

"No."

"Using this information against him in any way?"

Caroline rolled her eyes. "Of course not."

A pause lingered for a few moments. "I think you should ask for a million."

Caroline sat up straight. "What? Who are you, and what have you done with my mother?"

"Oh, relax. I'm just kidding."

"Good. I was about to remind you that the love of money is the root of all evil." It was a Bible verse her mom quoted whenever a corrupt politician was outed or a corporate scandal made the news.

"I'm well aware of that. What do you think you should do?"

"I don't know." She leaned over onto the counter again. "I mean, I didn't ask for it. He's offering it of his own free will, and I could buy a house or invest it for later on, even donate a lot of it."

"All true. Lots of possibilities to consider. Speaking of which, what did you decide to do about your contract? Or don't you know yet?"

Caroline groaned inside. "I still don't know. I can't seem to make up my mind. I really miss it out there, and you and Dad, but three more years is a good offer and great experience."

"We miss you, too. But you choose what you want. Not what we want. And certainly not what Dillon wants."

"Don't relationships require sacrifice?" Caroline's tone was tentative.

"Of course. But it should be mutual. Do you think he even looked for jobs in Providence?"

"He left Texas."

"I'm sure he wants you in his life. But that's different than wanting to build a life with you. Honey, we'll support whatever you decide, but just make sure you don't get lost by doing what someone else thinks you should."

"Okay, thanks, Mom."

She was about to hang up when Mom continued. "Caroline, you're wrong about one thing. You're not worth two hundred and fifty thousand dollars. Why don't you look up Luke 12:6–7 and try that on for size?"

Of course her mom had a verse for the moment. What else was new? She couldn't help but let out a little laugh before she promised to look it up and call later.

After hanging up, Caroline pulled up her Bible app, something she'd admittedly not done enough of lately, then scrolled through Luke until she found the passage.

"What is the price of five sparrows—two copper coins? Yet God does not forget a single one of them. And the very hairs on your head are all numbered. So don't be afraid; you are more valuable to God than a whole flock of sparrows."

She allowed the words to settle afresh on her. She still felt the pull inside, tearing her.

Mocking her.

But maybe she could learn to let go of the rope.

CHAPTER 41

"All I know is this is a disaster, and if you had just done what I'd asked you to, I wouldn't be in this mess." Tom's voice pounded into Chris's eardrum.

It was true, and Chris knew it. Yesterday, the debacle had made it into three of Boston's more prominent newspapers, all of which were laid out in front of him on the kitchen island in Tom's guesthouse. Long gone was the hope it would just remain a quiet, local story. "I'm sorry, what else can I say?" His voice sounded raspy.

"You said I had nothing to worry about. She wasn't a problem. Clearly you were wrong. And clearly, I can't count on you anymore."

Heat filled his cheeks. Chris believed Caroline when she'd told him she hadn't sent the letter in, but what did that matter now? The damage had been done and going down that road with Tom was absolutely pointless. And so was apologizing more or trying to convince him of his dependability.

Tom would only want answers, solutions, and thankfully—maybe—he had something. One last hope of salvaging whatever he could. He grabbed the back of his neck and paced the kitchen. "I think I can fix it. Or, at least, smooth things over."

"I'm all ears."

He took a deep breath. Then one more. "How about a partnership between The Williams Hotel Group and NPS?" He closed his eyes and winced as he waited for Tom's reply.

"You have got to be kidding me."

"Hear me out. The letter's been published. Everyone knows Chadwick wanted it donated. If you move forward, that doesn't look good for you. But there's no real reason you should have to hand over what you bought legally and have invested millions in restoring."

"Call me back when you're ready to discuss something I'm not already aware of."

"Tom, a partnership solves both problems. *The Chadwick Hotel, A Newport Preservation Society Experience,* or something like that. Let Marketing come up with something snazzy. But the bottom line is, you own 75 percent, they own 25 percent—you come out looking good, generous even. All the damage goes away. You run the hotel, all the operating decisions are yours, they get 25 percent of the profit and access to the property for a few events here and there. Everyone's happy." His heart was pounding now. *Please like it. Please like it.*

"I'm supposed to hand over 25 percent of my profit and that's supposed to make me happy?"

"I realize it's a compromise, but I think damage control will cost more than that if you let this go on. Again." He tapped his fingers on the counter.

"I think that girl has put you up to all this."

"She has nothing to do with it." And he meant that. Mostly. This wasn't about her, not really. It was about rescuing the project. Fixing what was broken. No, he didn't like how things went down at the wedding a couple weeks ago. He still cared about Caroline, but this wouldn't affect things between them one way or another. If it would, well, that would be a different story. Whatever, she was probably pack-ing her bags for LA now, anyway. It would, however, affect his reputation as a contractor, and right now, that's all he had.

"And I expect you'll want to finish the project."

Tom seemed to read his mind. Chris hunched over and rested his forearm on the counter. "I'd like to see it through, yes." He had to.

"Getting another contractor up to speed in time, if this featherbrained idea of yours even works, is out of the ques-tion." He paused. "But after that, I think it would be best if you moved on, and you can forget about that bonus."

A boulder landed on his back. He couldn't say it came as a total shock, but it still crushed his resolve, and he started to feel sick to his stomach. Eleven years of work—good, solid work—and now what?

Blythe's wedding had set him back far more than he'd wanted, and without that bonus to compensate for it, he was pretty much right back where he was a year ago. And with no salary, well, he'd be going even farther backward just to live. Plus, he'd have to buy a new truck, the one he drove belonged to the company.

He closed his eyes and swallowed hard. Basically, he had eight weeks, give or take, to finish the hotel and line up a new job, or he was toast. He took another deep breath. "I understand." It was all he could manage to say, and it wasn't true. But if he said what he really wanted to say to Tom right now, there would be no chance of him ever landing work again.

"You'll take care of NPS? See if they're on board and will agree to making this whole thing go away?"

"I'll set up a meeting as soon as we hang up." His voice sounded small.

"Fine." With that, the call ended.

Chris ran his hand through his hair, then sat on one of the kitchen barstools. Why hadn't he just told the electricians to throw the box away? Why had he even opened it?

Hollowness filled him and his throat tightened. He wouldn't be human not to feel the impact of this now, like someone had pushed him right back into the valley he'd been climbing out of for the last thirteen years. No traction. Nothing to grab on to. No way out. If he had more faith, he'd remind himself that God could redeem the broken things in our lives. But when? Hadn't Chris put in enough effort? Done his part? What more did God want from him?

The grout in the tile backsplash behind the stove was chipping. If he were a better man, he'd fix it as a thank-you to Tom for letting him stay here. Now he just wanted to watch it deteriorate. Rip it out, even. If this was where integrity and hard work had landed him, then perhaps that was the better route.

He laid his head in his hands and closed his eyes for a few minutes. Maybe longer, he didn't really know. There was only one thing left he could do now. He fumbled through his phone until he found the number for NPS, then asked the receptionist to connect him to Audrey. It only took a couple seconds for her to pick up.

"Ms. Brooks, Chris Stratton calling. I have something I'd like to discuss with you. Is there any chance you could set up a board meeting? I know it's a lot to ask, but I'd really appreciate it, and I think you'll be interested in what I have to say."

...

Linda, is there any way you could meet me for coffee in the morning? It's important (but not so important that you should leave Maddox home alone if he isn't feeling well).

The morning after this unexpected text, Linda sat in Bellevue Coffee, listening to the story of Jack's "generous" offer. She couldn't believe she had ever loved a man who would behave this way. "What are you going to do?"

Caroline twirled her cup between her palms. "I don't know. It's such a lot of money, and I could do good things with it. I could give part, or all of it, to a women's crisis center or an adoption support group. Part of me thinks that something like that would serve justice."

Linda nodded. "What do your parents think?"

"Some of what they think is probably not repeatable in polite company."

Both of them laughed at that. Linda said, "I'll bet."

"And the other person I asked—"

"Chris?"

She leaned back a bit, then shook her head slowly. "Someone else. He thinks it's pretty straightforward. Jack offered it so I should take it, to help me get started. But I wanted to hear your thoughts on it before I make my final decision. After all, you are involved in this, too."

She wants to hear my thoughts.

The importance of this moment could not be overstated. Linda reflected back on her twenty-one-year-old self. The one who was living in a new city, alone, terrified, and ashamed. She wished she could go back and speak to that frightened girl. To let her know that things would be all right, that she was doing the right thing, that yes this was so hard she didn't think she could make it. But she would make it. They both would.

"When I was pregnant with you, he wanted to help me, 'take care of the problem,' as he put it, and sent me a hundred-dollar bill." Linda quirked an eyebrow. "It seems your valuation has increased exponentially in the past few years. I would say that makes you a really good investment."

"I guess so." Caroline laughed. She sat for a moment, taking in what she'd just learned. "One hundred dollars, really? I never knew that." Her expression slowly darkened, until there was the hint of tears.

Linda reached over and lifted her chin, so she was looking directly into her eyes. "Your life was worth more than a hundred dollars, and your integrity is worth more than a quarter million. Walk away and don't look back. Your true value, Caroline, is so much more than any of this. The very hairs on your head are numbered by God Himself."

Caroline nodded slowly. "That's what Mom says, too. I think the two of you may be right."

"I guarantee it."

"Thank you." Caroline reached across and hugged her. "I'm really glad to find out that my birth mom is someone as awesome as you."

Linda savored the embrace for all it was worth. "And I am so very proud of the young woman you've become."

She returned to her car and drove toward home. For the first part of the ride, she seethed. How dare he? By the time she arrived home, every bit of anger had dissolved into pity. Jack had no idea what he was missing.

CHAPTER 42

It was a rather simple process for such a dramatic and life-altering document. Caroline signed her name across the bottom of the page, then reached for the envelope Jack's attorney had provided. Now all she had to do was seal it up and take it to the post office before they closed, and she could cross it off her Saturday to-do list.

She was about to start all of that when her phone buzzed in the back pocket of her jeans. She reached for it with the intention of declining the call, but Dillon's name flashed across caller ID. Her heart started to beat a little faster. She couldn't let him go to voice mail. This was something that needed to be discussed in a live conversation.

"Hi." She sat down on a kitchen stool.

"Hey, so I think I figured out what the tax implications would be on that quarter of a million dollars. For federal, we're talking—"

"Dillon—" She cut in, then took a deep breath. "I'm not taking it."

"What? Why?"

"I don't want it." She shifted her weight. "Well, obviously I want it, but I can't take it. It doesn't feel right."

"I don't understand. He offered it to you. It's pretty clear cut, isn't it?"

"In some ways, I suppose. But I can't take it without feeling icky."

"That seems kind of irrational to me."

"Maybe it is." She bit her lower lip and her stomach clenched. It was time to say what she knew in her heart to be true. What she should have said a while ago but hadn't been able to. "Dillon, I've also been thinking a lot about us. I miss California, but regardless of where either of us live, I think it would be better to move on." She paused. "Apart." Her heart was pounding now.

He was quiet for a few moments. "Oh. I see."

"I'm sorry, Dillon. I really do wish you all the best."

He let out a long sigh. "Yeah. You too, Caroline. All the best."

She hung up and put her phone back in her pocket, then allowed herself a moment for her heart to steady. When it finally did, a small ache surfaced, like the letdown of waking from a dream and discovering it was just an illusion.

But if you didn't realize you were pursuing an illusion, then you were not awake, not alive, not able to seek what was real and true and good. Not able to enjoy what you had in the very moment you possessed it.

She reached for the envelope, sealed it, and prepared to send off her rejection of rejection. Her rejection of what wasn't real or true or good.

And she did so with confidence that her account was full.

...

Caroline pulled the stack of papers from the printer downstairs, then started flipping through them as she walked back up to her office. That was, until she bumped right into someone, a rather tall and solid someone, and dropped the entire stack on the floor. *Ouch.*

"Excuse me, I'm so sorry."

"It's okay." She knelt to collect her papers. When she finished, she stood and looked to see whom she'd bumped into. "Chris, what are you doing here?" She very well may have been less surprised to see John Chadwick himself.

"I just had a meeting with Audrey and the board." He pointed back to the boardroom.

"Oh really? Is your boss calling a truce?" Her tone was on the snarky side and not at all what she'd intended. She shook her head and placed a hand on his forearm. "I'm sorry, that didn't come out right."

"I'm trying to work out a deal, and I think we're on to something." He nodded a few times, but then his expression shifted. "But after the Chadwick's opening, I will no longer be working for Tom Williams."

"Have you saved enough for your uncle's construction company?" Judging by the look on his face, she already knew the answer.

"No, I'm not exactly leaving by choice."

"Oh." The reality of what she'd suspected hurt when it landed. "I see. I'm really sorry."

"Yeah, well, it is the way it is." He shrugged.

"I really didn't send the letter to Aiden." Now she just sounded defensive. Great.

"I know. Gloria found it in the scanner. Audrey just told me."

Caroline nodded and pressed her lips together. "I bet you regret ever meeting me."

"I regret that this all happened for nothing." He looked around before continuing, and when he did his voice was softer. "If things were different between us, then, well, at least I'd have that. But it all seems like such a waste." He shifted his weight. "At least something good will come out of it for NPS. Good luck, Caroline. I hope things go well for you back in LA."

His smile seemed forced as he walked out the office's side door. Caroline thought about following him to the parking lot but just stood there for a few moments, unable to move. What good would it do, anyway?

She headed back toward the stairs when she spotted Audrey coming out of the boardroom. "Audrey," she called as she walked over to her. "May I ask what all that was about with Chris Stratton?"

"Of course. There's going to be a partnership between us and The Williams Hotel Group. Given all that's happened—the letter and the fact that it's not legally binding—we all feel the best way to move forward is for the hotel to open, but with certain provisions. We will get 25 percent of the profits, access to the property for events, and there will be information about the Chadwicks and photos of Chadwick Place on display in the lobby. How does this sound: The Chadwick, a Newport Preservation Society Hotel by The Williams Hotel Group. That's what we agreed on. Not bad, huh?"

Not bad? It was brilliant. Tom Williams should be leaping for joy. "I think it's fantastic. It's a perfect solution."

"I think I misjudged that Stratton fellow. He's pretty sharp. Not bad looking either." She winked at Caroline before she walked back toward her office.

Caroline rolled her eyes. *Tell me something I don't know.*

CHAPTER 43

"This came for you." Even as Linda handed Maddox the envelope, she wondered if she should have tossed it instead.

College flyers filled the mailboxes of high school seniors, and every day Linda agonized over whether to throw them away or show them to him. This envelope had an official-looking Westmont College Baseball insignia for the return address. He looked up from his English Lit project, currently scattered across the kitchen table. "Huh. This doesn't look like one of those 'please apply to our school' kind of things."

"Agreed." But what else could it be?

Over the course of the past months, Maddox had smiled and congratulated his friends with each and every college acceptance letter. Some got into their dream schools, a couple of teammates got baseball scholarships. He was happy for them, but this aspiration had been, for present at least, denied him.

For his freshman year, Maddox would stay close to home and attend a local junior college. After that, if things were still going well, he could look into transferring to a bigger school, and in one of the new and exciting locations he had always dreamed about.

He tore open the envelope. A couple minutes later, he slid it back across the table. "Read this." His voice sounded choked.

Dear Maddox,

Mike and Liz Chapman are dear friends of mine. From the very beginning they have been sharing your journey and how it intersected with their daughter, Caroline. We've all been praying for you and your recovery.

Last week, Caroline texted me some videos your mother had shared with her, so I could see what "a good baseball player my brother is." I was impressed.

I understand that you have not been able to workout to a great capacity but are hoping to play for your junior college next year. That is a great plan. I would be more than happy to speak with you in the future if you are interested in making a transfer.

I can't promise a spot on the roster, but I would like to keep in touch if you're interested. You sound like the kind of young man I want on my team.

Wishing you all the best for your continued health and educational endeavors.

George Shields
Westmont Baseball

"Can you believe that?"

Linda shook her head. "Honestly, it never even crossed my mind."

"Mine either." He reached for the letter and held it up to the light, just as he'd done with the Steve Kleen photo all those months ago. "I should tell Caroline about it and thank her for texting him. While I'm at it, I'll see if she's talked to Chris lately. I keep telling her that he's a cool guy."

"You've been telling her that? When?"

"We text a lot. Chris, too. I've been trying to help him out, you know, one guy to another. I've been putting in a good word with my sister."

Linda laughed. "I don't know that you should try to insert yourself into Caroline's love life."

"Of course I should. We share the same DNA. Do you think I want part of my DNA married to some loser? Absolutely not."

"Oh, Maddox, it's good to see the old you starting to show up again. Even if you are obnoxious."

"Obnoxious? Mom, that's the nicest thing you've said to me in a long time."

...

It was just after 9:00 p.m. when the girls from Caroline's new "post-college" church group left her house. She was the oldest by several years, but the only other groups with people her own age were for married couples.

She stood at her kitchen sink rinsing the mugs they'd used when she felt something rub up against her leg. A screech flew out of her mouth as she jumped back, and she nearly dropped one of the mugs in the process. "Oh, it's just you." She took a moment to catch her breath. "You startled me, Olive. Did you decide to come out of hiding now that everyone's gone?" It had only been a week and she was still getting used to having a cat in the house.

Just then, an overhead light burned out. *Oh well, that's just lovely.* She finished putting the mugs into the dishwasher, then made her way down to the basement in search of a new bulb. The last time she'd done this, Chris was upstairs. Waiting to kiss her. She pushed the thought aside as she moved a bottle of glass cleaner.

She'd been doing that a lot lately, pushing aside thoughts of Chris. Maddox was no help, constantly reminding her what a "cool guy" Chris was. She did call him once.

Almost. She hung up before it could connect. Maybe she should have let the call go through. At least tried to smooth things over.

No, he'd probably moved on by now, with that saucy red-head from Blythe's wedding. Oh well, she had a cat.

After bringing the bulb upstairs, she found the step stool in the closet. "This will be better, don't you think?" She finished screwing it in, then looked at Olive and smiled. "Much better."

But about three seconds later, the smile faded and was replaced by an onslaught of queasiness. *Oh, good heavens, I'm talking to a cat. This is unacceptable.*

But, really, what could she do now? She couldn't push it aside anymore. Couldn't avoid it. And she didn't want to.

But she had nothing to offer.

If she had taken Jack's money, she could have given it to Chris, helped him fill the gap for his uncle's construction company. There wasn't even one chocolate chip cookie left on the platter from tonight's Bible study.

She tried to formulate a plan. But there was no plan. All she could do was show up.

Hands empty.

Heart longing.

And if it didn't work, then she and Olive would live happily ever after. She got into the car, even though it was nearly nine thirty now. No one would be there. This whole thing was probably pointless, anyway.

She parked her car, then slipped through the gate, and to her surprise, the lights were on and music emerged from inside. *Oh, hallelujah!* Fresh energy infused her, at least enough to quiet the admonition competing for her attention.

When Caroline walked into the Chadwick, a tall bru-nette buzzed around the hotel lobby, directing movers here and there. "Philip, those curtains need to be hung three inches higher at least." She pointed toward a frustrated- and tired-looking man, balancing on a step stool, then she turned toward Caroline. "Can I help you?"

"I hope so. I'm looking for Chris Stratton."

"I'm sorry, it's just us, the cleaning crew and the movers, tonight. Is there something I can do for you?"

Her heart fell a tad. "No, that's okay. Thanks." She offered a smile, then walked back to her car... then ran back to her car. There was one more thing she could try, if it wasn't too late. She buckled her seat belt, then started the drive, her stomach quivering more and more the closer she got to her destination.

When she arrived, the entrance was blocked by a large iron gate. One that had been wide open the last time she was here. Perhaps it was prophetic. There was a keypad, but she had no idea what to press or how to call anyone inside.

There was only one option, one that hopefully wouldn't land her in jail, but desperate times and all that. She pulled her car out of the driveway, parked on the street, then walked over to the stone wall that surrounded the grounds. She looked around but didn't see anyone.

The wall wasn't very tall, and the stones provided decent footholds, so up she went. When she made it to the top, she kicked one leg over, then the other, then shimmied down the other side. No one seemed to notice, and a dog hadn't appeared out of nowhere to rip her to shreds. *Phew.*

She straightened her blouse, returned her purse to her arm, then paced down the long driveway. When she finally got to the guesthouse, she saw Chris's truck parked in front and couldn't quite decide if she was relieved or not. Her heart was pounding, either way.

She stood in front of the door and knocked a few times, trying to convince herself to calm down.

"It's open." Chris's voice came from inside.

She mustered her confidence, then turned the knob. It was dark inside, and she didn't see anyone when she first opened the door, so she took a few steps inside, closed the door behind her, and took a few more steps until she found him in the den.

"Hi."

"Hi." He looked up quickly, then stood a little straighter. "I'm surprised to see you. How did you get past the gate?" He placed a small stack of books into a box, next to the photo of his dad and him.

"I climbed the wall."

He let out a little chuckle. "I figured you'd be doing the same thing as me—packing, not scaling fences."

"It's a hobby. Anyway, I wanted to tell you that I'm actually not going back to LA. I signed on for three more years."

Chris stopped and looked up again. "Oh? Well, congratulations on the new contract. I'm glad one of us is happily employed." He smiled at her, but she could detect an air of sadness behind it.

"You haven't found anything yet?"

"I applied to a few hotel groups and never heard back. Makes me think Tom put the word out. Kind of annoying, to tell you the truth. I worked for him for eleven years. And he took all the credit for the good publicity on the Chadwick deal."

"I'm really sorry." It was all she had, and it wouldn't do anything to help. Not in any concrete way, at least.

"I'll get to where I want to be eventually. It'll just take a little longer now. I'm tempted to ask my—" He stopped and shook his head. "Never mind."

"Your uncle?"

"It wouldn't do any good."

She shrugged a shoulder and smirked. "Simple coffee would be nice."

"Ouch. I had that coming, didn't I?"

"It was good advice."

He raised his eyebrows. "I think it would take a miracle for me to even be able to talk to him, let alone ask for help. I was planning on handing him the money, taking the company, and being done with it. End of story."

"I happen to know a Carpenter who specializes in miracles." It sounded a bit hokey after she'd said it. Thankfully, Chris didn't give any clues if he felt the same way.

Her heart picked up its pace, and she scooted a little closer. "And if it doesn't work out the way you want, I would be interested in the services of a competent and courteous handyman whenever I need a lightbulb changed, a faucet repaired, or a driveway shoveled."

He turned to face her, then laughed. "Oh really?"

"Yes." She pressed her lips together and crept closer still, a sudden rush flowing through her. She hadn't actually thought this part through or prepared her heart for the real possibility that this was all too little, too late. Could he actually get past the unintended consequences of her actions? The last time she stood in this room, he'd told her she was worth the risk. Had he really meant it?

She took a deep breath and pressed on. "And in exchange, maybe some cookie dough parties? And baseball games?"

"Is that all?" He inched toward her as well, but his eyes narrowed, and she couldn't quite decipher his tone.

Another deep breath. Another nudge to keep going. Another beat of her heart asking for more. "No. Long walks on the beach? Candlelit dinners? Kisses?"

"Even though we're mortal enemies?" This time a sliver of a smile emerged, and her cheeks warmed as a result.

"Frenemies. But I hope not for long."

He looked toward the ceiling and tilted his head back and forth. "Hmmm, let me think about it."

"I know it's a little below your pay grade."

He looked right into her eyes, then put his hands on her hips and pulled her close to him. "You're not below anyone's pay grade." He brushed her hair back off her face, then slid his fingers down her cheek. The flicker in his eyes was unmistakable, and before she could catch her breath, his lips touched hers, like he'd been wanting this as much as she had.

When he pulled back, he nodded slowly. Deliberately. "Yeah, I can definitely live with that."

She felt light inside as she rested against his gray T-shirt, and a mischievous smile glided across her face. "Good, because my landlord said I could paint downstairs."

"Um, that might cost you an apple crisp."

She tilted her head to the side. "I think I can manage that."

He leaned in and kissed her again, then held her chin in his hand. "You have a deal."

CHAPTER 44

The warm May afternoon was a welcome change from all the rain last week, but the conversation Chris just had wasn't quite as sunny as he was hoping.

"I'm pretty limited when it comes to loan to value, man." Dave, a commercial banker representing Southern Massachusetts and Rhode Island, had told him. "Eighty percent is as high as I can go."

It was exactly what Chris had expected him to say, although the disappointment still churned in his gut, along with the burger he just ate. He got in his truck, then headed for the highway. It was time for Plan C. If that didn't reveal how desperate Chris was, desperate or crazy, he didn't know what would. Or maybe…it was something else he was starting to feel. Hope for a miracle? Probably just indigestion.

Twenty minutes later, he pulled into one of the two client parking spaces belonging to Stratton Construction Company. It had been a while since he'd been here. The office looked good from the outside, but he wasn't here to survey the exterior.

"Chris. You're the last person I expected to drop by." Jim looked up from a set of blueprints sprawled across his desk, then motioned toward a chair. "Have a seat. How've you been since Blythe's wedding?"

Chris remained standing. "I'm not here to catch up, Jim. I'm here to see if you're ready to retire. Play golf at your country club. Take Dianne on a cruise." The words sounded sharp, too sharp. He needed to be careful. He wasn't in a position to be arrogant.

"Retire, huh? What would make you think that? All those holidays you've spent with us recently, all those Sunday brunches you've come to? You probably heard me talking about retirement at one of those."

Chris clenched his jaw. "You know full well why I don't come." He let out a breath. *Easy, man. This is not the way to start.*

"I know why you think you don't come. If you'd listen to me for five minutes, maybe you'd finally accept the truth." Jim leaned over his desk, his hands propping him up.

Forget it. Seven seconds of being nice to this guy was all Chris could manage. "Listen to you explain why you bought my dad's company at a fraction of what it was worth and took advantage of a widow, your sister-in-law, who was in a difficult position? Not to mention completely disregard my dad's intention to give me half the company when I graduated from college? Ignoring the fact that I would have taken it over when he died so my mom didn't have to worry about money? No, I'm sorry, I don't have the stomach for that." Thirteen years' worth of anger threatened to erupt from deep within. His heart pounded, his neck tightened, his shoulders tensed.

"You think you know everything."

"I know enough." This was a waste of time. He hadn't come here to relive the past. Just secure his future. Now that it was clear that wasn't going to happen, he turned to leave. "Never mind."

"Sit down, Chris."

He stopped, his feet digging into the floor. "No, thank you."

"Christopher James, I said sit down." He stabbed his forefinger at the chair opposite his desk.

Chris hated hearing his middle name, chosen by his dad as a tribute to that jerk across the desk. He glared at Jim for a moment, then pulled out the chair and sat down, grinding his teeth.

"We need to settle a few things once and for all. If you want to come in here and talk about buying this company, we can. But we'll do so under one condition. Got it? I've had my fill of this nonsense." He didn't wait for a response. Instead, he took a breath and got right into it.

"First, I offered your mom every penny Dianne and I had at the time. And then some. We refinanced our house at 12 percent interest to make up the difference. I did it because I loved my brother and his family. You were only nineteen, for goodness' sake. The last thing I wanted was for you to throw away a college degree so you could take over a failing company. "

"Oh, please." Again, Chris's temper simmered. He leaned forward and grabbed the chair's arm.

"Quiet. Chris, your dad was an amazing man, a heck of a contractor. He could build anything, fix anything, and could spot an uneven door frame from clear across the room. But he was no businessman. I'd given him several loans over the years, no interest by the way, and when he died, the company was in major financial trouble. I don't think it would have lasted another year.

"In reality, I paid your mom well over what it was worth. To help her pay off the house, to help you kids, and to save this company. My intention was to have you work here once you graduated, earn equity over time. But you were too mad and stubborn to listen to anyone, so I figured I'd let you do your own thing. Give you space to work things out in your own way, on your own timeline."

Chris's heart was still pounding, his anger still burning. This didn't make sense. It didn't register with anything he'd known to be true. He pressed his lips together and shook his head.

Jim took another deep breath. "Second, I've been sending your mom a check every month for the last ten years or so, ever since the company got back on track. Not a lot, I admit, but she wouldn't accept any more. I've offered to send a paint crew to her house, have some guys freshen up the landscaping, anything she needs. But she always says no because she's afraid you'll get mad. You don't have to like me, Chris. You don't have to come to brunch or join me on the golf course. But you do need to finally accept the truth. That's my condition."

Jim leaned back and locked eyes with Chris for a few seconds, then took a couple steps to a filing cabinet in the corner of his office. He pulled a file out and laid it open in front of Chris. It was a profit and loss statement from the year his dad had died.

Chris didn't want to look. He didn't want to believe his uncle, that his dad had been in financial trouble, couldn't run his own company. In Chris's eyes, his dad could do anything. Was everything a man should be. Finally, Chris forced himself to face what was in front of him. His throat tightened. His uncle was right. The company was in the red. Big time.

"Things have really turned around since then. Last year, we expanded into Rhode Island."

"Does that mean you're increasing the price?" Chris's tone was more subdued now.

"No, we agreed on a number and I'll honor that."

His gut sank a little more. "Well, I actually don't have that much right now." He swallowed. "Between what I've saved and the loan I can get, I'm at 90 percent. I was hoping..."—he exhaled a breath of humility—"you'd be willing to loan me the rest."

Jim stared at him in silence, seeming to consider the request, then shook his head. "No."

Chris's burger threatened to reappear. "I figured." He ran his hands down the sides of his jeans and prepared himself for Plan D. More like Plan X. "Well, I'm in a bit of a bind, so would you consider hiring me until I have the rest?"

Again, Jim shook his head. "I don't want you working for me."

He felt the little momentum he had left drain from his cheeks. He leaned forward to stand and was about to tell Jim he'd see him in a few years—maybe—when Jim cut in.

"As it turns out, Chris, I am ready to retire, so I don't want you as an employee. But I don't think starting out with so much debt is the right way for you to go. So here's what I will do."

Chris leaned back in his chair, his heartbeat accelerating. "I'm listening."

"You purchase 90 percent of the company; I retain 10 percent as a passive investor. You get full control and if you want to buy me out down the road, we'll talk again."

Chris widened his eyes. It wasn't at all what he was expecting. The act of generosity from his uncle, certainly, but the similarity between this deal and what he'd arranged for Tom and NPS. Maybe their business philosophies weren't that far off after all. "Does that mean you still want your name on the sign?"

"No. It's all yours. I'm proud of you for saving like you did. For working so hard all these years. That's what it takes to run this company, and I have no doubt you'll do a fine job." He walked over to Chris and put a hand on his shoulder. "Your dad would have been proud of you, too."

Chris didn't flinch, although that was his first instinct. He kept his gaze to the floor. "Thanks."

"On second thought, I have two conditions." Jim took his hand from Chris and stood up straight. "You call your aunt Dianne and take her out for coffee or whatever. Lunch. Something. You and your sisters have been the only kids she's ever loved, and she deserves better from you. Agreed?"

A knot twisted in his gut. "Agreed."

"Good." Jim sat at his desk chair again, then let out a loud exhale and wiped his forehead. "I'm getting old." A small smile crept across his face. "A cruise sounds nice right about now."

"Bon voyage." Chris allowed a small smile to form as well and felt a little ice melt inside as he did.

Jim chuckled, then after a brief pause, he cleared his throat. "So, what do you need, the last three years of financials?"

"Yeah. That would be great." Chris reached into his pocket and pulled out his buddy's business card. "Can you send them over to Dave?"

Jim reached for the card, looked at it for a second, then nodded. "I'll have it done by this afternoon." He got to his feet again and extended a hand.

Chris hesitated, swallowed a lump that had been growing the last several minutes, then stood and shook Jim's hand. It was strong, firm, solid. "Thanks, Jim."

"You got it. And anything else you need, you hear me?"

Chris nodded again and allowed his uncle to pat his back a couple times. "I really appreciate it." It was the most genuine thing he'd said to Jim's face in the last thirteen years. "And." He took one more deep breath. "I'm sorry for taking so long to hear your side." The words were clunky on the way out, but as soon as they emerged, a noticeable peace held him steady.

"Me too." Jim nodded. "We really missed the time with you. But I also owe you an apology, and I should have said this years ago. I should have talked to you before offering to buy the company from your mom. Man to man. It was disrespectful of me, and I'm sorry. But all those years gave me time to build this company up, and your experience with Tom prepared you to take over. So, let's call it even, shall we?"

"Even." The one word he never thought he'd say to Jim.

Chris got into his truck, pulled out of the parking lot, and headed back toward Newport. He'd been wrong, about a lot, and it hit like a wrecking ball. So much time, so much anger, so much pain. But now, even though the loss of his father still hurt, Chris felt different. And not because of the circumstances, or even the relationship with his uncle. It was something deeper. Something once broken, something years of effort couldn't fix, now whole. Like a holy gift hidden within the wreckage.

He couldn't help but smile. The next time he'd come to Stratton Construction Company headquarters, he'd finally do so as the company's majority owner. And the first thing he'd do was send over a crew to fix up his mom's house.

CHAPTER 45

Like the rest of the mothers on graduation day, Linda was proud and anxious. Unlike most of the other mothers—whose anxiety stemmed mostly from the fear that their kid would trip across the stage—Linda's fear came from elsewhere.

Today would be Maddox's first foray into a crowd since his transplant. Because graduation was outdoors and since Maddox's numbers were looking good, the doctors had agreed to allow this under a couple of conditions. The first was no handshakes, hugs, or other close contact with anyone. With the exception of the principal, who shook everyone's hand as he presented their diploma. Maddox carried antibacterial hand wipes in his pocket and was instructed to deploy one immediately upon returning to his seat.

The second, and the one that killed Maddox, was he had to wear a face mask. He would be allowed to remove it before walking across the stage for the sake of the pictures, but he had to put it back on after returning to his seat (and wiping his hands with the wipe). After being told this condition, Maddox had originally said that he wasn't going to walk.

This lasted a couple of days, during which time word got around. On day two, Keaton, Parker, and a large number of other kids, picketed on their front lawn. Their signs said things like, "Maddox Riley unfair to classmates," "Maddox Riley disrupts graduation, shame on him," "Graduating seniors demand the presence of Maddox Riley." The whole family watched the parade, laughing at each new sign, until Maddox finally relented.

By design, he had skipped graduation rehearsal, and they intentionally arrived later than the lineup call to minimize his exposure to classmates. Cars were overflowing from the parking lot and out into the street, but this was not a problem. A special parking spot had been designated beside the gym. They pulled up to find a large *Reserved for Maddox Riley* sign duct-taped to an orange construction cone.

As Brent pulled into the spot, Maddox said, "This is so lame. I shouldn't be doing this."

Linda looked at the line of students that snaked down the sidewalk. She couldn't believe what she was seeing. She pointed toward them. "Oh yes, you should. Look!"

"What the—? I can't believe it." Maddox opened the car door and rushed toward his classmates almost before Brent had the car in park. Linda followed, smiling ear to ear, as her son approached his graduating class—every single member of which was wearing a face mask.

A cheer went through the crowd as he approached. "Welcome back, Maddox," and "Nice to see you, Maddox," and other words of welcome were being shouted all around.

Keaton and Parker emerged from the crowd, Keaton holding something behind his back. He glanced from Maddox to Linda. "Mrs. R., we knew you were concerned about the whole hugging, handshaking thing, so don't worry, we've solved your problem." He produced a cardboard sign on a string, clearly meant to be worn around Maddox's neck.

Look but don't touch.

"Keaton, I—" Linda was just getting ready to say she didn't think the sign was appropriate when all three Riley men burst out laughing.

"That is hysterical." Maddox proudly pulled the contraption over his head—careful not to disturb his graduation cap. "Thanks, guys."

"Yes, thanks," Linda finally managed, still not sure she fully approved of this.

"Don't worry, Mrs. R., we'll remind him to take it off when he takes off his mask. Wouldn't want to mess up your pictures."

"Thank you, Keaton. That would be much appreciated."

"Yeah, that's what my mother said."

And just like that, Maddox and his friends went to find their place in line for the ceremony. "Well, Maddox is settled. We'd best go find our seats," Brent said.

They made their way through the crowd toward Caroline and Chris and the seats they were saving. Caroline stood and gave Linda a hug. "This is so exciting, isn't it?"

"Yes, it is. Thank you so much for coming."

"Are you kidding? I wouldn't have missed this for anything." Caroline sat down and adjusted a large poster board leaning against her chair.

"What is that?" Linda asked.

"Oh, I made this." Caroline held it up. It was a sign that said, *Way to go Maddox* around a giant blow up of one of his baby pictures. She looked at Linda and shrugged. "Do you think it'll embarrass him terribly?"

"Possibly. All the more reason to do it."

Caroline laughed. "Just what I was thinking."

The graduation progressed through the usual welcomes, songs, and speeches. Then the class lined up row by row, waiting for their names to be called.

The line was in alphabetical order, so Maddox was toward the back of the class. When "Maddox Paul Riley" was called over the speaker, the entire student body erupted in applause, as did the rest of the audience. Linda clapped and screamed and sobbed all in one big confusing moment. Caroline held her sign over her head and shouted, "Woo, woo, woo."

Maddox crossed the stage, shook the principal's hand, then took his diploma. Just as the crowd went quiet, Caroline shouted, "Way to go, little brother!"

There was a smattering of laughter in the audience. Maddox turned toward the audience and held his diploma high with his left hand. With his right, he pointed directly at Caroline. "Thanks, Sis." Once again, the crowd went wild.

Just when Linda had believed she couldn't cry anymore, she discovered she was wrong. She sobbed her way through the rest of the ceremony, and nothing she could do would stop it.

CHAPTER 46

It was a day for the history books. Caroline stood on the front drive at the Chadwick Hotel and watched Audrey Brooks and Tom Williams cut a ribbon with an oversized pair of scissors. She clapped along with the rest of the substantial crowd, which included the hotel's first guests in for Memorial Day weekend, when someone nudged her arm.

"Hey." Chris put an arm around her waist.

"Hi, I didn't know if you'd actually come." But she was definitely glad he did. Her heart fluttered as soon as she saw him.

"I built the place. I figured I'd come check things out."

"Does Tom know you're here?"

He shook his head, then shrugged a shoulder. "Oh well. Guess what I got today." He reached into the pocket of his khaki shorts with his free hand, then held up a set of keys, flashed a smile, and waggled his eyebrows. "Four hundred and seventy-five horsepower, twenty-inch chrome wheels, and the logo goes on next week."

"Boys and their trucks. Can I drive it?" She grinned.

"Not if it's snowing. But I do have a very important question to ask you."

She narrowed her eyes. "Oh yeah? What's that?"

He turned to face her, his expression more serious. "I want to do something for the employees and their families, get things started on the right foot. I was thinking of a company summer barbeque."

"Fun! I love that idea. A bounce house for the kids? Maybe rent out one of the beach picnic areas?"

"Exactly. So you'll help me organize it?"

She tilted her head to the side. "That depends. Will you install the closet organizer I just bought?"

He nodded. "Sure. I'll even throw in a long walk on the beach." He leaned in a little closer. "And a few kisses."

"Deal." She pointed toward the hotel. "Let's go see what you built."

They started to walk inside together, but when they got to the front door, a man stepped in front of them.

"Tom, it's good to see you." Chris stood up straight. "This is Caroline Chapman. Caroline, Tom Williams."

Tom nodded in her direction and offered a small smile, but nothing more. "Chris, can I have a quick word with you?"

"Sure."

Caroline attempted to pull her hand from Chris's so she could give the men some privacy, but he held on tight, keeping her by his side.

Tom leaned back a bit. "I may have been a tad hasty in my decision to let you go. Would you consider coming back?"

"I appreciate that, Tom." Chris paused for a moment. "Not as your employee, but if you need a contractor, you can reach me at Stratton Construction Company, and I'll see what I can do." He used his other hand to pat the side of Tom's arm. "And, Tom, I don't know if I've ever said this to you or if I'll ever get the chance again—thank you. I've learned a lot these last eleven years and I'm grateful."

"Oh." Tom's eyes widened a bit, then he gave a slow nod. "I'm glad to hear it. And thank you."

Chris led Caroline into the hotel lobby. The two of them poked around each room on the ground level, then stood on the back terrace. The summer crowd was returning to Newport and the beach just on the other side of Cliff Walk was starting to fill up.

"So, what do you think?" Chris turned to face Caroline.

"I still think that chandelier would have been a nice touch."

"Oh, brother." He rolled his eyes. "Not this again."

Caroline gave a sly smile. "If I had a thousand dollars to spare, I'd definitely stay here."

"I'm never going to live this down, am I?"

"Nope."

"Hmm." He scrunched his mouth to the side. "Well, I suppose that's better than being run over."

Caroline laughed, then poked a finger onto his chest. "Don't think I won't."

"I have a better idea." He wrapped one arm around her waist, then the other. "How about we just stick to cookie dough parties and baseball games and apple crisp...and lots and lots of kisses."

She let him pull her close and put her hands on his shoulders. "You can plan on it."

EPILOGUE

Caroline looked around the ballroom. This year's annual Newport Preservation Society fundraiser was going smoothly so far, so she allowed herself a moment to step out onto the Chadwick's terrace for a bit of a breather, and to give her cheeks a break from smiling so much. The late-August air was warm, but the ocean breeze coming from just beyond the hotel's lawn provided more than enough refreshment. Hopefully it wouldn't make her hair frizz.

"Hi, there. Sorry I'm late." A deep voice came from behind her. She recognized it instantly, but it still made her jump a little.

She turned to see Chris standing a few feet away, looking crisp and handsome in his tux. "Well, hello. Glad you could make it."

"Wouldn't miss it. I just had to dodge a few bullets from Gloria on the way in." He took another step toward her, then planted a kiss on her lips. "You did it again. Another successful fundraiser."

She tilted her head to the side and scrunched her eyebrows. "Did you doubt it?"

"Never."

"Good. The hotel looks great, too. I freely admit, you did an amazing job."

"Did you doubt it?"

"Things got a little dicey toward the end." She smiled and her heart fluttered as she did. "But I wouldn't want to be anywhere else."

"I do recall saying we made a good team. As proven by this 'magical event in the perfect setting.'" He quoted Aiden's latest article, then rolled his eyes and laughed.

"Yes, we do."

"That reminds me. I have something for you." He reached into the pocket of his tuxedo jacket, pulled out an envelope, then handed it to her.

"What's this?"

"Now that you're an official resident, I thought you should have one."

She opened the envelope and glanced inside, then wished she hadn't. "No. No. No. I'm sorry, but I am not putting a Red Sox sticker on my car."

"I'm just kidding. That's for my truck." After a good laugh, he took the envelope from her, returned it to his pocket, then held out a small red box. "Here. This one's for you."

"You're hilarious. What is this?"

"Open it." He nodded toward the box.

"I'm afraid to."

"What do you mean? I thought you always wanted a Patriots Super Bowl ring replica."

She pushed the box back into his stomach. "That's not funny. You never were very good at telling jokes."

"Open it. Seriously." He grabbed her hand again, then placed the box in it.

She glared at him for a moment, then looked down at it. Should she? Did she even dare hope this was what she thought it was? She peeled back the lid slowly and cautiously.

Nope. Wrong again. It was a ring box, all right, but inside was a stainless-steel washer. She couldn't believe she'd fallen for it. "You're terrible, you know that? I think I will run you over."

"Well, if you run me over." He inched forward, speaking softly now. "Then you can't have this." He stood just a few inches from her and held out an emerald-cut diamond ring. "And then you couldn't be the future Mrs. Stratton, now could you?"

She had to blink a few times to make sure she was seeing clearly. She had a hard time really believing it. Believing this was actually happening.

"So? Will you?" She heard Chris speak but could barely move. Or breathe. Her legs felt like Jell-O.

After a long pause, he leaned in and whispered, "It's a yes or no question."

Finally, she managed to break free from the trance she was under. "Yes!" Her voice squeaked when she spoke. "Of course I will."

"Good. Hey, Aiden," Chris yelled, although Caroline wasn't sure if Aiden was actually around or not. Probably hiding in the bushes somewhere. "She said yes!"

Caroline couldn't help but laugh, the excitement over-flowing from inside. She looked up at Chris and he was smiling, too, but not at her. He seemed to be searching for something...in the ballroom? She followed his gaze until her own landed on another surprise. Shock, rather. Her mom, dad, and the Rileys came out onto the terrace.

"Ah! Oh my gosh!" Her hand flew up to cover her gaping mouth.

"Congratulations!" Mom squealed and pulled Caroline into a hug.

"When did you two get here?" Her tone was a good octave higher than normal. For one thing, she'd never seen her dad in a tux, but that was beside the point.

"We flew in yesterday, and we're being treated to a lovely suite upstairs." Mom's eyes sparkled as she looked at Chris.

"I'm stunned." Caroline turned to Linda, then gave her a hug as well. "You said you all had plans tonight."

"We do have plans ... to be here. You didn't ask what they were, so technically I was telling the truth." Linda raised her eyebrows, then gave a coy smile.

"Well, everyone," Caroline stammered. "Apparently Chris and I are getting married, as of two seconds ago."

Mom tilted her head to the side. "We know. He took us all out to dinner last night and asked for our permission." She leaned in and whispered, "I honestly think Maddox was the most excited of all of us."

Again, Caroline's mouth hung open. "You all went out to dinner last night? Why wasn't I invited?"

"It would ruin the surprise. Duh." Chris shook his head at her.

"So everyone knew about this but me?"

"Pretty much." Chris smiled, obviously proud of his accomplishment.

Maddox, looking uncomfortable in his rented tux, placed a hand on Chris's shoulder. "My permission is technically still pending those Red Sox tickets, just in case you forgot."

"Maddox," Brent cut in. "Your permission is technically inconsequential, just in case you forgot."

"I'm kidding." Maddox flashed a goofy smile. "But seriously, we're still going right?"

"Of course." Chris wrapped one arm around Maddox's neck and other around Marshall's. "I have to admit, I'm pretty pumped about having two brothers close by. I've had my fill of females."

"Hey." Caroline fired a glare his way.

"Chris, you do realize you'll have two mothers-in-law, don't you?" Mom put her arm around Linda. "One on each coast."

Chris's smile faded. "Maddox, Marshall, you've got my back, right?"

"Absolutely." Marshall nodded.

"Until the end, bro." Maddox gave Chris's back a few pats.

Caroline rolled her eyes. "Um, hello? Do you actually want to marry me or just adopt them?"

"I want you, but it might be a good idea to start looking for a place with a few extra bedrooms." Chris winked, then reached out for her.

"Well, Chris," Caroline's dad stepped forward. "She does come with quite a crew, but we're all happy to have you in our family. Just take care of my Coffee Girl."

Chris gave Caroline's hand a squeeze. "Absolutely." He seemed to stare through her eyes and straight into her heart, causing it to dance. "You can plan on it."

DISCUSSION QUESTIONS

1. What is your natural reaction when life doesn't go according to the plans you made? What would you like it to be?

2. Can you describe a time when what you wanted most constantly felt like it was just beyond your grasp? What do you think God was trying to teach you through that?

3. Did Chris do the right thing with the letter from the attic? Should he have told Caroline right away? Or waited until it was authenticated? Or did it no longer matter when it was proven not legally binding? Was his loyalty to his boss honorable?

4. What character did you identify with the most? Why?

5. Describe a time you felt like you were deciding between two paths? How did you handle that?

6. How would you respond to a quarter-million-dollar settlement? Should Caroline have accepted it? Donated it? Walked away?

7. How has forgiveness impacted a significant relationship in your life? Or just your heart?

8. In what ways do you struggle to believe God redeems the broken things in our lives?

9. Do you ever find yourself trying to pretend to be better than you are? How does the pretense of perfection keep us from getting the help we need / giving others the help they need?

10. In what ways does living a life that matters and leaving a legacy impact your choices?

11. What is the difference between "covering up" mistakes and leaving them in the past? Are there times to tell and times to keep quiet? What differentiates the two?

12. How has a significant illness impacted your ability to choose faith over fear? How do you struggle with the fact that illness exists in a world created by a sovereign God who could fix it all?

ACKNOWLEDGEMENTS

Katie

Clay Beccue—Although the story evolved quite a bit, your original idea was brilliant, and we wouldn't be here without you.

Lauren Beccue—Thank you for inviting me to be part of this narrative. From years of "writing playdates" to our first co-written novel—the journey and the friendship have been treasured.

Lee Cushman—For encouraging me during the dry years, for telling me that I would write again, because "That is what you do." Thanks for being a man of integrity and love and generosity and hard work.

Melanie and Caroline—For being the most amazing daughters in the world, and also for being the best of friends and encouragers. I am so blessed! Thanks, also, for allowing me to embarrass you on a regular basis.

Griffin and Parrish families—For the love and support during the loss of Mom (and Aunt Kathryn and Uncle Harlan). It's been a rough few years. I am so thankful we have each other.

Kristyn, Kathleen, Lisa, Stacey, Brenna, Denice—For always encouraging me to keep writing.

The Goodland Book Club—Genessa, Shannon, Christy, Nikki, Christine, Leora, Cindy, Keely, Amy, Nancy, and

Robyn. Thank you for loving great books as much as I do, and for reminding me why I always wanted to write.

Most of all, thank you, Father in Heaven, for Your love and guidance through the Valley of the Shadow. Thank you for a renewed love of the written word and the joy of creating. Thank you for your constancy. Thank You for waiting with open arms to welcome my mama into her new forever home.

Lauren

First and foremost, thank you, God, for putting this desire in my heart, for clearing the path so I could pursue it, and for sustaining me through all the ups and downs of writing and life. Thank you for helping me understand the true definition of value and success. You are my source for both.

Katie, "Thank you" is not adequate. I am so grateful you agreed to do this project with me, and I truly appreciate your patience, guidance, and encouragement. Writing this book with you was an absolute delight. Looking forward to our next "playdate."

Clay, this book is a bit different than we first envisioned on that rainy walk on Martha's Vineyard, but thank you for the inspiration and for being my go-to source for all that Rhode Island research. All those times you cleaned the kitchen while I was writing didn't go unnoticed, either.

Zach, Addie, and Blythe, thanks for sharing me with Caroline and Chris. You three are my greatest treasures. Luke 12:6–7, 2 Thessalonians 3:5 ("Of course Mom had a verse for the moment. What else was new?").

To the rest of my family, especially Mom and Hilary, I'm so grateful for you. Your encouraging words kept me going, and your prayers and practical help meant the world to me. I also need to acknowledge my dad, who passed away in 2008.

His unwavering faith, constant support, and love of baseball had a huge impact on me, and consequently, this book.

Finally, to the Johansen family: I look back on those years of friendship with Laura with great fondness. Piano, family camps, swimming—all of it was more fun with her. Laura introduced me to the Christy Miller series, which were the first books I actually *loved* to read. That certainly contributed to my love of books as a whole, both reading and writing. I still have (and treasure!) that autographed picture of Tim Salmon you gave me for my birthday. Your kind and generous family has impacted my life for the better. Thank you.

Katie and Lauren

Josh and Collette, thank you both for all your work, especially the beautiful cover.

Julee, we appreciate all your feedback and the stellar editing that made this book what it is. It just wouldn't be the same with all that smiling and nodding!

Marjorie, thank you for your sharp eye and attention to detail.

Carrie Padgett, thank you for your keen eye in the final proofread, and for years of writing encouragement and friendship.

Ginny, thank you for all you did to get this book from our computers to readers' hands. You were a pleasure to work with.

To all who took the time to read and endorse our book, thank you for your kind words. They meant so much to us!

To Janet and everyone at Books & Such, thank you for your representation and motivating us to work so hard.

Made in the USA
Columbia, SC
27 August 2020

18082827R00205